TAINTED: LANCE AND MARY

CLIFFSIDE BAY SERIES
BOOK FIVE

TESS THOMPSON

PRAISE FOR TESS THOMPSON

"I frequently found myself getting lost in the characters and forgetting that I was reading a book." - ***Camille Di Maio, Bestselling author of The Memory of Us.***

"Highly recommended." - ***Christine Nolfi, Award winning author of The Sweet Lake Series.***

"I loved this book!" - ***Karen McQuestion, Bestselling author of Hello Love and Good Man, Dalton.***

Traded: Brody and Kara:

"I loved the sweetness of Tess Thompson's writing - the camaraderie and long-lasting friendships make you want to move to Cliffside and become one of the gang! Rated Hallmark for romance!" - ***Stephanie Little BookPage***

"This story was well written. You felt what the characters were going through. It's one of those "I got to know what happens next" books. So intriguing you won't want to put it down." - ***Lena Loves Books***

"This story has so much going on, but it intertwines within itself. You get second chance, lost loves, and new love. I could not put this book down! I am excited to start this series and have love for this little Bayside town that I am now fond off!" - ***Crystal's Book World***

"This is a small town romance story at its best and I look forward to the next book in the series." - ***Gillek2, Vine Voice***

"This is one of those books that make you love to be a reader and fan of the author." -***Pamela Lunder, Vine Voice***

Blue Midnight:

"This is a beautiful book with an unexpected twist that takes the story from romance to mystery and back again. I've already started the 2nd book in the series!" - ***Mama O***

"This beautiful book captured my attention and never let it go. I did not want it to end and so very much look forward to reading the next book." - ***Pris Shartle***

"I enjoyed this new book cover to cover. I read it on my long flight home from Ireland and it helped the time fly by, I wish it had been longer so my whole flight could have been lost to this lovely novel about second chances and finding the truth. Written with wisdom and humor this novel shares the raw emotions a new divorce can leave behind." - ***J. Sorenson***

"Tess Thompson is definitely one of my auto-buy authors! I love her writing style. Her characters are so real to life that you just can't put the book down once you start! Blue Midnight makes you believe in second chances. It makes you believe that everyone deserves an HEA. I loved the twists and turns in this book, the mystery and suspense, the family dynamics and the restoration of trust and security." - ***Angela MacIntyre***

"Tess writes books with real characters in them, characters with flaws and baggage and gives them a second chance. (Real people, some remind me of myself and my girlfriends.) Then she cleverly and thoroughly develops those characters and makes you feel deeply for them. Characters are complex and multi-faceted, and the plot seems to unfold naturally, and never feels contrived." - ***K. Lescinsky***

Caramel and Magnolias:

"Nobody writes characters like Tess Thompson. It's like she looks into our lives and creates her characters based on our best friends, our lovers, and our neighbors. Caramel and Magnolias, and the authors debut novel Riversong, have some of the best characters I've ever had a chance to fall in love with. I don't like leaving spoilers in reviews so just trust me, Nicholas Sparks has nothing on Tess Thompson, her writing flows so smoothly you can't help but to want to read on!" ***- T. M. Frazier***

"I love Tess Thompson's books because I love good writing. Her prose is clean and tight, which are increasingly rare qualities, and manages to evoke a full range of emotions with both subtlety and power. Her fiction goes well beyond art imitating life. Thompson's characters are alive and fully-realized, the action is believable, and the story unfolds with the right balance of tension and exuberance. CARAMEL AND MAGNOLIAS is a pleasure to read." ***- Tsuruoka***

"The author has an incredible way of painting an image with her words. Her storytelling is beautiful, and leaves you wanting more! I love that the story is about friendship (2 best friends) and love. The characters are richly drawn and I found myself rooting for them from the very beginning. I think you will, too!" **- *Fogvision***

"I got swept off my feet, my heartstrings were pulled, I held my breath, and tightened my muscles in suspense. Tess paints stunning scenery with her words and draws you in to the lives of her characters."- ***T. Bean***

Duet For Three Hands:

"Tears trickled down the side of my face when I reached the end of this road. Not because the story left me feeling sad or disappointed, no. Rather, because I already missed them. My friends. Though it isn't goodbye, but see you later. And so I will sit impatiently waiting, with desperate eagerness to hear where life has taken you, what burdens have you downtrodden, and what triumphs warm your heart. And in the meantime, I will go out and live, keeping your lessons and friendship and love close, the light to guide me through any darkness. And to the author I say thank you. My heart, my soul -all of me - needed these words, these friends, this love. I am forever changed by the beauty of your talent." - ***Lisa M.Gott***

"I am a great fan of Tess Thompson's books and this new one definitely shows her branching out with an engaging enjoyable historical drama/love story. She is a true pro in the way she weaves her storyline, develops true to life characters that you love! The background and setting is so picturesque and visible just from her words. Each book shows her expanding, growing and excelling in her art. Yet another one not to miss. Buy it you won't be disappointed. The ONLY disappointment is when it ends!!!" - ***Sparky's Last***

"There are some definite villains in this book. Ohhhh, how I loved to hate them. But I have to give Thompson credit because they never came off as caricatures or one dimensional. They all felt authentic to me and (sadly) I could easily picture them. I loved to love some and loved to hate others." - ***The Baking Bookworm***

"I stayed up the entire night reading Duet For Three Hands and unbeknownst to myself, I fell asleep in the middle of reading the book. I literally woke up the next morning with Tyler the Kindle beside me (thankfully, still safe and intact) with no ounce of battery left. I shouldn't have worried about deadlines because, guess what? Duet For Three Hands was the epitome of unputdownable." - ***The Bookish Owl***

Miller's Secret

"From the very first page, I was captivated by this wonderful tale. The cast of characters amazing - very fleshed out and multi-dimensional. The descriptions were perfect - just enough to make you feel like you were transported back to the 20's and 40's.... This book was the perfect escape, filled with so many twists and turns I was on the edge of my seat for the entire read." - ***Hilary Grossman***

"The sad story of a freezing-cold orphan looking out the window at his rich benefactors on Christmas Eve started me off with Horatio-Alger expectations for this book. But I quickly got pulled into a completely different world--the complex five-character braid that the plot weaves. The three men and two women characters are so alive I felt I could walk up and start talking to any one of them, and I'd love to have lunch with Henry. Then the plot quickly turned sinister enough to keep me turning the pages.

Class is set against class, poor and rich struggle for happiness and security, yet it is love all but one of them are hungry for. ......Where does love come from? What do you do about it? The story kept me going, and gave me hope. For a little bonus, there are Thompson's delightful observations, like: "You'd never know we could make something this good out of the milk from an animal who eats hats." A really good read!" - ***Kay in Seattle***

"She paints vivid word pictures such that I could smell the ocean and hear the doves. Then there are the stories within a story that twist and turn until they all come together in the end. I really had a hard time putting it down. Five stars aren't enough!"

- ***M.R. Williams***

ALSO BY TESS THOMPSON

CLIFFSIDE BAY

Traded: Brody and Kara

Deleted: Jackson and Maggie

Jaded: Zane and Honor

Marred: Kyle and Violet

Tainted: Lance and Mary

Cliffside Bay Christmas, The Season of Cats and Babies (Cliffside Bay Novella to be read after Tainted)

Missed: Rafael and Lisa

Healed: Stone and Pepper

Cliffside Bay Christmas Wedding (Cliffside Bay Novella to be read after Healed)

Chateau Wedding (Cliffside Bay Novella to be read after Christmas Wedding)

Scarred: Trey and Autumn

Jilted: Nico and Sophie

Kissed (Cliffside Bay Novella to be read after Jilted)

Departed: David and Sara

BLUE MOUNTAIN SERIES

Blue Mountain Bundle, Books 1,2,3

Blue Midnight

Blue Moon

Blue Ink

Blue String

EMERSON PASS

The School Mistress of Emerson Pass

The Sugar Queen of Emerson Pass

RIVER VALLEY

Riversong

Riverbend

Riverstar

Riversnow

Riverstorm

Tommy's Wish

River Valley Bundle, Books 1-4

LEGLEY BAY

Caramel and Magnolias

Tea and Primroses

STANDALONES

The Santa Trial

Duet for Three Hands

Miller's Secret

TAINTED: LANCE AND MARY

CLIFFSIDE BAY SERIES
BOOK FIVE

TESS THOMPSON

For my Bonus Son,
Jeremy Strom.
My favorite "nice" guy.
Like my hero, he's smart, sweet, loyal, and funny.

1

Lance

TEN SECONDS BEFORE the clock struck midnight and tossed them into a new year, Lance Mullen had only one wish. He wanted to kiss Mary Hansen. Not a friendly peck on her alabaster cheek or a chaste brush of lips. No, his kiss must steal her breath and quicken her pulse and weaken her knees. He must make her swoon.

This was not a task for the shy or meek. Only a hero could rouse her from her half slumber.

It would take the kiss of the greatest love story ever written.

Around him, his friends began to chant the countdown.

Ten…

Mary stood next to him in Zane and Honor's crowded living room. All night she'd stayed near, so close he could smell the subtle scent of her perfume and bask in the heat that radiated from her skin. She tugged the sleeve of his jacket.

"Lance, you have to count."

Nine, eight...

He looked down at her. *His* pulse quickened, *his* knees weakened at the mere sight of her. With an oval face and one of those well-defined jawlines he found so attractive, she reminded him of fine china, meticulously honed into beautiful lines and curves. Tonight, she wore a dark blue velvet dress that clung to her slender waist and hips. Her caramel-hued hair was swept up into a pile on top of her head, exposing her long neck, the tips of her delicate ears, and the birthmark on her neck that reminded him of a question mark. All evening he'd longed to trace the birthmark with his finger as if it might unleash the answer to her heart. Yet, he wondered, too, would she shatter under his touch?

She played with the gold bangles around her wrist and counted down the seconds with the rest of his friends. *Seven, six...*

She smiled up at him with eyes as dull as a child's crayon. *Five, four...*

One day she'd told him that all interesting characters in novels have a secret.

He had one.

He was in love with Mary Hansen. No one knew, not even his best friends. She was tainted in their eyes, prickly and cold.

Unlike a hero in Mary's favorite novels, his secret did not make him interesting. More like pathetic.

Three, two, one...

Confetti floated and danced around him. "Auld Lang Syne" played from the speakers. His best friends and his brother kissed their wives—everyone married now but him. Maggie and Violet were pregnant. He knew his sister-in-law, Kara, wouldn't be far behind. He was ashamed that their happiness made him sad. More than it should? Maybe. Was he wrong to want a love of his own? A woman to cherish and dogs and babies and the busy, messy lives his friends had made for themselves? If it was wrong, if he should not yearn for more when he had so much, then he was guilty. His new house and all the money in the bank and his expensive cars and clothes meant little when you woke up alone.

He wanted to wake up with Mary Hansen.

The passage into her heart was as mysterious as the Agatha Christie novels she lovingly displayed on the *Staff Picks* table of their bookstore. That said, he knew more than most about the damaged beauty by his side. During their late nights of easy friendship, she'd slowly revealed herself to him as they prepared to open the revamped bookstore. The plot? Six years ago, her baby daughter had died, followed closely by her mother's death. Then, her husband had admitted to having an affair while she was pregnant. The subtext? Trained as a librarian, she lived only in the pages of the novels she coveted. They were her link to the living world.

Mary turned to him and played with the collar of his shirt. "Sir Lancelot."

"Yes?" She labeled everyone by characters in books. He was Sir Lancelot. Every time she called him that, his heart fluttered. However, she was not his Guinevere but his Sleeping Beauty. If only he could waken her.

"You're supposed to kiss me or it's bad luck." She held up her cheek.

This was his chance. *Do it. Be bold.*

"It has to be on the lips," he said. "Or it doesn't count."

"I'm not sure that's true, but just in case, you better do it." She pursed her lips, playful.

She was about to know he was not playing.

He pressed his lips to hers, not hard like he wanted but with just the slightest of pressure, and kissed her. To his surprise, she softened against his mouth. She kissed him back! Yes, there was no question. Her lips moved, mimicking the flutter of the confetti that tickled his ear. He lingered at her mouth, lost. My God, she tasted of champagne. Another stanza of music passed.

Still, he could not let go. He slipped one arm around her waist. She kept her arms at her sides but allowed him to pull her small-boned frame against his broad chest. Overwhelmed by the scent of her perfume and her hair, he kissed her harder. A spark of light exploded behind his eyes. An engine rumbled through his stomach.

She pulled away, flushed and breathing hard. "What was that?" she whispered.

"A kiss."

"Why did you do that?" She splayed her fingers against the base of her neck, as if a collar choked her.

"I'm sorry. I got carried away."

She looked down and rearranged the bangles on her arm. "It's fine. Just a kiss between friends."

Suspicions confirmed. He was a sick man. Not with a physical ailment, by the grace of God, but with a mental malady he'd named after himself. *The Lance Syndrome. Men who fall for women who are either married, gay, emotionally unavailable, or not interested due to lack of physical attraction.*

"I want to go," she said.

His heart no longer fluttered at her words. Once again, he'd blown it.

A few minutes later, he pulled out of Honor and Zane's driveway and headed down the hill toward town. Mary sat beside him, stiff and quiet. He'd frightened her with his unwanted kiss. He could kick himself. Here it was the first day of the new year and he had nothing but the same mistakes stretched out in front of him like a road map to his own personal hell. New year. Same mistakes. New woman with which to make same mistakes.

Nice. Tori Hawthorne, the woman who'd wrecked his life, had once called him *vanilla melba toast* during a fight. He was the guy you called when you needed a warm smile, genuine encouragement, or to kill a spider. Not the guy who pressed you against the wall and kissed away all reason.

Everyone knew nice got you nowhere in life.

His father had always said a man's greatest strength was also his greatest weakness. Lance was a good man, a compassionate person. He was sick to death of himself. Sure, it was great to be empathetic and nonjudgmental, but it made life more complicated. Seeing beyond a person's public face made almost everyone understandable, even lovable. He could see a person's innate character, the person they'd been before life whittled away at their trust and courage.

It was as if he stood on a glass floor and could see what lay below when others saw only a shiny reflection of themselves. One couldn't truly see another if they looked exclusively with their eyes. Only a heart could see through glass.

He saw Mary with his heart. Behind her reticence and aloofness, those layers of porcelain, was a woman who had suffered great losses yet continued onward, fighting the darkness that wanted to pull her under. To him, this was the true definition of character. She was strong and brave. His friends didn't understand. They couldn't see beyond her cracked glass floor.

Make small talk. Get through the awkwardness. Back to friend zone.

"What's the famous medical manual? You know, the one on my mother's desk?" Mary knew every book ever published. She was a walking database of books.

"The Merck Manual," she said.

Lance snapped his fingers. "Right, that's it."

He imagined *The Lance Syndrome* listed in the Merck Manual. Along with the description of the syndrome, photographs of the women he'd once loved displayed as exhibits A though F. His last conquest, Exhibit F, Tori Thayne Hawthorne, best described as *married.* A footnote at the bottom of the page would include details such as, *the boss's daughter who subsequently got him fired from his upwardly mobile job as a hedge fund manager in one of the most prestigious firms in New York City.*

Never one to fail quietly, no, not Lance Mullen. He went out with a splash big enough to empty his famous brother's swimming pool. Lost the girl and the job and his eye twitch and everything else he'd built over the past eight years of eighty-hour work weeks by falling in love with his boss's married daughter.

His brother, Brody, had convinced him to come to Cliffside Bay. Start fresh.

So, he had. He began again in Cliffside Bay. He'd had a beautiful house built on the corner of Brody's property. The Dogs and their wives had welcomed him back into the fold, delighted he had finally moved to town. He thought he'd made the right decision for his life. However, one couldn't shake fundamental flaws just because one moved across the country and constructed a beach house.

Wherever he went, there he was.

Exhibit G was his current work in progress. *Mary Hansen.* She might be his finest disaster to date. Mary fell under two categories. She was emotionally unavailable *and* put him squarely in the friend zone. Only his most self-destructive work contained women who fell into more than one category.

She shifted in her seat, smoothing her hands down the front of her dress. Damn that clingy blue dress coupled with the pair of nude sandals that showed off her long legs. Mary Hansen was one sexy librarian.

He should never have asked her to be his date. Not when he knew his feelings were so far out of the *friend zone* it was practically another planet.

Mary looked over at him. Her eyes sparkled in the lights of a passing car. "I don't want to go home."

"You don't?" If only she meant, *I want you to take me home and rip off my clothes.*

"No, it's just a little after midnight. Now that half your friends are pregnant or have small children, that was a tame New Years' Eve celebration."

"Everything's changed." He'd felt it keenly all evening. He

was going to be alone the rest of his life, thanks to *The Lance Syndrome.*

"Let's buy a bottle of tequila and make margaritas," she said.

"You drink margaritas?"

"I used to. I used to be fun, believe it or not."

"I think you're fun now," he said.

"I'm not."

"You are," Lance said. *More than you know.*

"I want to be fun again. I want to have fun. Do you know how long it's been since I cut loose?"

"Is that a rhetorical question?"

She laughed. "Yes. I don't want to go home to my empty house. Not tonight. I hate New Year's Eve. I just want to forget my life for a few hours."

"I have tequila at my house."

He turned onto the road that took them out of town and up the hillside toward the Mullen property.

"I feel like drinking too much and dancing in my underwear," Mary said.

He coughed. "What?"

"You *are* awake," she said.

He was awake *now*. The thought of her dancing in her panties was enough to keep him from sleeping for weeks.

"You've never danced in your underwear," he said. "No way."

"Once. In college. After too many tequila shots."

"I can't picture it." *Maybe you could demonstrate later.*

"Librarians know how to party," she said.

He laughed. "That's a party I'd love to go to."

"Seriously, the country song's true. Tequila does make your clothes fall off. And other things." The last part was said under her breath.

"What does that mean?" he asked.

"Never mind." She punched his shoulder. "Keep your eyes on the road."

They turned into the Mullen property. The head of Brody's security team, Rafael, was off for the night, but Taylor, the night guy waved them through.

"I'd hate to be as famous as Brody. Well, famous at all," Mary said.

"It's the price he had to pay to play football." In the past tense. Brody would never play again. A neck injury had forced him into retirement at age thirty-one.

He drove by Brody's house, then past the driveway that led to Mary's dad's place. Her father had married the Mullens' longtime housekeeper, Flora, essentially their second mother, and built a cottage where they planned to stay part of the year. Currently, they were in Oregon at their other house and wouldn't be back until next month. Mary was staying at their place while they were gone.

"Any luck finding a house?" he asked.

"Nothing's for sale or rent. I've *got* to find something before Dad and Flora come back. I cramp their style."

"I still think we should make the rooms above the store into an apartment. Like Zane's apartment above The Oar."

"Maybe. I don't know. Something about living above a bookstore in that tiny space reiterates the fact that I'm doomed to a life of cats and spinsterhood."

You don't have to be.

He turned into the third driveway. His house wasn't far from the cliff, but not so close it would fall into the ocean. He'd made sure of that. Like trading stocks, one had to measure the risks versus the rewards.

They walked up his stone pathway to the front door. He'd left the yard lights on, but the stones were craggy and uneven. Perfect excuse to take Mary's arm. How she walked in those heels was as intriguing as the woman herself.

He kept hold of her as they ambled up the stairs to the front door of his Cape Cod–style home. Once inside, he turned on a few lamps with a command on his phone.

"Oh, Lance, it's gorgeous."

His designer, Trey Mattson, had put the finishing touches on his house that afternoon. The white couch was now adorned with blue pillows that mimicked the color of the ocean on a summer day. Paintings of the Italian seaside hung on the walls.

The living room and kitchen were one great room, strategically designed to face the ocean. Tonight, the giant windows acted as mirrors, catching their reflections. During daylight, however, they looked directly out to the ocean. Wide-planed, distressed hardwood floors throughout contrasted with white walls and light furniture with pops of blue in pillows, bowls, and vases. At the kitchen island were five stools for five Dogs.

"Did the table for the dining room come?" she asked.

"Yes, finally." He pointed toward the closed door to the dining room, next to the stairs that led up to the second floor. "You can look at it later." He'd bought an enormous table with enough seating for all of his friends and family. Someday, he would host a holiday meal. A vision of the two of them together with a couple of kids flashed before his eyes. How he wished it could be true.

"Oh, Lance, the view from this window is unbelievable." She stepped out of her sandals and placed them neatly by the door to the patio.

"I'll never tire of it," he said. The window was in fact a door, much like a garage. During warm months, the entire door rolled upward and disappeared, making the living room and deck into one space.

"I love the high beams and light walls. Everything seems so clean and fresh." She swept her hand over the back of his white couch. "And the bits of blue are lovely. My favorite color."

"Mine too. Anyway, we can thank Trey for all of this. I can barely pick out a pair of shoes let alone decorate an entire house."

Lance had asked Trey for the ultimate seaside escape—a sanctuary from the world. He hadn't said it out loud, but he wanted a place where he could feel at peace. A home where he could forget what happened in New York and let all the expectations he'd had for his life drift away in the ocean breeze. This house should grant him peace. Something had to.

"I love the floors," she said.

"Brody said they're manly but also pretty, like me."

"That's not nice."

"It's fine. Just brotherly ribbing."

"You're handsome, not pretty," she said.

"I guess so." Embarrassed, his ears burned. For years the Dogs had teased him about being too pretty for a guy. Secretly, it offended him. He'd grown a short beard just to counteract the prettiness. It did nothing to disguise his delicate features. "Now, about that drink."

"Yes, let's get this party started."

He laughed at how awkward those words sounded coming out of her mouth. In all the months they'd spent together, he'd never known her to have more than a glass of wine. At the shop, she drank apple cinnamon herbal tea all day long. "I'm always cold," she'd told him one time when he'd teased her about her tea addiction.

In the kitchen he found a bottle of tequila in the pantry. "I don't have margarita mix, but I have lemonade. Will that do?"

"That'll do just fine." She sat, rather primly, on the oversized chair by the fireplace. *That dress.* That dress needed to come off.

"You want to borrow a shirt and a pair of my boxer shorts?" he asked.

"You read my mind." She crossed the room in her bare feet over to where he had opened the bottle of tequila and the lemonade carton. "Here, I'll do this while you fetch me something to wear. This dress is like a cobra around my middle."

"I can imagine." He'd like to be a cobra around her middle.

When he returned with a soft t-shirt and a pair of his boxer shorts, two glasses of the lemonade tequila concoction waited on the coffee table. She excused herself to change in the downstairs bathroom. *Do not think of her naked.*

She returned a few minutes later with her dress over one arm and placed it on the back of a chair. "I just thought of something. You won't be able to drive me home if we have too many drinks."

"It's too far to walk in the dark. You can sleep in the guest room. No one's stayed there yet. I figured it would be Kyle's room, but now he's married, and I'll probably never see him again." He spoke casually, oh so cool, like there was no agenda.

"Especially with another baby on the way."

He looked at her closely. Had her voice quivered when she'd mentioned a baby?

She grabbed her drink. "I need a straw. Do you have straws?"

"I do. For when Dakota and Jubie come over. Kids love straws."

"I love straws," she said.

"I never knew that."

"We've never had drinks before."

He left his drink on the coffee table and went into the kitchen to get her a straw. He grabbed only one. Men didn't drink from straws. Even nice men.

She thanked him and stuck it into her drink, then took a long suck as he sank into the corner of his L-shaped couch. "I have something to say." Her eyes shone in the light from the fireplace. Now that he thought about it, she might have been a little drunk at the party. "Thanks for hiring me to manage the bookstore. I have a purpose I wouldn't have if not for your generosity." She cut herself off and raised her glass. "Anyway, to the new year."

"To the new year."

She curled up in the oversized chair looking comfortable, not to mention sexy as hell, in his shirt.

"Speaking of the store," he said. "I closed the books this morning. We made a profit our first month. It's much better than I expected."

"The holidays helped. Next month might be terrible."

"Don't be such a pessimist," he said. "Having trivia night and book clubs and all the other stuff you thought of will bring people in during slower months. Plus, customers love how you help them find just the right book for them." Every time a new customer had come in looking for a gift, she'd rattled off a few questions and then presented them with several books sure to please.

"I love finding people the right book." She was talking faster than her usual measured pace. He worried over how quickly she was downing her drink, but there wasn't much he could do to stop her. "I looked at my stock account today. How are you making me all this money?"

"I've been pleased," he said. More than pleased. Over the past few months, he'd increased her wealth by ten thousand dollars. She didn't have much to start out with, unlike his former clients who invested millions. "I watch the market closely, that's all."

"Not all. You're a genius."

"That's what my boss used to say." Back when he was a rising star at the firm. Before he was summarily fired.

Her glass was almost empty. She wasn't kidding when she said she was in the mood to have a few drinks.

He moved to stand by the fire. Her hazel eyes glittered with energy when she met his gaze. And her cheeks were flushed a bright pink. This was not *self-contained Mary*. Tonight, she was *all sexy librarian Mary*.

"How about another?" She uncurled her long legs and got up from the chair, then crossed over to the kitchen. "I made a pitcher."

"I'm good for now." He might have to look after her later. Best to stay sober.

Moments later, she was back in her spot, guzzling her drink.

"Be careful," he said gently. "You're not much of a drinker, are you?"

"Not really. But do you ever just get sick of being who you are?"

"Almost every day." *Definitely today.*

"What would you change?" she asked.

He rattled the ice around his nearly empty glass. "I'd like to be more like Kyle and Zane. More of an alpha type guy."

"You mean because of women?"

"What else reason would there be? It's always about a woman."

"A woman? Or women?" She pulled a pin from her hair and her hair cascaded around her shoulders. "It has to be the latter if you're going to be a romance book alpha male."

"Do you like that type?" he asked.

"I have no idea. I don't think about men. I have no interest in ever letting myself get hurt that way again."

"Are you ever lonely?"

"I didn't think so." Indecision played across her features. She was obviously wrestling with what to say next. "Until recently."

"How recently?"

"Tonight. When you kissed me..." She looked up at the ceiling. Her eyelashes fluttered. "Your kiss unsettled me."

"Is that good?" *Act like it was nothing.* He strolled over to the couch and sat with his legs stretched out on the coffee table. *Mr. Casual.*

"Yes. *Our* kiss, to be more accurate. I believe I kissed you back, making it *ours*." She crossed her legs. "Which is weird."

"Because it was nice?" he asked, a flare of hope in his chest.

She rested her neck on the back of her chair and stared at the ceiling. "Nice isn't how I would describe it. More like, hot."

He swallowed and gripped his glass in both hands, afraid he might drop it onto his new couch. The ice cubes had melted into slivers.

"It surprised me," she said.

"Why?"

"Because I don't think of you that way. You're my pal. My best pal."

The friend zone. Damn it all.

"But now I feel a little confused," she said.

"You do?"

"I do, yes." She tilted her head, studying him. "Are you?"

"Not in the same way."

"I don't follow."

"I think about you." *How's that for an understatement?*

"You think about me? Like that?"

"It's impossible not to. Given how gorgeous you are. I mean, seriously, that dress tonight. I'm a man, not a zombie."

"Oh." She stared at him for a second, then finished her drink with a noisy slurp and got up for more. Surprisingly, she walked in a straight line all the way to the kitchen. When she returned, she stood near the couch and examined him as if they had come upon each other on the street and she was trying to place where she knew him from. "You've surprised me twice tonight. That never happens. People don't usually surprise me."

"Most people are much more than they appear on the surface," he said.

She shook her glass at him. "You've taught me that. It's humbling to hear what you see in others that most people miss. I love that about you."

"Yeah?" She loved that about him. She'd narrowed in on this trait. She saw him for who he was.

She slapped her left knee. "I'm vowing right here and now to make this a better year. I can't be sad forever. I mean, it's been six years since I lost Meme and my mother, and my husband left me for that barista skank."

Skank. He'd never heard her use that word before. Tequila loosened her tongue.

Mary slurped up her drink. In hindsight, the choice of a straw might not have been wise.

"It was like everything was mine one minute and poof it all

disappeared in the next." She waved her hand in front of her face like she was swatting away mosquitos. "But I have to stop being like this. I have to start living."

"You suffered a terrible loss. It's understandable that you withdrew." *What a stupid thing to say. Trite and ridiculous.*

"You want to know something?" she asked.

He nodded.

"Reading novels—my old friends—has been the only thing that gets me through the day. I can get lost in a story and forget for a while. Or, sometimes, the story mirrors something in my own life and helps me cry and grieve and feel less alone. But you know what? I'm not really living. Dammit, my mother would be truly disappointed in me." She placed her empty glass on the coffee table and wandered over to the bank of windows. "Do you know how long it's been since I had sex?"

He almost choked on his drink.

"The last time was with my husband. Can you believe that? Good old Chad the Cheater." She giggled as she turned to face him. "Do you know he's married and has three kids? Three. Can you imagine how that hurts?"

She'd shared this with him before, but he didn't remind her. He would let her talk for as long as she needed.

"I could, yes," he said.

"How stupid is it to have an incompetent cervix? I mean, seriously? Of all things. My Meme never had a chance because of my incompetence."

He had no idea what to say. She'd gone into labor at only twenty-two weeks. The baby wasn't developed enough. Despite heroic efforts of the hospital staff, tiny Meme had died in Mary's arms.

She turned back to the window. Her breath steamed up the glass as she spoke. "And wouldn't you know it, life goes on. Unfortunately. So, you just have to get up every single stupid day and pretend like you're present in the world when all the time you're just a ghost floating amongst the living. And in the middle of all the soul-crushing grief, you're pissed as hell too—witnessing all the lucky ones with their precious families and happy marriages—those adorable babies at the supermarket all fat and pink. It all eats away at you until all that's left is this angry, bitter shell. You hate yourself for it. Honestly, you do. You want to be gracious and graceful and believe that God is good, but you can't. You rage against Him. You hate all the happy people."

Lance joined her by the windows. Her reflection in the glass appeared ghostlike and eerie. He wanted to take her in his arms and hold her, comfort her, but remained at a distance.

"Now you know. I'm an awful person," she said.

"No. Not awful. Hurting."

"Damn, Lance, how are you so good all the time? How do you always know what to say so that I feel understood instead of judged?"

"I'm not good all the time. You know how I wrecked my life. No one to blame but myself."

"I blame the boss's daughter." She rested the side of her head against his shoulder. "I could never blame you for anything. You're too good for this world."

He wrapped his arm around her shoulder.

Mary jerked away. "No, I'm not doing this. I'm not ruining our fun night. This is the beginning of a new year. We're going for broke." She scurried across to the kitchen and grabbed the pitcher of drinks. "You've got to catch up. It's terrible manners to let a lady get drunk while you remain sensible and sober."

"Sensible and sober? God, I sound like an old man." He fetched his drink from the coffee table and finished the dregs. "Here, give me that pitcher. I don't trust you."

She laughed. "Because I'm drunk?"

"Yes, and my furniture's white." He poured them both a new drink. "I'm worried you're going to be sick."

"No way. I ate a huge dinner. I'm fine." She fell back onto the couch and planted her legs on the coffee table. Her toenails were painted pink and reminded him of perfect seashells. "My mom always made me come up with New Year's resolutions. Did you guys do those?"

"Sure. My mom was always big on making goals. I mean, not that we stuck to them, but yeah." He took the chair she'd vacated earlier, afraid if he sat by her he might lose it and pull her onto his lap.

"Do you have any for this year?" Mary asked.

"Read more." He grinned at her. "Someone suggested that." She'd given him a stack of some of her favorite books for a Christmas present.

"What else?" she asked.

"I'd like to find someone. The right someone. I guess that's not a resolution, but a wish."

Her voice softened. "Those are different things, yes." She fiddled with the hem of her t-shirt before she leapt up. "We need music. Something cheery."

He found his phone and turned on the Bluetooth speakers. A pop song came on, sexy and up-tempo.

"Is this the dancing-on-the-table portion of the evening?" He leaned back in his chair like he was ready to watch a show.

In front of the fireplace, she swayed to the music and flashed him a saucy grin. "What? You think I won't do it?"

"I *know* you won't do it."

"Really? Well, how about this?" She put aside her drink and stepped onto the coffee table. With her arms stretched out above her head, she moved her hips in a circle one way and then the other. Maybe she was right. Librarians knew how to party.

"Didn't you say something about underwear?" The comment flew from his mouth without proper evaluation of the consequences.

Her hip gyration commenced. With an evil glint in her eyes, she gazed at him. "You don't think I'll do it."

"I don't."

"Oh, I'm doing it all right. And you have to watch. No turning away now."

"There's no way in hell I'm turning away," he said gruffly.

She slipped the shorts down her hips and let them drop to the tabletop. Like a professional stripper, she stepped out of them and kicked them across the room to where he sat.

"Told you I'd do it." She turned in a circle, displaying her perky bottom in pair of red bikini panties. "Do you like them? They're red for New Year's Eve."

He swallowed. "I don't see any dancing."

She tossed her hair behind her shoulders. "I've decided it's hot in here with the fire and all. So, I'm upping the game. What do I get if I take off the t-shirt too?"

"First take it off and then I'll tell you."

She smiled, sexier than any woman he'd ever seen, and lifted her shirt, inch by excruciatingly slow inch, up her torso and over her head.

The bra was red and lacy and scooped low over her round breasts. Damn, she was gorgeous.

"The bra matches the panties," he said. "Nice."

"Of course. Bra and panties have to match. Especially on New Year's Eve." She tossed the shirt to him. "Now, pay up."

"What do you want?" His voice cracked.

"I want you to dance with me."

"With or without clothes?"

"Your choice."

As if planned, a ballad came on the stereo. He unbuttoned his shirt and peeled off his socks. In just his jeans, he moved across the room like an invisible ribbon pulled him to her. When he reached her, he lifted her from the table and set her on the floor. He put his arms around her waist. She placed her hands on his neck and drew him nearer. The scent of her perfume made him heady as they swayed to the music.

After a few minutes, she trailed her fingertips down his torso until she reached his stomach. "You've been hiding your abs from me."

"They've been there." *Waiting for you.* He ran his fingertips up the length of her legs. Her skin was silk. His thumbs slipped under her panties and caressed the sides of her hips.

She sighed against him. "I want you to kiss me again."

He pressed his mouth to the nape of her neck before working his way up to her mouth but stopped before he kissed her. "Are you sure this is what you want?"

"Yes," she whispered. "I want all of you."

She was drunk. He knew this was wrong. But he had to have her.

"Do you want me?" she asked.

"God yes." He twisted a lock of her hair around his finger. "You have no idea how much." He kissed her, finally, rough and hard. She responded with the same raw passion.

When they fell apart, breathless, she looked up at him. "I'm on the pill and I'm allergic to latex."

"I'm clean. You don't have to worry."

"But this has to be sex only." She played with the lock of hair that fell over his forehead. "Just tonight. Never again."

"Why?" He reached under her bra with an indolent finger, smiling when he felt her shudder.

"I can't be with someone nice. We're a terrible match. I'm mean and bitter."

"Maybe I'm not as nice as I seem. The things I want to do to you are definitely not nice." He moved his hands to brush the bare skin above her tailbone.

"It's been so long. I may have forgotten how."

"I'd like to say I'll be gentle, but that's a lie." With one quick movement, he wrapped her legs around his waist and shoved her against the wall. He kissed her mouth with increased urgency as his dexterous fingers unsnapped her bra.

"One night. That's all it can be." She groaned as he swept his thumb over her nipple.

"No more talking." He tossed her onto the soft rug in front of the fireplace and covered her body with his.

As the first light of dawn crept under the shades, Lance held Mary as she fell asleep. Her hair tickled his chest and she breathed in long, steady breaths. He stared at the ceiling, unable to sleep despite having made love to her three times in two hours. After the first time on the floor in the living room, he'd taken her upstairs to his bedroom. No sooner had they reached his room than she'd shoved him onto the bed and straddled him.

He'd never been with a woman as wild. Frankly, he'd never been as wild. They'd both acted like savage animals. Would she regret it? What would it mean when she woke? Did they go back to being friends? Was she serious about the one-night thing?

Was it just the booze? Had he set himself up for a full-fledged Exhibit G?

Sex changed things for him. It was an intimate act that brought relationships to a deeper level. He would not be able to forget how she'd surrendered herself to him. Nor could he forget what it had felt like to surrender to her.

He must have fallen asleep because the next thing he knew he was alone in bed. Sitting up, he scanned the room. Mary was in the high-backed chair in the corner with her face buried in her drawn-up knees. Was she crying? He crossed over to her and perched on the arm of the chair and stroked her hair. "What's the matter?"

She looked up, her face wet with tears. "This is all my fault."

"I seem to remember being there too."

"I've ruined it now. We can't be friends. Not after what we did."

"Is that all you want? To be friends?"

"What else would I want?" she asked.

"Something more? Dating maybe?"

She swiped at her eyes and drew in a long, shaky breath. "I told you I'm not interested in a relationship. This whole thing was a mistake. I drank too much. Tequila makes me crazy, obviously."

His stomach churned. Why had he hoped she might feel for him the way he feels for her? The descent into reality hurt more when he allowed himself hope. *I'm an idiot.*

"Don't look at me that way," she said. "This is not what you want. Not me."

"If you say so." He couldn't keep the pain out of his voice. *Exhibit G.* Right in front of his face.

"I can't walk out of here thinking our friendship is ruined."

He looked at her, softening. If he cared about her, he would assure her that all was well. That was the only thing to do. This was a new addition to a long list of mistakes he'd made with women. "Our friendship isn't ruined. We'll just pretend like it never happened."

"Really? Can we?" Her expression brightened.

"Of course. Don't think twice about it."

She threw her arms around him and he held her for a moment. How could she walk away from a chance for love? It was all he wanted. But it didn't matter. She'd been clear from the beginning. One night of passion, then back to friends. He released her from his embrace. "Come on. I'll take you home."

2

Mary

AT HER DESK in the bookstore, Mary turned the page of the *New York Times* article on the latest celebrity scandal. The husband of a supermodel had been outed for his affair with the nanny. There was a picture of the nanny, triumphant, as she smiled leaving her apartment. Mary shook her head in disgust. Another man succumbs. Another woman weeps. The girl was not as attractive as the famous, rich supermodel. Men married to powerful women so often cheated with someone subservient: the nanny, the assistant, the personal trainer. Was it the man's ego that needed to be fed? She shook away the image of her ex-husband and the neighborhood barista.

She stuffed the paper into the trash bin. Here was just one more piece of evidence that she was right. To give your heart to a man was reckless and stupid. She would never do it again. Not even to Lance Mullen. Her stomach turned over at the thought of him. She glanced at her daily calendar. February fifteenth. Six weeks into the new year and she could count on one hand the number of times she'd seen him since the night they'd spent in his bed. He'd lied to her. Things had changed between them. He avoided her. Their easy friendship was over, replaced by a stiff politeness. She suspected he regretted the sex as much as she did. He'd moved on like it meant nothing, which of course it hadn't. Those were her terms, after all. He was dating someone from the city according to Violet. Mary had spotted him coming out of The Oar with a tall blond woman just last week. He'd clearly moved on and wasn't interested in being close friends like they were before she so foolishly drank too much and slept with him.

A harsh voice whispered in her ear.

It was more than that and you know it. You tricked him.

She missed him more than she thought possible. There was the other worry too. A big worry in the form of a missed period. She looked down at her handbag on the floor by her feet. A pregnancy test, still in its box, poked out of the side pocket. With her foot, she shoved her purse under her desk.

If he knew what she'd done, how she'd lied to him, he would never forgive her.

The old-fashioned bell over the front door rang, announcing a customer. Lance had insisted they keep the bell from the previous version of the town's bookstore. An homage to the past, he'd said.

Lance was everywhere in this shop. No matter where she looked, he was there.

A young woman came in and headed for the fiction section. Mary let her wander for a few minutes before she approached. Often, customers enjoyed browsing without interference from the staff. Others, though, welcomed advice about which book might be perfect for them. The way this one hesitated, Mary figured her for the latter.

"May I help you find something?" Mary asked. The young woman looked familiar. She had long raven hair and big eyes, and her curvaceous body was shown to great advantage in skintight jeans and a leather jacket.

"Yes, I'm looking for a romance," she said.

"One of my favorite genres," Mary said. "Historical or contemporary?"

"Contemporary. Maybe a billionaire story. Or, a single dad and the nanny."

Nanny? A specific trope. As always, people's tastes in books fascinated her.

Nanny. That's where she knew this woman. She'd been Kyle's night nanny. Mel something. Violet hadn't liked her. Mary led her over to the romance section. "I love the billionaire romances too—such a guilty pleasure to imagine ourselves lucky enough to have a billionaire fall in love with us."

Mel smiled and tossed her shiny hair over one shoulder. "Exactly. I haven't had the best luck with romance lately, so I thought a good book might do the trick."

"I understand perfectly." Mary picked out a few titles for her, along with several from the single dad trope. "You'll enjoy this author. It's steamy, though. Do you mind that?"

"I have to get it somewhere," Mel said.

Mary nodded, embarrassed. A moment from the night she'd spent with Lance flashed in front of her eyes. If she'd just stuck with reading a romance instead of participating in the hottest night of her life, she might not have made such a mess of things. He might be at the store with her instead of avoiding her.

"I'm also looking for a thriller or two," Mel said. "Something intense."

Mary thought for a moment about what to recommend. Usually men asked for thrillers, not young women. She wandered over to the thriller section and picked out a few. "These will keep you up all night turning pages."

"Good. I can't sleep lately anyway."

"You used to work for Kyle, isn't that right?" Mary asked as she rang up Mel's books.

"That's right. You know him?" Mel's piercing gaze sent a shiver up the back of her spine.

"Yes, I'm good friends with Violet."

A look of distaste traveled over the girl's pretty features. "The other nanny."

"Now wife." Mary watched her carefully, looking for clues. Why didn't she like Violet?

Mel's eyes widened. "Wife? I hadn't heard."

"Yes. They eloped a few weeks ago."

"Eloped? But why?"

"I'm not sure." This was a lie, but Mary didn't feel comfortable sharing Violet's pregnancy with Mel. It wasn't her news to share. Not that they'd tried to keep it secret. Kyle told everyone he saw that his wife was having a baby. Mary found it touching. Kyle was more than she could have wished for her first friend in Cliffside Bay. When they found out they were unexpectedly pregnant, Violet had wanted a ceremony before she started showing, but instead decided it was more practical to get married at city hall and have a wedding after she had her figure back.

"When?" Mel asked.

"Just after Christmas," Mary said.

Mel studied her hands, the muscles of her face contorting like she might cry.

Mary busied herself with finding a bag for the books.

The young woman wiped the corners of her eyes before looking up at her. "Do you ever wonder why life's so hard?"

"Yes, sometimes." *All the time*. "But for the worst times, there are always books. They can get a person through a lot." Except for the loss of a child. Not even the finest-told tale could alleviate that pain.

"I don't know if that's true," Mel said. "Sometimes books just point out all the things you don't have."

"Or, we live inside them. Escape into the pages." She patted the bag of books on the counter. "Start with these. If you enjoy them, come back and I'll find more for you."

Mel picked up the stack of paperbacks and brought them to her chest like a shield. "Thanks. These will teach me a lot, I'm sure."

Mary watched her cross the store and slip out onto the sidewalk. *Teach me a lot? What an odd thing to say.* She didn't have time to contemplate it further because another customer came in asking for a book about pregnancy. As she led them over to the non-fiction section, she couldn't put aside her fear. She had to take the pregnancy test tonight. Denial was not bringing her menstrual period. It had been six weeks since the night with Lance. She hadn't had a period in the new year. Which could only mean one thing.

The next morning, Mary stumbled out onto the patio of her dad's cottage. The sun had suddenly appeared after weeks of rain. Every tree and plant sparkled with rain water. She squinted into the sun, her eyes tired and dry from crying herself to sleep.

She looked back to the wand in her hand. This was the fourth pregnancy test. When the first test had shown a positive result the night before, she'd bought three more, praying that she wouldn't run into anyone she knew at the drugstore.

Four tests didn't lie. She gripped the railing, afraid she might faint.

It was the kiss that had done it. An epic kiss. A kiss from the greatest love story ever written.

No one penetrated the armor she'd made for herself. Those screws were tightened as far as they would go. Until Lance. Gorgeous, kind, special Lance. He'd loosened them with that kiss. Desire, not for any man, but for Lance, had seeped through the cracks and set her on fire.

After the kiss and all the way down the steps and into

Lance's car, she'd chastised herself, knowing that her response had been in direct proportion to her loneliness. She hadn't been touched by a man in six years. She liked it that way. No love equaled no chance of pain. It made sense, she reasoned, that a handsome man's kiss would've aroused a lonely woman. Nothing to worry over.

She had plenty of worries now.

What was she going to do? She had no health insurance. This would be a high-risk pregnancy because of her stupid cervix. How would she pay for it?

And then there was Lance. Sweet Lance. Not knowing how she'd tricked him, he would do the right thing and offer to pay for everything. That was Lance. How awkward it would make absolutely every single aspect of her life. His family hated her, for good reason. She'd been awful when her father had decided to marry Flora about five minutes after their reunion. But this? Deliberately getting pregnant? This was unforgiveable.

Yes, she'd tricked the best guy in the entire universe into getting her pregnant.

She wrung her hands and paced up and down the patio. There was no way around it. She had to go into town and see Doctor Jackson Waller. Everyone in this town seemed to be closer than the six degrees of separation—it was more like three degrees. Jackson was one of Lance's best friends. They called themselves the Dogs, which honestly, made her roll her eyes. Grown men shouldn't be as close as they all were. It was weird.

You're just jealous and you know it.

I must tell Lance I'm pregnant. There was no way around that. However, she couldn't tell him of her trickery. Her deliberate deception. He must never know.

She could remember the exact moment she'd made the decision, despite the cloud of tequila that had fogged her brain and skewed her judgement. With her head in her hands, she replayed it in her mind.

It had been during the third drink from the lemonade and tequila pitcher.

She'd looked over at him, sprawled on the couch, his long legs and muscular torso displayed in those jeans that hugged his tight butt. His eyes had sparkled in the light from the fireplace. *My God, he's gorgeous. The man could be a movie star,* she'd thought.

She loved his mind too. Brilliant and quick. Still, even with all his gifts and talents and looks, he was the best person she'd ever known.

Her thoughts tumbled to the earlier misery of the evening. Like photographs, she replayed the moments that had pierced her heart: Violet and Maggie pregnant, glowing with happiness. Pink-cheeked Dakota and Jubie chasing streamers. Mollie Blue laughing as she gazed up at Violet.

Like then, she'd been filled with such jealousy, such rage. She wanted a baby. Why couldn't she and Lance be like the rest of them? In love and pregnant?

She'd known the answer, of course. He would never love her. No one could, but especially not pure-hearted Lance. Not the way she was now, cold and bitter. She'd had no illusions they could ever be a couple. God hated her too much to give her a man like Lance.

But Lance could get her pregnant. God could give her a baby for the one He'd taken. Yes, this was the answer. She would seduce him tonight. Right now. He'd kissed her earlier. He'd wanted her. She hadn't known that until then. He could give her a precious baby. He would never have to know. Then she would leave town, run away to raise him or her on her own. *No one* would ever have to know.

Now, the deck seemed to sway under her shame. What had she done?

When she'd woken in his arms the next morning and the humiliating light of day slipped into the room, she known she'd made a terrible mistake. Yes, she'd tricked him. But there was something worse. The truth was evident. She'd been in denial.

She was in love with sweet, sexy Lance Mullen. How could she not be? The way he'd touched her like she was the most beautiful woman in the world had given her hope that he might feel the same way about her. No one could make love to her that way without genuine feelings. And holy God, the rough, tender, wild way he'd touched her had inflamed her, caused her to forget everything but the need for more. More Lance.

He was her favorite person. They talked easily and deeply about every aspect of their lives. She could be herself with him and never fear judgement or shame. He made her laugh. He made her remember she was still a young woman. His quick intellect evoked her admiration.

She could breathe when he was near.

For years, every breath had cost her, pained her chest like an out of shape runner on a steep slope. Lance was oxygen. With him, the pain eased.

And now she knew. The passion between them could burn down the world.

Why then, was she unable to let herself be in a romantic relationship with him?

The answer was simple. She couldn't trust him. Even Lance. Especially Lance. Not after Chad's betrayal. They were everywhere—lying spouses. Men who cheated on their successful, beautiful wives with the nanny or ran away with the best friend or decided they needed a threesome with the buxom secretary and her twin sister. Okay, maybe not that last one, but the others happened every day. Chad had seemed like a decent man, like a man besotted when she made her way down the aisle on their wedding day. But as Meme fought for her life, he'd been in the arms of the barista who'd made his double tall mocha every day. Chad, with his mocha paunch and thinning hairline, had nailed a twenty-year-old coffee jerk that had a tattoo of the sun on her left shoulder. He'd said he hated tattoos. Another thing he'd lied about.

And, there was the very real fact that Lance had slept with

another man's wife. There was a fissure in his goodness. A crevice that could be exploited, given the right set of circumstances.

If that could happen, it was no leap to think that Lance would succumb over time. Would it be his assistant or the cute young grocery clerk or Zane's adorable sister Sophie? One of them would pull him away from her. It was only a matter of time.

And when that day came, she would die. She did not have the strength to survive that much pain. Not again. Not with the way she felt about Lance. His betrayal would be too much to bear. She could not risk it.

So that awful morning, she'd run away, hoping that her ridiculous plan would not come to fruition. *No baby, please God.*

She sobbed into her hands. What had gotten into her? A half a bottle of booze, that's what. In that moment, drunk from tequila, the plan had seemed to make perfect sense. So, she'd lied to him about being on the pill. She was certainly not allergic to latex.

She loathed herself. How could she do this to Lance who had been nothing but kind to her? How could she have done this to the man she loved more than life itself?

Because I'm a bad person. No wonder God hates me.

Mary's stomach seemed to fall to the floor when Lance answered the door. She took a quick assessment. Damp hair, and he smelled of soap and his spicy aftershave. He'd recently showered. He'd shaved off his beard, which made him look younger but no less handsome. She ached to throw herself into his arms.

"Please, come in," he said, stiff and strange like they didn't know everything about each other.

She followed him into the living room. She blinked against the bright light. Sunshine streamed through his big windows.

Outside, the ocean was deep blue under a cloudless sky. A rare sunny day in February.

"Can I make you an espresso?" he asked.

"Some water would be nice." She glanced at the kitchen counter. Two wine glasses, one with a lipstick stain, stood next to an empty bottle. The girl had been here.

"Have a seat," he said.

She hated how formal he sounded. Their old rapport had vanished.

He brought her a glass of water and sat down on the couch. "What's going on? Something with work?"

"No, the store's fine." *Even though you haven't been in to see me for weeks.*

"Sorry I've been a little MIA. I've been busy with my business."

And with the blond.

"It's fine," she said.

"Violet told me she took Dakota to one of the story hours and he loved it," Lance said. "Another one of your great ideas."

She flooded with warmth at the compliment. This is what she missed most—how Lance made her feel good about herself. But no, she must not get distracted. She must do what she came here to do.

"I have something to tell you." Her mouth was without moisture. She took a quick drink of water and wet her lips.

"Sure." A tiny muscle by his right eye twitched. She'd noticed it when she'd first met him, but it had gone away over time. Had she brought it back?

A surge of guilt turned her stomach. "I don't even know how to say this." She clasped her hands together.

His expression changed to concern in an instant. "What's wrong?"

"It's just that I have a problem. We have a problem. A kind of big one."

"You're scaring me," he said.

"I'm pregnant. It's yours. I mean, obviously. I haven't been with anyone else."

His skin drained of color, but his full lips looked almost purple, like they'd been stained with grape juice. "Pregnant. Did you say pregnant?"

She pulled the wand from her jacket pocket. "See here."

Lance continued to stare at her like he'd heard her wrong. "But I thought you were on the pill?"

"Sometimes they fail." God, she was such a liar. She half expected a bolt of lightning to strike her dead.

"Like with Violet and Kyle," he said under his breath. "She was on the pill too."

"It happens, like one percent of the time," Mary said.

"Such small odds. How weird that it happened to us too."

"Something in the water?" she asked with a laugh that came out as a squeak.

He got up from the couch and went to the window and looked out at the view before turning back to her. "Pregnant. I'm in shock. Forgive me."

Forgive you? If you only knew.

"I'm not sure what to do," she said.

"What to do?" His brow wrinkled. A flash of color returned to his cheeks. "You don't mean an abortion? Don't even tell me you're thinking about that as an option."

He'd immediately ruled out an abortion. She wasn't surprised, but still, it was a relief to hear him say it. "No, no. Not that. I can't do that." Mary swallowed the lump in her throat. "But it's complicated because of my cervix. It'll be treated as a high-risk pregnancy. And I don't have insurance, so I'm worried about the money."

He blinked. "You don't have insurance?"

She flushed, self-conscious. "Too expensive. And then there's my father. He doesn't think I should ever try and have another baby after what happened the first time. There's your brother and Kara. They already hate me. The fact that I'm going to have their niece or nephew is probably their worst nightmare. I don't know what Flora will think other than probably be annoyed that I've ruined her precious Lance's life. Your mother will be disappointed you're involved with someone like me."

Lance scowled. "I'm not sure any of what you just said is accurate, other than your father, whom I don't know well enough to make a judgement. My brother and Kara are not like that, especially when it comes to family."

"Your friends and family despise me," Mary said. "Except for Violet, they'll all be horrified. I'm an outsider."

"You underestimate my friends."

"Maybe." If they only knew the truth, they'd hate her even more than they already did.

He tented his hands in front of his face, like he did when he was thinking through a problem. For what seemed like an hour, he didn't say anything. When he looked up, his eyes sparkled with obvious pleasure at his solution. "There's only one thing to do."

She waited.

"We have to get married."

Her mouth dropped open. "Are you insane? We can't get married."

He paced between the coffee table and the fireplace. "Hear me out. I have insurance. If you marry me, you can be added to my policy. They honor preexisting conditions now, so you'll be covered, even if you're high-risk."

"Insurance is no reason to marry someone."

"In our case, it is. There's a baby at stake here. I want you to have the best medical care possible."

"My dad won't understand a quickie marriage," she said.

"What's to understand? We fell in love and decided to spontaneously elope. Later, we tell them you're pregnant. No one needs to know the details or timeline. We'll go to Vegas and come back married."

She couldn't process all this as quickly as he obviously could.

How did a man immediately come up with a complicated plan like this? "We shouldn't get married."

"Why not?"

"Because you don't love me." *And because I'm a bad person who got pregnant on purpose.*

A flicker of emotion crossed his face. Anger, resentment?

"We can get married, and once the baby comes, get a divorce," he said.

"How will that not make more of a mess than we're already in?"

"Insurance, Mary. Think about it. The child will be raised in separate households whether we get married or not."

She nodded and squeezed her hands together. Insurance would make all the difference in the world. She might even get better medical treatment. Doctors liked to be paid.

"If it's a fake marriage, then it's not like either one of us gets hurt when we get a quickie divorce," he said.

"But you're...you have a life. You *should* have a life not saddled with the stigma of divorce."

"There's no stigma anymore. Half of marriages end up in divorce."

Like her marriage. Now, she'd have two failed marriages. *This is your fault. Don't you go feeling sorry for yourself.*

"What if the baby comes early like before?" he asked. "Do you know how much the NICU costs without insurance? This is the only solution."

"Is it? Really? Because it sounds insane." What *she* had done was insane. What did she expect would follow next?

"People have gotten married for lesser reasons than this."

"I suppose."

"After we're divorced, we'll still be great friends, which will be good for our child. We can share custody. We'll make it work."

"This feels too fast. You're not thinking through everything."

"What have I left out?" he asked.

"What about your life? You said you wanted to meet someone and get married, have a family. How will you do that with me hanging around?"

"I'm not about to shirk my responsibilities for selfish reasons. I'll take care of you and the baby. You can count on that."

"This is extreme. Marriage? A *fake* marriage is a trope in a romance novel. Real people don't do this. As your friend, I would advise against it." She tried to smile but it was delivered in the form of a sob. If he only knew her guilt in this plot. Or that she desperately loved him.

His expression remained uncharacteristically stubborn as he put his arms around her. "I'm not about to let you deal with this alone. We made a mistake that night. It takes two to tango and all that. Now we're going to have to adjust our lives to deal with it."

"But your life is ahead of you and I've ruined it. You know as well as I do this is my fault. I got drunk and threw myself at you." *And pretended to be on the pill.*

He drew back to look at her, the muscles under his high cheekbones flexing, as if trying to figure out what to say next. "I had feelings for you. I had them for months. I was hoping you felt it too—that we could become more than friends."

"Is that why you've been avoiding me?" she asked.

"Yes. Frankly, it hurt when you left that morning without so much as a thought to giving this a chance. Given how much you seemed to enjoy our evening together, it shocked me when you basically shut me down the next morning."

Images from the night in his bed flashed before her. She covered her burning face with her hands. Why did he have to remind her?

"You walked away without so much as a cup of *goodbye* coffee," he said. "So yeah, I've been hurt and mad."

He had feelings for her. Past tense. She'd squelched them with her erratic behavior. *Just as well. I'm not right for him. I'm a liar. If there was any chance for us, I ruined it. Like I do everything.*

"I told you from the beginning I wasn't interested in a relationship," she said.

He put his hands up in the air. "Sue me. I was hoping you'd change your mind."

"Oh." She had no idea what to say. His anger made her want to sink into the floor and disappear. Lance had never once raised his voice in annoyance or irritation during their months of friendship.

"Don't worry, I'm over it," Lance said. "I get it loud and clear that you don't feel that way about me. But listen, you did *not* do this alone." Lance grabbed both her hands. "Please, you have to be reasonable. This is the best choice."

"It isn't 1950." She moved away from him and leaned against the wall, afraid her knees might buckle.

"As far as I'm concerned, it may as well be. This is *my* child we're talking about. My baby. And you're a friend I care about very much. What else could I possibly do?"

She hugged herself. A little person was inside her, cells dividing faster than her spinning thoughts. She looked up at Lance's compassionate face. He returned her gaze, his blue eyes the color of a stormy night sky. Relief saturated the tides of panic. Lance was here for her. Having him by her side meant she would not have to do this alone.

"I'm scared." She fought with all her might to keep the tears from overpowering her control, but her bottom lip rebelled with a pitiful tremble. She'd promised herself she'd be strong and independent. Yet, here was Lance Mullen being a prince. What had she expected? He stepped up without question or thought to his own needs. Lance was a great man. Had she ruined his life?

She started to cry in little bursts that almost sounded like laughter.

He pulled her into his arms. "We'll get the best doctors in California. I'll make sure of it. They'll do that thing you told me about."

"The surgical cerclage?"

"Yes. The one that sews everything up nice and tight."

"You remember that?" She'd told him that if the doctors had known about her problems, they would have performed a surgery that closed her cervix, thus preventing preterm labor. Now that they knew her condition, a cerclage would most likely save the baby.

"I remember," Lance said. "I remember everything you tell me. I'm not letting anything happen to you or the baby. Our baby."

She rested her face against his strong chest. Why did it have to feel so right in his embrace? "You're so good."

"I wish that were true. You know I've made stupid, selfish choices. One that cost me everything. But that doesn't mean I can't do the right thing now. Let me do this. Please, marry me."

She looked straight into his eyes. "Are you sure?"

"Yes, I'm sure."

"It's the right thing for the baby. I know that's true."

"Good. Now go home and pack your bag. We're going to Vegas."

For the first time since she confirmed her pregnancy, she smiled. A second later, she sobered. "Wait a minute. What about your girlfriend?"

"Let me worry about that."

"Is it serious with her?" She held her breath. *Please say no.*

"God no. She's not even my girlfriend. I've just been dating her. It's nothing. Not compared to this. Trust me."

Not compared to this. That was the understatement of the century.

By that afternoon, they were on a first-class flight to Las Vegas. The flight attendant, blond and pretty with a flirtatious smile just for Lance, delivered champagne. Lance returned both glasses and asked the girl for two sparkling waters instead.

"My wife's pregnant," he said. "Which means I don't drink either."

"Oh, you poor thing." The flirtatious smile for Lance was immediately replaced by an indulgent grimace for Mary. "Are you nauseated?"

"No, I'm fine, thank you," Mary said. "But I wouldn't mind something to snack on when you have a chance."

"Chips or fruit or both?" she asked.

"Both." Mary looked over at Lance when the flight attendant walked away with their glasses of champagne.

"Wife?" she asked.

"I'm practicing saying it. This is my wife, Mary. Hey, are you taking my last name?"

"Stop joking around. What we're about to do is serious and borderline insane."

"You're taking the fun out of our wedding day," he said.

She shifted her weight to get a better look at him. "You *should* have the champagne. I'd down the bottle if I could, knowing what we're about to do."

"No. I need to keep a clear head. I've never gotten married before." He swept the front section of his shiny brown hair away from his forehead. As usual, it flopped right back into place, just shy of his left eyebrow. She almost shivered, remembering how the silky strands had felt slipping through her fingers.

"It's amazingly easy. Much harder to get a divorce," she said.

The plane shivered as they climbed altitude. Mary's stomach lurched. The flight attendant's question might have cursed her. It was too soon to be nauseous though. With Meme it hadn't started until the eighth week.

"Are you feeling all right?" Lance asked, his brow wrinkled in concern.

"Yes, I'm fine."

The flight attendant brought their drinks and snacks. Mary reached for the bag of chips, suddenly ravenous.

"Here, let me," Lance ripped a neat corner off the bag and

poured the chips onto a napkin. "These things can be a bugger to get open."

"I'm pregnant not incapacitated," she said, teasing. *Ah, dear Lance.* He would be such a good husband and father. *If only this were real.*

She crunched a chip, more happily than was decent. They were almost as good as the sex had been with Lance. "I normally don't even like chips."

"What isn't there to love?" he asked.

"Too much salt and grease. I guess the little garbanzo bean likes them." She crunched, enjoying the salt on her tongue. "I might blow up like a balloon, you know."

"Did you the last time?" Lance asked.

"No, I was Olive Oyl with a basketball stomach. Not a good look."

"You're built like a supermodel. You'll look amazing pregnant."

She rolled her eyes. "You don't have to lie to me just because you got me in trouble."

He swept an errant strand of hair away from her face. "You're beautiful."

"Stop it." She broke his gaze and searched for a bite-sized chip amongst the pile. Guilt crawled up the back of her spine.

After a moment, he asked another question. "What was your first wedding like?"

She licked salt from her upper lip and dotted her mouth with a cocktail napkin. "Over the top, which is embarrassing considering how it turned out. I was spoiled rotten and my mom was the type who loved a party. The minute we told them we were getting married she was on the phone booking appointments." She glanced out the window. They flew above the cloud cover now. Blue sky stretched out before them.

"Did you have a pretty dress?" he asked.

Only Lance would ask about the dress. No other man would even think about that. "Very pretty. It had an A-line skirt and tons of tulle and lace. I felt like a princess. If I'd only known, I would've saved my dad's money." She tucked her hair behind her ears. "My mother never knew how our marriage turned out. I was thankful for that. What he did would've broken her heart. She was very idealistic and romantic. Like I used to be." A detail from the night Chad left her came to her. "At the door, with his suitcases in hand, he left me with one parting shot. 'If you'd ever separated from your mommy, maybe we would've had a chance.'"

"Unnecessarily cruel, given the fact that he cheated on his pregnant wife, then left her while she was grieving her baby and her mother. I could kill him with my bare hands, I swear."

She patted his arm, touched by the glimmer of indignation in his eyes. "It's okay now."

"Of all the subjects we've delved into, you've never really told me much about him," Lance said.

"Maybe I've forgotten almost everything about him at this point." She bit into another chip, thinking of a way to describe him. "I usually say he was like George Wickham from *Pride and Prejudice*, but you haven't read that one yet."

"My mother and Flora are constantly watching the movie."

"The one with Colin Firth?"

"Yes. Apparently, he's dreamy," Lance said.

"Yes, he is."

"Wickham is the charming one, right? The military guy who lies to Elizabeth?" He laughed at her astonished expression. "It wasn't my fault. They made me watch it with them one night. It was good, but don't tell the Dogs. I'll never hear the end of it."

"Even so, the book is always better."

"So you say. Anyway, it's in my stack. Which, I'm happy to report is one book shorter."

"Which *did* you read first?" Since their ill-fated night, she hadn't gotten any updates on Lance's literary education.

"*The Great Gatsby*." He grimaced.

"No, you didn't like it?"

"Not at all."

"How is that possible?"

"I hate books with sad endings. It was thoroughly depressing."

Mary couldn't argue with that statement. "It's considered by some to be the greatest American novel ever written."

"Yes," he said, drily. "You mentioned that. Anyway, back to Chad. Tell me what he was like."

"Maybe you knew someone at your old job like this. The consummate sales guy? Quick witted. Charming."

"Sure. My boss. Howard Thayne."

"Victoria's father?" *Victoria.* His boss's married daughter.

"The very same." Lance rubbed his forehead like there was a dirty spot that needed cleaning. "She takes after her father."

Mary tucked that away to think about later.

What was the best way to describe her ex-husband? She found it difficult to paint a picture of someone. There was the physical description, of course, but that mattered much less than conveying their essence. How did you narrow down one's fundamental core into an understandable couple of sentences? This is what she loved about great writing, which is why she was a reader and not a writer. "Chad was keenly aware of other people's weaknesses and was fast to exploit them to get what he wanted. The moment he knew your currency, he figured a way to give it to you—*if* it benefited him."

"He doesn't sound like your type," Lance said.

"I was different back then, less able to discern charm from substance. We were in college when we met, and I was shy and naïve. His outgoing personality attracted me. He was fun and flirtatious, kind of like Kyle, only without the giant heart." She leaned her head against Lance's shoulder, remembering the early times with Chad. He had often told her she was pretty. *Thin, not like the other cows on campus,* she'd heard him tell his friend one day when he didn't know she was in the room. She cringed, remembering how that had pleased her, instead of providing evidence of his poor character. "I was flattered. The popular frat boy liked me. Succumbing to flattery never ends well for the flattered." She crumpled up her chip bag and stuffed it into her empty glass. "The frat boy and the librarian. Talk about a story that didn't end well."

"The frat boy and the *sexy* librarian," Lance said.

"Funny." She turned away, unsure what to say.

"Sorry. Am I just supposed to pretend I don't know how sexy you are?" he asked in her ear.

She flushed with heat. How could she want a man as much as she wanted this one? "Lance, please."

"I'm sorry. I don't mean to embarrass you." He brushed a crumb from next to her mouth. "Anyway, it should've been the other way around. The smartest, loveliest girl on campus liked *him*."

The way Lance spoke to her reminded Mary of her mother. She was like that, always so sure everyone should fall at Mary's feet, overwhelmed by her talent and beauty. It never seemed to occur to her that not everyone saw her daughter in quite the same way. Unconditional love was one thing, but this was a step further. Blind love, perhaps?

Love? Did Lance still have feelings for her that extended beyond friendship? Her stomach plummeted at the thought. He'd said he was over it. Dare she hope that he was lying? Lying? *She* was the liar. Best to remember how they arrived in this mess.

The flight attendant brought their meals. Surprisingly, the food looked appetizing. "I'm not used to first class," she whispered. "But I could *get* used to it."

"Now that I can, I always fly first class," Lance said, grinning. "My dad was extremely frugal. When we were old enough to sit alone, he always made us fly coach while he and my mom sat up here."

"Really?" Lance and Brody's father had been a quarterback

and then a sports announcer. She knew they'd had a lot of money.

"Yes. He said until we could pay for our own first-class tickets, we would remain in coach. They used to wave at us from up here and smile wickedly."

"I admire wealthy people who can instill a work ethic in their children," she said.

"That was my dad. Then there was Flora."

"Was she scary?" Mary asked.

"Terrifying. She took the raising of us very seriously. Not one to suffer fools, she put up with no nonsense." He frowned and tugged on his ear. "The minute we got out of line she put us right back in. That said, she could be almost suffocating in her need to be useful. Our parents were easy-going, but Flora was a total helicopter parent. Looking back, it makes sense."

"You mean because she had to give up her baby?"

"Right."

"It's hard to believe she never told your family about her past, given how close you all are," Mary said.

"She was ashamed. It took a health scare to make her realize how badly she wanted to find him."

"Which led her to my dad."

"Does it still bother you?" he asked.

"Not as much. He's happy. I'm ashamed about how I acted. Plus, it really put me on the wrong foot with Kara and Brody."

"We can fix that."

She cut her chicken into small pieces. "You're the ultimate optimist, aren't you?"

"Maybe." He speared a piece of broccoli and waved it at her. "Have you gone out to see Cameron yet?"

Cameron Post. Her long-lost brother. He lived on a farm near the coastal town of Stowaway, just an hour north of Cliffside Bay. She'd met him a few times before Flora and Dax's wedding, but hadn't had the inclination to pursue much of a relationship. She couldn't explain why, other than a stubbornness to accept that he even existed.

"I know I should," she said. "But I'm a bad person."

"You're not a bad person," he said. "However, it might surprise you how much a relationship with a brother enhances your life."

"It's different. You and Brody grew up together."

"I was thinking of Zane and Sophie. They didn't find each other until later."

"Well, yeah, but they're so alike.."

"I'd take you to Cameron's sometime if that would help."

"Maybe." Would it help? Having him by her side might ease some of her anxiety. "Cameron makes me nervous, if you want to know the truth."

Lance didn't say anything other than shoot her a questioning look as he took another bite of his broccoli.

"He's too tall, for one thing," she said.

"That's not why. What's the real reason?"

"He's angry and resentful toward me. I got Dad all my life and he got cheated."

"Are you projecting?" Lance asked.

"You're impossible."

"What?" Lance grinned. "You might feel guilty, so you're projecting that onto him."

She glanced across the aisle. An older couple were drinking wine and doing a crossword puzzle together. "I miss wine."

"Am I that annoying?"

She looked over at him. "You're the opposite of annoying." *You make it so I can breathe.*

His thick lashes went to half-mast over his blue-grey eyes.

She went back to dissecting the chicken. They ate without conversing for a few minutes.

When he was done with his meal, Lance set it aside and looked over at her. "That chicken wasn't half bad."

Mary agreed as she set her napkin over her finished meal.

"Speaking of chicken, what are we telling our families about our nuptials?" he asked.

"What does that have to do with chicken?"

"Because when we get home, you'll be moving in with me. And as a good wife, cooking for me." He looked at her, deadpan, before breaking into a grin.

"I don't think you want me to cook." She hadn't gotten this far in the plan. One step at a time. Get married. Go home.

"You don't have to cook," he said. "I'll cook."

"Do you know how to cook?"

"No. Flora didn't allow anyone in the kitchen but her."

That woman.

"I'm moving in with you? Like right away?" she asked.

"We'll be married and having a baby. You *have* to live with me."

"Why? It's not like we're trying to convince immigration to let me stay in the country. Our insurance company isn't going to care."

"If our friends and family think it's a marriage of convenience, they're not going to give you the support you deserve."

"Oh my God, because they all hate me?"

He let out a breath. "I miss wine too."

"Don't change the subject."

"Okay, yes, it's because they don't like you. If they knew we married for the insurance, you'll remain an outsider. I don't want you to be an outsider. I want you to have the support of the Wags."

"What the heck is a Wag?"

"That's what the girls call themselves. Maggie, Kara, Honor, and Violet. The Wags to the Dog's tails."

She rolled her eyes. "Seriously?"

"Don't make fun. Those ladies have found a family in one another."

She didn't comment further. Jealousy was such an ugly companion. But there it was, crowding into Mary's seat, crushing her. She wanted to be accepted by them, but they hated her. She was an outsider and always would be.

"Whether they think our marriage is legit or not won't make a bit of difference in whether they like me."

"I disagree," Lance said. "They'll rally if they think I love you."

"I don't need them."

"All women need friends. Especially when you're pregnant and most especially given the special circumstances. Those ladies will be there for you." He folded his used napkin into a neat square and placed it next to his plate. "Also, it will keep our parents from freaking out. None of them will approve of what we're doing unless they think we're madly in love."

This was probably true. Her father would think a marriage of convenience was a dreadful idea. He'd worry over custody rights and financial obligation if he understood it was merely a business transaction. He didn't know Lance the way she did. Whether they were in love or not, Lance would never abandon her or the baby.

There was also the embarrassment factor. Despite it being socially acceptable to be pregnant out of wedlock, even from a man you weren't in a relationship with, the idea made Mary cringe. Being an unwed mother wasn't on her list of life goals. She should have remembered that during her intoxicated scheme.

"What's that term people use to describe the father of an unwed mother's baby?" Mary asked.

An amused guffaw burst from Lance's lips. "You mean *baby daddy*."

"Right. And I'd be your *baby mama*. Is that correct?"

He nodded, the corners of his eyes crinkled in suppressed laughter.

"I don't want to be your baby mama and I most certainly do not want to call you, Lance Mullen, prince amongst men, a baby daddy."

"Are you agreeing with me, then?" he asked. "We pretend to be swept away by love." His eyes twinkled as he snapped his fingers. "I have the perfect excuse about why we didn't want a wedding."

"You're finding lying a little too easy. Do I need to sleep with one eye open?"

"This isn't a thriller," he said.

She sucked in her bottom lip, amused. "No, wrong genre entirely. A night of drunken sex leads to a baby and a marriage of convenience. It's a romance trope if there ever was one." Why had she said that? Implying that this would lead them to a real love affair was preposterous. Yes, it did happen in the romance novels she devoured. But not in real life. Real life was more like literary fiction. Sad endings, flawed heroes, doomed fates.

"I've never read a romance novel," Lance said. "Maybe I should. As you know, I love happy endings."

This is not a romance novel. She was incapable of trust or belief in a *happy-ever-after*.

"Well, this isn't a romance novel. We need to keep our heads," she said.

"If this *was* a romance novel, would I pose for a photo without my shirt?"

"You have the abs for it." *Dammit. Stop doing that. It'll only encourage him.* But his abs were worthy of a sexy cover. She almost shivered remembering how she'd trailed kisses from his chest to his stomach. He'd clenched his muscles the further south she went.

"I'd rather see your gorgeous face on the cover," he said.

"Lance."

"What?" His eyes widened in a look of innocence.

"Stop it."

"Stop what?"

"Saying nice things," she said.

He tapped his upper lip with his fingertips and peered at her with such intensity she had to look away.

"Is that why you can't fall in love with me? Because I'm too nice?"

She fussed with the shade over the window, stricken by the vulnerability in his voice. *I am in love with you.*

"That's what Honor told me one time. She said I have no luck with women because I'm too nice. If that's true, I don't understand anything about women."

Mary turned back to him. "I'm not sure if it's true."

"In general, or us specifically?" he asked.

"Your fine character has nothing to do with why I can't fall in love with you. It's me. I can't allow myself to care that deeply for a man. Not again." She squeezed his forearm with cold fingers. "It's important that you understand that."

His eyes had darkened to the color of a stormy midnight sky. "I'm nothing like your ex-husband."

"All men are like my ex-husband. Eventually. Given the right circumstances."

"My dad wasn't."

"You think that, but you don't know for sure. He was a professional athlete." *Don't be naïve.*

His thick lashes fluttered as he seemed to consider her position. "You're wrong. I can promise you. You don't know the men in my family. Not the way you think you do."

She moved her dirty plate from one side of the seat tray to the other. Lance was certain he knew the men in his family and even himself. However, he was wrong. Handsome men cheated. Rich men cheated. Lance was both and so was his brother. It was only a matter of time before Kara filed for divorce. Would it be a nanny or a maid? Maybe even his adorable manager, Honor, who was married to his best friend, Zane. Honor and Zane. Talk about two people destined to cheat on each other. They were both so good looking and obviously interested in sex. Soon, one of them would get antsy. Next, another broken family to add to a long list.

"People are flawed," she said. "Even people with good intentions eventually hurt each other."

"What about your dad? Did he cheat on your mom?" Lance asked.

She hesitated and took in a deep breath. "Yes. Even my dad."

"Are you sure? How do you know?" Lance's eyes widened in shock. *So naïve. His disbelief's genuine.*

"My mom told me. I was a baby when it happened. It was some woman at the hospital where he did his residency. Meanwhile, my mom was home suffering with postpartum depression."

The flight attendant delivered another set of drinks to the couple across from them.

"How did they get through it?" Lance asked.

"I don't know. My mom said he regretted it—that it was a momentary weakness on his part. A short affair, whatever that means. She blamed herself and the depression. 'I didn't take a shower for months, Mary.' That was her excuse for him. She said they married young. My father hadn't fully grown up when they found out they were having me. And there were self-esteem issues because of his childhood. You know, all the same excuses women come up with to forgive the men they love."

"She had to dig deep, maybe, to save her marriage and her family. People make mistakes. Forgiving someone and moving on takes great strength."

"I guess." Mary needed more water. The effort to keep from crying had sucked all the moisture from her mouth.

"Why did she tell you, I wonder?" Lance asked.

"You'll laugh when you hear this one. It was right before I married Chad. Not a cautionary tale, mind you, but advice about the ups and downs of marriage. Weathering storms together, I think is how she put it."

Lance shook his head as expressions of disgust and disbelief crossed his face. "That's quite a storm."

"Chad had his affair before we even had a storm to weather.

Then continued it while we buried our child." She stopped, gathering herself. "I'll never get over that. I can't. Even if he'd wanted to stay with me, I wouldn't have been able to forgive him. I'm not like my mother."

"Have you forgiven your dad?" Lance asked.

"I try not to think about it."

"But do you?"

"The whole thing made me wonder if I knew him at all. If it's possible to know anyone. Like *truly* know them."

"Not everyone has secrets. Not everyone's capable of cheating," he said. "Look at my friends and their wives."

"Unproven."

"What's that mean?" Lance asked.

"I think Kyle's cheating on Violet with that nanny. Mel. She was in the other day looking for romance books about rich single dads who fall in love with their nanny."

"No way. One hundred percent wrong."

She shrugged. "I hope you're right because Violet deserves so much better."

"I feel sorry for you," Lance said.

"Why? Because I'm realistic?"

"No, because you've allowed your past hurt to keep you from trusting people. Not everyone's weak. Some men know how to fight for love."

"We can agree to disagree," she said.

He raised his eyebrows. "Fine. For now."

"You shouldn't be so smug. It's very bad manners." She poked his shoulder and smiled. Why did her stomach have to flip over every time he looked into her eyes?

The flight attendant took their dishes and returned with cookies. The plane shook. Behind them someone gasped.

"There's one thing I wanted to get straight," Mary said. "When we divorce, we just agree to child support. I don't want any of your money or your house. California is a fifty-fifty state. It won't matter how long we're married." She had brought this point up to her father when he told her he was marrying Flora. That had not been their finest daughter-father moment.

He nodded. "I'm not worried about any of that. All I care about right now is making sure you and the baby have the medical support you need. We'll worry about the rest of it after the baby comes."

"All right, fine. You realize we're starting this marriage out with you getting everything you want." She smiled. "It can't possibly continue."

"I'll keep that in mind. However, there is one more thing."

"Now what?"

"If everyone's going to believe this is a real marriage, you need a dress."

"A dress? You mean, a wedding dress? Don't be ridiculous."

"I brought a suit."

She threw up her hands. "What's the matter with you? How did you even think of that?"

He flashed a boyish grin. "I'm a details guy, what can I say?"

"Well, we don't have time to find a proper dress. Not in Vegas anyway. We'll just look for something white or whitish."

"I looked it up before we left. There's a couture shop. I made an appointment for us. Tomorrow at ten. We'll have a nice breakfast and then head over there."

"You can't just walk in and buy a gown off the rack."

"The clerk I spoke to—very soothing voice by the way—assured me that given your body type and height, it's likely they have some floor samples for sale you might like. Last season's, but I didn't think you'd mind."

She stared at him, flabbergasted. "I hardly need a couture dress for a fake wedding."

"Only the best for my fake wife."

"You're impossible."

He smoothed a lock of her hair away from her cheek and looked into her eyes. "I get it that this situation isn't ideal. But we've always had a great time together and enjoyed each other's company. There's no reason to stop now. We should try and have some fun. It's good for the baby if his mother's experiencing joy."

"You don't know that." Her heart fluttered, lost in his eyes. She could swim in them forever.

"Do you have evidence to the contrary?"

"No," she said.

"Good, then eat your cookie. Garbanzo needs the calories."

Lance Mullen was a Sir Lancelot if she'd ever met one.

Sir Lancelot and Miss. Havisham. What a pair they were.

3

Lance

EXHIBIT G WAS turning into much more than a two-sentence entry under the definition of the *Lance Syndrome*. He'd taken his insanity to a whole new level.

He had a plan. Simple and straightforward. *Marry Mary Hansen. Charm her into falling in love with me. Have a beautiful baby. Live happily ever after.*

At first, her news had stunned him into paralysis. To be clear, he would have insisted they marry regardless of his feelings. She needed his medical insurance. Marriage was a totally reasonable and practical solution. The part where it slipped into possible irrationality was his intention to wear down her defenses until she trusted him. Which, if that happened, he felt sure she would realize how perfect they were together. She would be trapped in his house, so to speak, and perhaps would see that her affection for him was bigger than just friendship.

She'd said once that he was her best friend. That was the

foundation of every good marriage. Not to mention how they'd burned a hole through the atmosphere the night they'd spent together.

This pregnancy was a sign. Mary was the woman he wanted and needed. He needed only for her to see it too. And, most importantly, to prove to her that he was loyal. Cheating on her would be the last thing he would ever do. Since he met her, he'd barely looked at another woman. Last night he'd told Missy, the woman he'd dated a few times, he wasn't interested in pursuing anything further. Sadly, he'd told her, he was stuck on someone else and it wasn't fair to lead her on. She'd thanked him for his honesty, finished her wine, and quite civilly walked out of his house.

That was before he knew Mary was pregnant—before he had any hope that fate might connect them in this phenomenal way. The game had changed. He had a chance now.

A married man did not betray his wife. He cherished her and protected her. He shielded her from harm. Mullen men did not need to fuel their egos through conquests, especially when they were blessed with an exceptional woman by their side. The strength of a man was measured by faithfulness and the ability to remain a steady and loving companion through the ups and downs of marriage. He was that man.

They checked into the hotel a little after eight that evening. He'd asked for a room with two beds, but all they had available was a honeymoon suite. The irony. Mary found the room equally amusing, but he could tell she was worried about the cost. The moment they walked into the suite, she wrapped her arms around her waist like she did when she was nervous. "How much is this a night?"

He mumbled not to worry about it. His bookish girl had no idea how much he was worth. Of all the intimate details they'd shared about their lives, he'd kept that detail to himself. He wasn't sure why, other than it felt tacky to mention it to a woman who so obviously cared nothing about money, other than it allowed her to buy books. Anyway, he didn't like to talk about money. His mother had taught him it was gauche.

"I want to pay half," she said.

"Don't be ridiculous."

"But Lance, this isn't right." She rummaged through her bag. "I'll write you a check."

"No way. Not happening."

Uncharacteristically, she gave up, leaving the room to use the restroom with a worried furrow etched across her forehead. He would erase that furrow. Give him time. He would. Money was not something she would ever have to worry about if she were married to him.

Although his brother had helped, he'd earned every penny of his fortune through blood, sweat, and tears.

Lance had spent five years living in a studio apartment in Brooklyn, eating pasta for dinner and spending money only on clothes for work and an occasional trip home to see his family. Everything else he'd put in the bank until he felt the market was right to invest. He'd studied high risk companies for years. After he'd identified six high-tech stocks he'd felt were outliers, not fully understood or evaluated accurately by the market, which made the shares cheap, he'd made his move. At the same time, he'd asked Brody, Kyle, and Honor if they had any play money they wouldn't mind losing. He'd told them it was risky—they were likely to end up with none of it back. *Also,* he'd added, *it might take years, so only send what you can afford to lose.* They knew his instincts were uncanny. Brody said Lance had a sixth sense about stocks, despite the conventional wisdom of the market, and wrote a fat check. *Worth the risk,* Kyle had said. Even though he'd had the money set aside for a boat. *Who needs a boat,* Lance had told him. *Just get a friend with a boat.*

Brody wouldn't have agreed unless Lance had agreed to take

fifty percent of whatever he'd earned from his initial investment. "Your fee," he'd said. "If it wasn't for you, I'd never know about any of this." He'd made Lance sign a legal document agreeing to the terms. Brody had also given him a separate amount for Honor. Brody and Lance didn't tell her. If they made money, great, she'd be set for retirement. If not, she never had to know.

It took four years, but Lance had been right. All but one skyrocketed, as he'd suspected they would. Like his brother knew where to throw the football, he had an instinct for the stock market. It was like an old man who could always tell you when it was going to rain. He'd sold them when his instincts had told him the stocks couldn't grow higher and in fact might tumble. He'd made Kyle enough to buy a hundred boats and Honor's sacrifice—her shoe budget for a year—could buy more pairs of shoes than she could ever wear. Brody's investment had become many, many millions. The account Brody had set up for Honor for her retirement had made so much that Lance talked Brody into dividing the money. Half had been placed in a retirement fund; the other half he continued to manage for Honor without her knowledge. She had no idea either account existed. Brody had planned on telling her about the account next Christmas, but now that he'd been forced into retirement, his need for a manager would soon be over. A four-million-dollar severance package should suffice.

After managing his own initial windfall, Lance had subsequently tweaked his portfolio until he was now worth millions. He was rich. Like the stocks he invested in, he was a sleeper. His wife would never have to worry.

However, after her declaration about making sure he gave her no financial support other than for the baby, his gut told him to keep quiet. There was no time for a prenuptial agreement. Not that he needed one. Mary wasn't the type to take advantage of him. Maybe it wouldn't matter. Perhaps she would soon be in love with him and they could have a real marriage.

She came out of the bathroom wearing the hotel robe. Her

hair was wet, and her face scrubbed of makeup. "I needed a shower in the worst way. The hot water felt good."

"What would you like from room service?" It was after eight and he imagined she was hungry. They hadn't eaten since lunch on the plane. Looking at her closely, she seemed a little pale.

"Room service? It's so expensive," she said.

"Not here."

"You're a liar," she said, laughing. "Maybe a salad?"

He called down to room service, ordering a steak and a Cobb salad. When he finished, she was on the couch with her arm over her eyes. "You okay?"

"I'm just so tired." She said with her arm still over her eyes.

"Stay awake for some food and then I'll put you to bed."

"You're going to be such a good father," she said under her breath.

He instructed her to rest while he did a few tasks on his computer. For one, he wanted to order a few e-books on pregnancy. He needed to know what to watch out for, especially given her health concerns. The moment they got home and announced their marriage, he would ask Jackson or his dad, "Doc," to find them the best OB-GYN in San Francisco.

Mary snoozed on the couch while he read the first chapter of the pregnancy book. He flipped through the pages, growing more and more amazed. A woman's body could produce a miracle.

When room service came, he had them set the food up on the table. After Lance took the cloches off the plates, the aroma of grilled steak filled the room. Mary sat up and sniffed. "That smells so good." She ambled over to the table and stared down at the steak. "My mouth's watering."

"You have it," he said.

"I'm craving red meat, I guess."

He grabbed the salad and dug in before she could change her mind.

"Did you know you're supposed to be taking prenatal vitamins?" he asked.

"I got some at the drugstore."

"Good. I was worried when I read that in the book."

"You have a book?"

"While you were sleeping, I ordered that *what to expect* book."

"That's a good one." She smiled but her eyes were gloomy. What troubled her? The baby? Him? The future?

He returned her smile and set a piece of avocado on her plate. "Eat that. It's the good kind of fat."

She did so, but not without an affectionate smirk. Whether she could ever love him or trust him was immaterial. His priority was taking care of Mary and their baby. For the first time in his life, he knew his exact purpose.

Lance sat on a posh, firm loveseat in the lobby of the wedding dress shop. Upon their arrival, Mary had disappeared into a dressing room with Layla, the shop's owner. Layla was bone thin with an asymmetrical blond bob cut so precisely he imagined she could cut glass with the ends. Dressed in a fitted black dress and stiletto heels, she was a mixture of a private school head mistress and an editor of a fashion magazine. All of which would have made her terrifying if not for the gleam of obvious adoration for her job, the dresses, and her client.

Although alone, he felt the presence of the half dozen headless mannequins displayed in the windows, as if they might come alive and dance around the polished floor. What else could they do but dance, dressed as they were. The room smelled of dried roses. Not unpleasant exactly, other than it reminded him of his childhood spinster neighbor, Miss Spinella. She, along with her teeth-baring, sausage-shaped dog, had been distinctly unpleasant. He shivered, remembering the way she and Sausage

Dog had stared at them from her upstairs windows whenever he and Brody had played in the backyard.

Soft jazz played from hidden speakers. Along the walls were rows of dresses in white, blush, and cream, with varying degrees of sparkle, lace, and skirt circumference. He had no idea which Mary would choose and didn't care. His bride would look stunning in any of them. He wanted Mary to have whichever one she loved the most. He'd told Layla over the phone not to tell Mary the price of any of the dresses. She'd murmured a note of approval.

While he waited, he searched for wedding chapels via his phone. There were a lot. I mean, yes, it was Vegas, but how would he choose? And, why were they obsessed with Elvis here? A half dozen featured something Elvis, including an impersonator who performed the ceremony.

He called a few that seemed nice, but they had no slots. One of them recommended he call the Golden Chapel off the main strip. He did so. They answered on the first ring. Yes, they had slots. "Just come on by when you are ready. First come, first served."

An hour later, Mary walked out of the back with a dress carrier in her hand, presumably with the perfect dress inside, if his bride's beaming face was any indication. "I found one. It fit like I'd ordered it myself."

Layla went behind the counter and typed something into the computer. "The minute I saw Mary," she said to Lance, "I knew I had the perfect dress for her. This dress came in last month for a young lady with an almost identical figure to Mary. Sadly, she cancelled her wedding and never picked up the dress. Well, as always when it comes to finding the ideal dress, it was meant to be."

Layla placed a piece of thick card stock paper on the counter. "Now there's the small matter of your bill."

Lance snatched the receipt before Mary had a chance to see

the amount. Fortunately, the row of tiaras in a display case had diverted her attention.

He gulped at the price. Couture was no joke. Not that the price mattered. If Mary was happy, he was happy.

"What about a veil?" he asked. "Every bride needs a veil."

"Mary said she didn't want one," Layla said. "But perhaps a tiara?"

"Do you want a tiara?" Lance asked.

"The dress is enough," she said.

"You're getting a tiara. Pick out which one you want," Lance said.

"There's no need," Mary said.

"We'll take that one." Lance pointed to the simple one in the corner, attracted to its delicate, intricate design and shiny diamond rhinestones. Something about it looked like Mary.

"That's my favorite too." Mary flashed him a shy smile and blushed. "It's not necessary, though."

"Excellent. Add that to the bill, please Layla."

Layla, still behind the computer, nodded. "Very good, sir."

"Can you recommend a place for Mary to have her hair and makeup done?" Lance asked Layla.

"Lance, I don't need that," Mary said.

"Every bride should have hair and makeup," Layla said with a firm lift of her chin. "Allow me." She picked up the receiver of the phone on the desk and dialed. "Yes, darling, it's me. I have a teensy-weensy favor. I have a bride in need of your services. That's right, for this afternoon. You'll adore her face. Exquisite bone structure. Wonderful, thank you. I'll send them over now."

Layla hung up the phone and smiled, clearly pleased with herself. "My friend Anthony had a cancellation. If you hurry, he'll get you in immediately." She smoothed her hands down the front of her dress. "I love when serendipity plays out before my eyes."

He glanced over at Mary. She threw up her hands and

laughed. "You're determined to give me a wedding and you've done it."

"Never underestimate my obsession with details." He offered his arm. "Come along. Let's take a cab over to Anthony."

"I wish you a magical wedding." Layla handed him a card. "Do text a photo if you have a chance. Mary, you'll be the most beautiful bride in all of Vegas."

Of that, he had no doubt.

Anthony was not as he'd imagined. Lance had pictured him slight and perfectly coiffed. Instead, he was a large man dressed in an old-fashioned suit, with a sleek layer of sweat on his full cheeks. Without fuss, he swept Mary into a chair. For a moment, he simply stared at her reflection in the mirror, like an art connoisseur at a gallery opening. Finally, he placed both hands in her hair and fanned it out over his arms. "It has to be up. Yes?" Anthony's voice was low and resonant, like an opera singer on his lunch break.

"Sure." Mary pulled the tiara out of her purse. "And there's this."

Anthony nodded in obvious approval before turning to Lance. "You, young man, have to go now. We'll send her back to the hotel when she's finished."

"Yes sir." Without thinking, he leaned down to give Mary a kiss on the forehead. At the same moment, she tilted her head upward. Lips landed on lips. Like magnets, they lingered for a second, then two. He must move away. Now. Yes, now. But her mouth was soft and pliant. She tasted slightly of strawberries.

She pulled away first.

Embarrassed, he stepped backward and bumped into the salon chair next to him. Thankfully, it was empty. "I'll see you back at the hotel."

"See you soon." She fiddled with the tiara in her lap without meeting his gaze.

No eye contact after a kiss? Not a good sign for removing Exhibit G from the medical manual.

It wasn't until he was nearly to their hotel that he remembered one final detail. They needed rings. "Take me to the finest jewelry store on the strip."

The cab driver took the toothpick out of his mouth and glanced at him in the rearview mirror. "Finest or least crooked?"

"Least crooked."

Several hours later, Lance prowled around the hotel suite bedroom like a nervous animal. Mary was in the other room, supposedly slipping into her dress, according to her text. He'd been in the shower when she'd returned from the salon and she'd told him not to come out until she was ready. While he dressed in his best suit, he could hear her moving around in the other room and the crinkle of tissue paper.

From outside the bedroom, Mary called out to him. "Have a drink. Your pacing is making me nervous."

He walked over to the door. "What's taking so long?"

"I'm almost ready. I had to call someone to help me zip up the dress."

"I could've done that."

"And break tradition?"

He took her advice and poured a scotch from the minibar, then stood at the window and looked out over Las Vegas. Haze, smog, and sunshine made the sky orange with hints of an impending apocalypse. He downed his drink and waited to be summoned. For the third time in as many minutes, he felt for the engagement ring in his jacket pocket. Still there. A smug smile curved his mouth. The ring was magical, elegant and sophisticated, with a princess diamond surrounded by tiny diamonds.

She'd think it was too big, but he didn't care. He wanted her to have a ring that matched her.

"All right, you can come out now," Mary called to him.

Nerves rumbled through his stomach. Why did this moment feel like the most important one of his life?

He entered the living room. Mary stood by the windows. Behind her, storm clouds gathered in an angry promise of rain. She clasped her hands together in front of her chest as her mouth twitched in a nervous smile. "I'm ready, finally."

Lance stared at her, unable to move, stunned by her splendor. She shone with a light so bright it crippled him.

"Do you like the dress?" she asked.

He nodded. Unshed tears choked his voice. Even if he could speak, how would he ever convey her loveliness? The dress was simple with skinny straps and lacy material that flowed gently from her waist to the floor. Her hair was up in a complicated twist paired with the tiara. Subtle makeup enhanced her delicate bone structure and almond shaped eyes.

"I think the dress cost a lot of money. She wouldn't tell me how much. It's simple but very pretty, don't you think?" Mary's voice had a tinny quality as the words tumbled from her mouth.

He drew closer and could see that she trembled.

"I'm suddenly petrified," she said.

God, how he loved her. Nothing in his life had prepared him for the agony of this love that ripped open his chest and consumed every piece of his soul.

He staggered toward her, like a drunk man. There was no poetry inside him that could do her justice.

Regardless, Mary needed words. She craved them. If he were to be worthy of her, he must find them. They must be epic. Like the kiss on New Year's Eve, they must startle her out of her sleeping state so that she might see him.

He drew in a deep breath. Outside the window, purple clouds sped across the sky. For a split second a sliver of sunlight appeared. Certainty washed over him. He must tell her the truth of his heart.

"I've been all over the world and have had the privilege to see the most magnificent works of art known to man. But never in my life have I seen anything as exquisite as you."

Mary's bottom lip trembled. "Thank you."

He dropped to one knee.

She jerked and stumbled backward, clearly startled. "What're you doing?"

Lance took the ring box from his jacket. "I have to tell you the truth. If there were no baby, I would still want to marry you. I'm in love with you. I've loved you so long now that I can't remember the time before you. It's you, only you, that I want. I know there's a chance you might never love me back. Nonetheless, I'm a risk taker. I'm betting on us. I believe after a time you'll come to see I'm the man to trust with your heart." He opened the box and presented the ring. Her eyes widened as the diamonds sparkled under the light. "Say you'll be my wife."

"This isn't the deal. This isn't what we agreed on."

"If you don't love me by the time the baby comes, then I'll let you go. We'll get divorced as planned."

"I'm broken. You know that."

"I don't care how broken you are. Everyone is in one way or another, including me. If we take our broken pieces and put them together, we can become whole. An impenetrable team. A perfect puzzle, still with cracks, but formed into something profound. Let me love you back together."

"Oh, Lance." She looked up to the ceiling and then back to him. Her hands clasped and unclasped. She sucked in a deep breath like a woman about to fall prey to a riptide. "You won't want me by the end of this pregnancy. There are things about me you don't know. Decisions I've made that might change your mind."

"Nothing, no man or act of God or decision from your past, will ever change my mind. I love you and I always will."

"You have to know the odds are stacked against us. The last thing I want is to hurt you, but I know deep down I will."

"I've made a fortune betting on the dark horse, the outlier. I'll take my chances."

"I might be your darkest horse yet."

"You're my dark horse, Mary Hansen. The finest of my choices." He took her left hand. "Will you marry me?"

"Promise me you'll forgive me if I hurt you."

"I promise."

"Then, yes."

After securing their marriage license, they had the driver take them over to the wedding chapel. When they arrived and went inside, they were greeted by a receptionist, given a plastic-coated number—fifty-four—and told to wait in the lobby with the other couples. While they waited, he looked around at the other couples. Some, like them, wore traditional wedding attire. Others were in street clothes and seemed to have consumed more than their share of libations, given the giggles and inappropriate displays of affection.

"Does that mean we're the fifty-fourth couple of the day or week or month?" Mary whispered.

"Week? Maybe? I don't know."

For the first time since he'd given it to her, she held up her hand to gaze at the ring. "Tell me this is a fake diamond. Please."

He shook his head. "Does that sound like me?"

"This must've cost a fortune. You don't have money to just toss around on gigantic rings. It's irresponsible."

He didn't say anything. The money discussion would come later.

She continued to look at her hand. "I can't help but love it. I'm enamored, which goes to show you how shallow I am."

"It looks nice on your hand. I knew it would."

She spread her hand over his knee. "My mom always said I had princess hands. When I was a kid, that was the only pretty thing about me."

"Impossible."

"No. Imagine skinny as a rail, buck teeth, and thick glasses."

"Sounds adorable."

She pushed her hand into his chest. "You're hopeless."

He played with her dangling earring, then brushed his fingertips down the silky skin of her neck. "I wish the whole world could see you right now."

"I just wish my mom could see me."

"I wish that too. I wish my dad was here. I miss him so much sometimes it's debilitating."

"It just hits you out of nowhere," she said. "And it's like the first time."

"Yes."

They looked into each other's eyes and an understanding passed between them. *This is true intimacy between two people. This is what I've looked for all my life.* How could she not know this was love?

"My dad would make a big fuss over you," Lance said. "He loved women."

"I would've have loved to meet him." She grabbed his hands. "But I know what a great man he was because I know you."

Their number was called.

"Let's do this." He stood and then pulled her to her feet and escorted her across the room and into the chapel.

Elvis, dressed in a white suit, stood at the front of the room. More specifically, this was Elvis after he'd eaten too many peanut butter and banana sandwiches. Mary squeezed his hand. "I'm nervous suddenly."

"Don't be. Elvis won't bite," Lance said.

"Come on up here, little lady." He *sounded* like Elvis. He looked like Elvis. Fake Elvis, fake marriage. *Fake it until you make it.* "Let's get you two hitched and off to the fun part." Elvis gestured for them to meet him in the front. A plump woman with pink hair sat to the side, knitting furiously. "That there's my wife, Melva. She's your witness and photographer."

Next, Elvis looked over their marriage license. "All good. Come this way so we can get a few photos."

Melva set aside her knitting and grabbed a camera. She had them pose in front of the arch in various positions. "I'll get these out to your email lickety-split," Melva said.

Elvis cleared his throat. "Dearly beloved, we are gathered here today..."

Five minutes later, they were married.

4

Mary

THE CAR MADE its way down the Las Vegas strip under a stormy sky. Mary was blind to the scenery. Instead, her mind replayed Lance's earlier confession. He loved her. He wanted a real marriage. A happily ever after.

At first, her heart had hummed with joy. Until the memory of what she'd done brought her crashing back to reality.

What would happen if she told him the truth? How would she even say it? *I lied to you about one of the most important decisions a person ever makes. I tricked you into getting me pregnant.* His feelings would rapidly change when he saw her for what she really was. A desperate, bitter, liar. She *must* tell him. It was the right thing to do, and the only solution to stifling his ridiculous notion that he loved her.

She accepted Lance's hand to help her to get out of the back of the car and waited under the awning of the hotel while he tipped the driver. A gust of wind rustled the skirt of her gown.

The distant sound of thunder caused her to shiver. Around her, people passed to enter the lobby of the hotel, many smiling at her. *Nothing like a woman in a wedding dress to melt the heart of the masses.*

A few minutes later, they walked into their suite. The table had been set for dinner. Tempting aromas of garlic and butter filled the room. Despite the emotional impact of the day, her stomach rumbled.

"I didn't know what you'd feel like, so I ordered a few different items," he said.

A steak, a pasta dish, fried chicken, and a hamburger were lined up on the side table.

"I'm starving," she said.

They sat down to the feast, sampling bits from each plate. They talked and joked about the day's events like it was an ordinary day. In his presence she forgot about everything but him. She could look at him all day in his blue suit that matched his eyes.

When they had their fill, he stood. "Will you dance with me?"

"Dance?"

"I want to dance with you while you're wearing that dress. Please?"

She agreed, reluctantly. The last thing she needed was to feel his arms around her, tempting her, reminding her of the night they'd spent together.

He pushed a button on his phone. Music played from the Bluetooth speaker on one of the side tables. She moved into his arms. "What is this song?"

"Frank Sinatra. 'The Way You Look Tonight'. My mom and dad had it at their wedding. I always thought I'd have it at mine. When I saw you in that dress, I knew it was truly the perfect song for tonight."

What was she going to do about this man? This perfect man. *Tell him what you did.*

"I have something to tell you," she said.

He looked down at her with such hope in his eyes that her courage failed her. She couldn't tell him. Not tonight. Maybe when they got home tomorrow.

"What is it?" he asked.

"Thank you for making this day special. No matter what, we'll be able to tell the baby about our wedding."

"And we'll have photographs." He pulled her closer as they swayed to the music.

She looked up at him. His full mouth curved into a smile. She shivered, remembering what it was like to kiss him. He caught her gaze in his. They stopped moving and simply stared into each other's eyes.

"I'm going to kiss you, unless you say not to," he said.

"I won't say no."

He pulled her even closer and kissed her, gently at first until her arms circled his neck. They kissed until the music stopped. She pulled away, breathless. "I should change," she said.

Lance let her go but reached for his phone. "One more photo before you take off the dress. Just to remember this moment." He made her stand by the window and snapped pictures with his phone. Finally, he relented and let her leave to change.

In the bedroom, she realized she couldn't get out of the dress without help and called out to him. He showed up in the doorway with a scotch in his hand. He'd taken off his jacket and tie and had rolled up his sleeves. Her breath caught. Had there ever been a more gorgeous man? She doubted it.

"What can I do for you?" Lance leaned against the doorway, his eyelids lowered to half-mast. He'd looked that way the night she'd danced for him on the table.

"I need you to unzip the dress."

"Ah yes. Another reason to thank Layla."

She smiled as she turned around to show him the back. "I think you have a crush on Layla." Earlier, she'd noted how he'd looked at the wedding shop owner with admiration. It had bothered her, wakened that awful monster inside her that fed on insecurity and distrust.

"There's only one woman I have a crush on," he whispered in her ear. His fingertips brushed her shoulders and down the length of her arms.

She shivered.

He unzipped the dress, torturing her by caressing the freed skin with his thumb as he made his way down her back. When it was completely unzipped, she turned back to him. "Thank you."

"Not so fast." He placed his fingers under the spaghetti straps and slid them from her shoulders. "You'll need me to help you with this next part." He peeled the dress from her torso until it pooled at her feet. "Hold on to my neck and I'll lift you."

She did as he asked. He lifted her up and out of the dress, before setting her on the ground. The dress crumpled to the floor, like a weary ragdoll. Mary's hands dropped to her sides. Naked now, other than undergarments and the high-heeled sandals, she stared back at him.

"Jesus. I thought you looked good in the dress." He drew her to him and ran a finger along the lacy edges of her bra. "You know how badly I've wanted to see you like this again?"

If he wanted her, she would let him take her. Just tonight. She'd have him for one more night. Tomorrow she would tell him the truth.

She looked up at him. "Do you remember that night? All the things you did to me?"

His eyes glittered in the dim room. "Hell yes. I remember everything. Every single moment." He traced her collarbone with his mouth. She gasped when his fingers unhooked her bra. "Do you?"

"Yes." She slid her bra off and tossed it toward the dress.

He put his fingers into her bun and pulled the pins loose. Her hair cascaded around them. He tugged her closer. Instead of kissing her mouth like she thought he would, he pressed his lips to the soft skin under her right ear. "Do you want me to do it all over again?"

Oh God.

With his free hand, he hovered just above the nipple of her left breast. Her swollen breasts ached for his touch. He spoke hoarsely into her ear. "Do you want me to tell you or should I show you?"

"Show me."

He lifted her into his arms and strode across the room. At the bed, he set her down with what she suspected was great restraint. He slid the sandals from her feet and gazed down at her. "Christ, you're gorgeous."

"Take off your clothes," she said. "Or I'll do it for you."

"You stay where you are." Within seconds, he'd discarded his shirt, pants, and socks. He joined her on the bed.

She ran her hands down his muscular torso. Yes, just as she remembered.

He groaned and pulled her under him. "You want to know what haunts me? The memory of your face the first time I made you..."

Her mouth went dry. She flicked her upper lip with her tongue.

"Do you remember the sounds you made?" he asked.

She nodded, flushing. Anyone within a fifty-mile radius probably heard her.

He pressed his finger against her mouth. "I remember what that wicked tongue of yours did to me. And the way your back arched, and your soft skin and hard thighs and perfect breasts. None of which a man could forget anytime soon." He traced a finger from the hollow of her throat to just above her left breast. "I remember what you looked like the second time and the third time too." His fingers stopped at the pulse in her neck. "I remember how your pulse raced." He whispered in her ear. "And how wet you were."

"Lance. My God."

"Do you want me to do it again?"

"Yes."

"Tell me. Say it," he said, roughly.

"I want you to do it again. Now. I've had enough words."

5

Lance

AT THE FRONT door of his house, Lance stopped and looked over at his bride. "You ready?"

Mary folded her arms across her chest and offered a stubborn shake of her head. "You're not carrying me inside. Absolutely not."

"Come on. Carrying the bride over the threshold's a tradition."

"Nothing about this union is traditional."

"You can't deny me this. We agreed we were going to have fun. Remember, that's good for the baby."

"Oh, for heaven's sake, *you're* such a baby. Go ahead."

He grinned and swept her up into his arms, kicked the door open with his foot, and stepped into the entryway of his house.

"Welcome home, wife."

"Thank you, husband. Now set me down. I have to pee."

While she used the facilities, he brought her bags and a few boxes in from the car. They'd stopped by her dad's cottage to pick up her clothes and a few other items, including a stack of books. Apparently, the rest of them were in storage up in Oregon. Some girls collected shoes. This girl collected books. If his plan worked and she fell in love with him, they were going to have to turn one of the empty rooms into a library. He could have a rolling ladder installed so she could stack them all the way to the ceiling.

On the drive home from the airport, they'd agreed to announce their marriage in person, starting with his mother, Doc, Brody, and Kara. His mother, coincidently, had asked him to come to dinner. When he'd mentioned bringing Mary, she'd politely agreed. If she only knew why. Her father and Flora were due to arrive back from Oregon in the morning. Mary had arranged to have breakfast with them at the cottage. She didn't add that Lance would be by her side.

The Dogs would have to wait until tomorrow.

By the time he'd lugged the last suitcase into the house, Mary was in the kitchen drinking water from a glass. She belonged in a kitchen like this one, refined and elegant.

"Where do you want to sleep?" he asked.

She almost choked on her water. "Sleep?"

"My room or the guest room? I mean, after last night, I thought you might like to sleep with me." He slid next to her and took her into his arms. "I'd like you to sleep with me."

"I don't know if that's a good idea." Her voice sounded hollow and shaky.

"Why?"

"Because...because I don't know how I feel."

"Then, I'll put your things in the guestroom. Just know the invitation's always open." He pecked her on the lips. "You'll fall in love with me yet, Mary Hansen."

———

When he turned up Doc's driveway for dinner, he looked over at Mary. "Remember why we're doing this. Don't be scared."

"I feel sick to my stomach. I've just never been good at lying."

"Let me do the talking," Lance said.

"Are you good at lying?"

"Not particularly."

They laughed as he parked next to his mother's sedan.

Mary shivered beside him and let out a long sigh. "I don't want to go in," she said.

"Me neither."

"Let's just get it over with."

His mother was at the stove when they entered the kitchen from the back patio. Since his mother's marriage to Doc last year, she'd managed to redecorate the house, including a new kitchen. She'd gone for a traditional look, with white cabinets and light granite countertops.

"Welcome, Mary," his mother said, hugging them both in turn. "It's not often one of my boys comes over for Saturday dinner, so it's an extra treat to have you. I made soup and a salad. And there's bread from the bakery and pie for dessert."

"Smells great," Lance said.

"Thank you. I'm learning slowly." His mother wasn't much of a cook. Flora had made every meal for their family for forty years while his mother was busy saving the world as a human rights lawyer.

"Good for you." Lance stepped nearer to the stove. On the counter were empty boxes of premade soup. "Mom, making soup doesn't mean opening a box."

"It does when I make it." She laughed and tapped her manicured nails on the countertop. "Who has time for cooking when there's so many books to read."

"I agree completely," Mary said. "Speaking of which, I brought you something." She pulled the latest paperback of his mother's favorite mystery series out of her bag. "Just came in today."

His mother's face lit up. "I cannot wait. Did you know there are rumors this might be the last of the series?"

"I'd heard that, yes. I'm hoping it's just gossip," Mary said. "I can't imagine life without this series to look forward to."

"Oh my gosh, me too," his mother said.

He stopped listening as the conversation veered into further discussion of books he'd never heard of. He wandered over to the beverage refrigerator and grabbed a beer.

Kara and Brody arrived, carrying a bouquet of flowers and several bottles of wine.

"What's Mary doing here?" Brody whispered in his ear as they slapped each other on the back in way of greeting.

"She's my date," Lance said.

"Dude, you don't have to save every stray cat," Brody said.

Lance ignored him, hugging Kara instead. "Good to see you."

"You too," Kara said.

The women greeted each other with a hug that wasn't a hug, as no actual body parts touched. He said a silent prayer. *Please God, don't let Mary get hurt.*

Doc arrived from the garage entrance, carrying a bag of groceries. A baguette teetered and fell from the bag. Brody snatched it before it hit the ground. Lance took a moment to study his brother. Since his retirement, he'd been down, but he seemed more like his old self tonight. He bustled behind the counter, giving his mom a big hug that lifted her partially off the ground and shaking Doc's hand with his usual vigor.

"Good of you to bring the wine," Doc said when he spotted the wine on the counter. "And you decanted it for me?" The corks had been removed and stuck back in half way.

"I cannot tell a lie," Brody said. "Kara did it."

"Good girl." Doc kissed Kara's cheek, then turned to give Mary a quick squeeze. "You both look beautiful tonight." His eyes narrowed, like he was suspicious. "Glowing."

"Who wants a glass besides Doc?" Brody asked from behind the island.

"I've got a beer," Lance said.

"You boys seem as nervous as Mexican jumping beans," his mother said. "Like you were when you were young and had done something naughty."

Lance peeled the label from his beer and avoided eye contact.

"Just a small bit for me," Mary said, beside him. They'd agreed she wouldn't make herself conspicuous by refusing wine. This night was about announcing a marriage, not a baby.

"Me too," Kara said.

When everyone had a drink, Doc invited them into the dining room. They all sat while he helped his wife deliver bowls of soup. Next to Lance, Mary trembled. Under the table, he set a hand on her knee. She placed her cold hand over his. As soon as his mother sat, he would come out with the news. Get it over with.

His brother beat him to the punch. As usual.

Brody clinked his glass with a fork and cleared his throat. "Kara's pregnant."

"Really?" his mother asked. "Am I dreaming?"

"No dream, Mom. It's for real," Brody said.

"Well done," Doc said. "Well done."

"When are you due?" his mother asked.

"Well, it's very early still," Kara said. "We shouldn't even be sharing since it's so early, but Brody couldn't wait."

"Let's just say we had a good New Year's Eve," Brody said.

"Brody!" Kara flushed pink. "End of September. Around the twenty-fourth."

"We're so psyched," Brody said.

How was this possible? Despite himself, given the circumstances, a jolt of joy surged through him. They would have babies at the same time. Cousins who would grow up together.

"That's great news," Lance said. "I've always wanted to be an uncle."

Under the table, he slipped Mary her ring. It was time.

"We have some news too. I know this will come as a bit of a shock." He wrapped his arm around Mary's shoulder. "We got married yesterday in Vegas."

"What did you say?" Brody's face had darkened in an instant. "Married?"

"Married? In Vegas." Kara asked.

Mary's shoulders stiffened. He held her tighter.

His mother appeared frozen in shock, with her glass of wine in midair.

Doc recovered faster than his wife. "Well, yes, it's a surprise, but congratulations."

"Have you been dating?" his mother asked.

Here come the lies. "We spent a lot of time together, you know, getting the store ready to open. A friendship grew into something more," Lance said. *Come on, buddy. Now's the time to pull out all the stops. Convince them this is the right thing.* His brother's intense stare threatened to wither him. He turned to his mother instead.

"We were together every day at the store and that would turn into having dinner together or ordering take out and talking for hours." All true.

He was surprised when Mary took up part of the story.

"As the months went on, we became closer and closer. Before I knew it, Lance had become my best friend. Not just here in town, but ever." Her voice shook like a student giving her first speech. "Since losing my child, I've struggled with depression." He kept his arm wrapped around her. "Books have been the only thing that truly gave me joy. Until Lance."

Was that true? He took his arm from around her shoulder to get a better view of her face.

"One day, right after the store opened, I dropped by to check on her. She was with a customer, so I stopped to watch, fascinated by how she always finds the perfect book for anyone who comes in. The customer was this older man. He told Mary how he'd lost his wife right after Thanksgiving and was having a hard time facing Christmas without her. Could Mary suggest some books that might distract him? She asked him a series of questions. What kind of books had he liked when he was a kid? Did he like thrillers or mysteries? That kind of thing. She took all this time with him, even talking to him about grief and sharing some of her own story. I realized two things in that moment. One, we'd opened more than just a bookstore. Mary makes it a place of healing and compassion. Choosing the right book for a customer makes it personal and God knows we need human connection in a world gone mad." He paused and drank from his water glass. "Second, I realized how deeply I'd fallen for her. I knew there wasn't anything or anyone that would keep me from her if she would have me."

So far, all true.

"But why keep a secret?" his mother asked.

"We just wanted to keep it to ourselves until we knew for sure what it was. Selfishly, I wanted to cement our bond before we involved everyone else."

"Why the sudden marriage?" His mother had her lawyer face on, which scared him.

"We just felt a sudden urgency to be married," Lance said.

"I don't get it," Brody said. "You got married without me there? Without Mom?"

"We didn't want to make a big fuss about it," Lance said.

"That's not like you," his mother said. "You'd want Brody and the Dogs there."

Lance glanced over at Kara, hoping for support. She nodded, understanding. "Maybe Mary didn't want a wedding. Not all women do."

"I'd already had one," Mary said. "It was an ordeal I didn't want to do again."

Brody's voice held the intensity of a rain cloud about to burst. "You were my best man. I was supposed to be yours."

"Honey," Kara said. Her words were unspoken but clear just the same. *It's not about you.*

Brody didn't take the hint. "Why didn't you tell me? Or the Dogs? We tell each other everything."

"I didn't need everyone weighing in with their opinion," Lance said. "Sometimes you guys can be overbearing. Especially with me. Plus, you've had a lot on your mind. I didn't want to bother you with this."

To his utter shock, Brody's eyes turned glassy with tears. "You wouldn't have bothered me."

"Brody, it's…it's complicated," Lance said.

"This is our fault," Kara said. "You didn't want everyone weighing in because you thought we'd disapprove." Before he could answer, Kara continued. "We've not been particularly welcoming to Mary. Isn't that right, Lance?"

"That's right," Lance said.

"It's as much my fault if not more," Mary said. "I acted terribly. My dad is all I have left. All I *had* left. Now I have Lance."

"And all of us," Kara said.

Brody's piercing gaze skirted back and forth between Lance and Mary. "Why not an engagement? Why not a proper wedding where your family and friends could celebrate with you?"

Mary shifted and knocked her bowl with her arm. Orange soup splashed onto the white tablecloth. The clatter of her fork against a water glass punctuated the tension that hung over the table. "We didn't have a proper wedding because I'm pregnant."

Lance's heart thudded. This was not the plan. No one moved or seemed to breathe for at least ten seconds.

"What did you say?" Brody asked.

"I said, I'm going to have a baby, but there are complications because of my health," Mary said, sounding near tears.

Lance glared at Brody from across the table.

Why couldn't you just leave it alone?

"You're right, Brody. Lance deserved a wedding with you

and the Dogs and all the family there. But there was a sense of urgency because I have an incompetent cervix." Her voice broke. "Which is why Meme was born at twenty-two weeks."

Brody's intense stare was replaced by one of confusion. However, the two medical professionals and his mother understood what an incompetent cervix meant.

"I'm so sorry," Kara said.

"I needed insurance." Mary swiped tears from the corners of her eyes. "Or risk losing the baby."

Mary crying was enough to undo him. Why did Brody have to make this harder? "Not that it's anyone's business, but that's why we decided to get married right away without any fuss. Mary's health and the health of the baby are more important than a wedding. I'm sorry if it's disappointing I did something without group consensus, Brody. But really, this is between Mary and me. I intend to do whatever it takes to take care of her and the baby."

His mother tented her hands over her chest, almost like a prayer. "You're absolutely right. A wedding is one event. A marriage and family are a lifetime. We're all in shock, that's all." She gave a tenuous smile. "After all, we didn't even know you were dating."

Lance moved his water glass an inch toward the left. The condensation dampened his fingers and the tablecloth. He'd love to toss the whole thing against the wall, right next to Brody's fat head. His brother had to accept he wasn't privy to his every thought or choice or action. He was a man, not a little boy. Somehow that seemed to be lost on his big brother.

"Whatever you need, we're here to support you," Doc said. "We're delighted to welcome you to the family, Mary. And two grandchildren. Cousins to grow up together. How special."

Kara nodded. "It's wonderful, really. We're happy if you're happy. Lance, you're in a little trouble for not inviting us to Vegas to at least be witnesses, but I'll get over it. Especially since you've now made me a sister and an aunt."

Doc reached over to Mary and patted her forearm. "With proper care you can have a full-term pregnancy. Jackson and I will make sure to find you a specialist in the city."

"I always wanted a big extended family. I was an only child without a single cousin. Do you know your due date?" Kara's smile from across the table warmed him and soothed some of the sting of his brother's reaction.

Mary's mouth lifted in a slight smile. "I believe it's around the same time as yours. End of September."

"No way? And Maggie and Violet are just a bit ahead of us. All the kids can grow up together. We're so blessed." Kara's eyes misted. "I'm sorry. My emotions are all over the place already."

"It's an amazing turn of events," Lance said.

"Yes, it is," Kara said.

He should have known Kara would come through for him. Kara had suffered great losses. She understood the broken parts in others.

He looked over at his mother. She granted him an indulgent smile before turning to Mary. "Have you told Flora and your father?"

"Tomorrow morning," Mary said.

"They'll be as happy as we are about the baby," Doc said.

"Of course they will be," his mother said. "As am I. Three grandchildren at once? It's more than I could hope for. I can see it already. I'll have to fight Flora for time with them." She raised her glass. "To Lance and Mary and babies."

Brody raised his glass, but his eyes maintained the familiar flinty sheen of the famous quarterback looking for a receiver in the end zone.

My life. Not his. I answer to my wife now, not my bossy big brother.

6

Mary

AFTER DINNER, Mary escaped to the bathroom, then slipped out to the patio for a respite. Exhausted and unaccustomed to spending so much time with other people, she longed for a warm bed and a good book. Instead, she stood near the railing and breathed the cool, damp air into her chest. A layer of thick fog obscured the view of both sea and sky. Lights from town and the other houses that decorated the hillside twinkled through the mist. An occasional hum of an engine penetrated the silence. On a winter evening in sleepy Cliffside Bay, most residents were nestled indoors. Even the noisy seagulls rested.

Like Honor and Zane's house, Doc owned one of the older houses in town. These homes perched on the hillside like stairsteps, with the view of the ocean as the primary architectural goal.

When she'd first come to Cliffside Bay, she'd been immediately smitten by the natural beauty of the landscape. Having lived on the coast in Oregon with its jutting monster rocks and rough surf, she hadn't thought the northern coast of California would suit her. Like many assumptions, including her initial idea of Lance Mullen, she was incorrect.

She'd expected Lance's view of her to be tainted by the others. He would come to her already disliking her. However, when she'd first met him at her father's wedding, Lance had appeared to be without prejudice. He'd stayed near her during the reception, even sitting with her at dinner and, later, asking her to dance. She'd presumed at the time that Flora had bullied him into babysitting her. Flora wasn't the type to leave something to chance. No, she would make sure witchy Mary didn't ruin the wedding by assigning the nicest man in the world to keep a close watch on her.

To this day, she wasn't sure if that assumption had been true. Regardless, Lance was kind to her that night. He was funny and charming in a quiet way. Her preferred type of person. One couldn't trust the most gregarious person in the room. Charisma didn't equal character.

Lance Mullen. How could she have known when she'd first met him at her father's wedding that he would become so integral to her life?

She'd had no intention of confessing to the pregnancy. When she'd seen how upset Brody was, she'd felt compelled to tell the truth. Once again, it came back to her lies. If she wasn't careful, she could cause a rift between the brothers. She would never forgive herself it that happened.

The door to the patio creaked, interrupting her thoughts. Kara stepped outside, carrying a blanket. "It's cold out here. I thought you might want this for your shoulders."

Mary thanked her and took the blanket, grateful for the warmth. As overheated as she'd been earlier when under interrogation, her stint on the patio had chilled her. "I didn't realize how cold I was."

"The dampness will do it," Kara said. "My mom always said it seeps into your bones."

"My mom hated the rain when we lived in Oregon," Mary said. "She always said she preferred the snow of the east coast over the endless gray."

"She had a point." Kara flipped a light switch and the gas fire pit came to life. "Want to sit?"

Mary agreed and pulled one of the chairs out from under the awning. Kara did the same.

When they were settled, Kara warmed her hands near the fire. "I'm not one to mince words," Kara said. "I'm sorry we got off to such a bad start. I should have tried harder to get to know you. I had no idea about...what you've been through."

"It's my fault," Mary said. "You and Brody were nice from the beginning and I acted awful. There's no excuse, really, other than I panicked. I thought I was going to lose my dad too. After everything, he was the only one I had left."

"I get it. I lost everyone I ever loved when I was forced to leave it all behind and move to a place I'd never been, knowing no one. If I'd had just one person left from my old life, I would've clung to them with everything I had."

The back of Mary's throat ached. What was it about being understood that made her want to cry?

"Lance is special to me. I always wanted a brother," Kara said. "It goes without saying that I want only the best for him. I've hoped and prayed for Lance to find his soulmate."

"You think we're soulmates?" Mary asked.

"Don't you?"

Mary studied Kara's profile. Shadows thrown from the fire made it impossible to decipher any subtext.

"I don't know if I believe in soulmates," Mary said.

A light came on from inside the house, illuminating the far end of the patio.

"The boys must be having a cigar," Kara said. "That light is Doc's study." Kara gestured toward the newly lit window just as someone opened it from the inside. "They don't want Janet to know they're smoking." Kara laughed. "She does, of course."

The faint scent of cigar smoke drifted out to them. Mary was about to ask Kara how she was feeling when Brody's emotionally charged voice carried out the window.

"You're in denial, man. She trapped you into this for your money."

"Give me a break," Lance said. "She doesn't even care about money, unless it's to buy more books."

"There's no way you love her. This was a one-night stand after a drunken New Year's Eve. Are you sure it's even yours?"

"Don't be an ass."

"Does she know you have twenty million dollars in bank?" Brody asked.

Twenty million dollars?

"This is a fifty-fifty state, you idiot. She could get half of your money. Half of the money you lived in a rathole for years to make."

"She's my wife. I love her. She's going to have my child. *Your* niece or nephew. What's the matter with you?

"I'm looking out for you! Dad would want me to." Brody's voice had raised to the level that half the neighborhood could probably hear him. "After what happened back in New York do really expect me to just stand aside and let another manipulative woman ruin your life? She could get half your house, which is on *my* property."

"I'm going to kill him," Kara said under her breath.

Mary couldn't move, stuck to the chair, barely breathing.

"I don't know what's wrong with him," Kara said. "He's protective of Lance. He doesn't trust people."

Mary managed to croak out a few words. "I didn't even know Lance had that kind of money."

Kara stared at her. "You didn't?"

"I had no idea."

Kara stood and held out her hand. "Come on. I'm getting you

inside. It's time to go home. I need to have a few words with my husband."

"I'll just stay here until Lance comes out." Wild boars from Africa would have to chase her back inside.

"I'll send him out with your bag." Kara knelt by Mary's chair. "Brody's overreacting. He's not good with surprises or change."

Mary wiped her eyes of the stupid tears that blinded her. "It's fine. I know it's my fault. If I'd acted differently in the beginning, things would be better between all of us."

"That's no excuse for him to act like this. I'm sorry. Truly."

"I'll be fine. Just, please, get Lance." *I just want Lance.*

"Okay. I'll call you tomorrow. Maybe we can have lunch?"

"Sure." Her mouth had turned to stone.

After Kara disappeared inside, Mary stared into the fire and let the tears come. Soon, Lance came out, carrying her bag.

He immediately fell to his knees beside her. "Kara told me you guys heard all that. I'm sorry."

"Can we go home?" She gave her eyes one final swipe, knowing but not caring that her makeup was probably smeared all over her face.

He held out his hand. "I have ice cream."

"What kind?" She let him help her to her feet.

"Salted caramel."

"No chocolate?"

"We can stop at the store. Whatever you want, I'll get you."

"Rocky road?"

"Consider it done."

Mary changed into soft cotton pajamas and washed her face before joining Lance in the living room. Two bowls of ice cream waited on the coffee table. He'd changed into sweatpants and a long-sleeved t-shirt. The room smelled slightly of his cologne and an orange blossom scented candle.

Night now, the room had transformed from a light and airy beach house to a cozy retreat. Outside, the sea presented black and silent. The gas fireplace and several candles cast shadows in the dim room. Classical acoustic guitar played from hidden speakers.

He patted the spot next to him on the couch. She settled in, letting him drape a soft cashmere blanket over her legs. He handed her the bowl of rocky road and a spoon.

"You want to talk about it?" he asked.

"Not especially."

He didn't push further. They ate from the bowls of ice cream and watched the fire.

"That was harder than I thought it would be," she said, finally. "Hearing how much he distrusts me."

"I'm sorry he hurt you." Lance's voice sounded hoarse.

A shouting match with your brother Snape could do that to a man. *Snape?* Not quite right for Brody, but it would do for now.

"Tomorrow with Flora and my dad might be worse," she said. "And now we're going to have to tell them about the baby. Now that's it's out with one set of parents, we have to tell the others."

"Flora will be excited about the baby."

"I've blown it with her too," Mary said. *Tainted.*

"They'll all come around. You'll see."

"And if they don't?"

"You have me." He put his empty bowl on the coffee table and draped an arm around the back of the couch so that he faced her. "You have my word. I'll always be here for you."

"What about if we divorce? Do you think they'll try and take the baby from me?" There. She'd said it. Biggest fear. Worst case scenario.

"Over my dead body." He played with the fringe on the blanket that covered her lap. "No one will have anything to say about this baby but you and me. No matter what the future holds for us, when it comes to our baby, we're a team. You can trust me."

"I can't lose another one."

"You won't. I'm not going to let anything happen to either one of you." He narrowed his eyes and looked up at the ceiling. She waited, assuming he had something to add. Instead, he looked back at her and smiled. "Eat your ice cream."

She ate another bite. The velvety dark chocolate soothed the back of her throat. She rested her head against his shoulder, a habit she'd formed in less than forty-eight hours. Lance was getting to her. He had her believing that she could trust him. If it weren't that there was a huge lie between them, maybe they had a chance.

The fact that he was worth so much money would only make matters worse. Once she told him what she'd done, he would think Brody was right. Right now, he didn't think her capable of lies, but he didn't know her.

I was drunk. Maybe that gives me a pass?

It wouldn't. Nothing could save this. She placed her hand over her flat stomach.

"I had no idea you were mega rich," she said. "Why didn't you tell me?"

"Yeah, about that." He ran his fingers through his hair like she sometimes did after wearing a tight ponytail for too long. "I didn't want you to know in case it scared you off the plan."

"Honestly, it might have. I don't want you to ever think this is about money for me," she said.

"Don't you think I know that?" He took her empty bowl and set it on the coffee table next to his, then placed his hand on her thigh. "I see you exactly as you are."

She took a second to gather herself. *Tell him what you did. Then he'll know how awful you really are.*

"But Lance, I can't do this."

"What?"

"Keep sleeping with you. It's not right and it's confusing."

"Are you mistaking confusion for feelings? You can't possibly respond to me the way you do and sit there and tell me you feel nothing for me."

"It's just sex for me. Nothing more." God would strike her dead for her lies. Or He should anyway.

Lance stood and went to the fireplace. With his back to her, he spoke quietly. "If that's all it is, then I agree. We should stop."

"I'm sorry, Lance. But I don't want what you want."

He whirled around to look at her. "But why? Can't you see who *I* am? Can't you see I would never hurt you?"

I see exactly. You don't see the monster I am.

"It's not you," she said. "This is about who I am. I can't do this. I don't *want* to do this."

His shoulders sagged. "I don't know why you're actively resisting a gift like this. For as long as I live, I'll never understand it."

"It's just that...there's something I should tell you."

"Stop. I get it. You don't love me, and you think you never will. I'm going to bed. Don't forget we have Flora and Dax in the morning." With that, he left the room. She heard his footsteps trudge up the stairs. When his bedroom door slammed shut, she let the tears come, sobbing silently into the blanket.

7

Lance

THEY ARRIVED AT Flora and Dax's the next morning a little after ten. Before he rang the doorbell, he looked over at Mary. She looked urban yet feminine in loose jeans and a pink sweater. "You remember the script?" he asked.

"Yes, you?"

"All I have to do is tell the truth, but yours might be harder to remember since it's made up."

"Lance." She placed a cold hand on his arm. "I'm sorry about last night."

"You already said that." Once during an awkward breakfast and once on the way over. This made three times. "It's okay. You ready?"

"I guess so." She sounded soft and sad, like her pink sweater.

He rested his chin on the top of her head and gave her a quick squeeze. "No matter what, I always have your back. Now, let's get this over with." He rang the doorbell.

Mary brought one hand to her mouth, like she was going to be sick.

The door flew open, revealing Flora, who greeted them with a delighted smile. "Lance, what're you doing here?"

"This and that," he said.

She looked at him and then back at Mary with a suspicious glint in her eyes. Flora never missed anything when it came to either of the Mullen brothers. As children, they couldn't even think about doing something naughty or she'd have them upstairs in their rooms thinking instead about the consequences of their actions.

"We have some news, Lance said.

"News? Intriguing." Flora asked them inside, running a hand through her salt and pepper curls. "We just arrived. The plane was late out of Portland this morning. Terrible fog. Dax is bringing in the bags." She grabbed Lance into a hug. "You look terrible."

"I do?"

"The five o'clock shadow makes you look like a homeless person." Her mouth pursed with disapproval. "Or a criminal."

"That sentiment seems to be going around," Lance said with a secret wink to Mary. She missed it, staring at her hands, obviously too nervous to heed his teasing.

"Mary, you look very well," Flora said as she patted Mary awkwardly on the shoulder. *Oh, brother, Flora. You can do better than that.*

"You as well," Mary said. "You've changed your makeup."

Flora wore her usual red lipstick, but her eyes were made up, quite attractively with a smoky shadow and mascara. "I had a makeover at that overly priced Nordstrom. Your father insisted. I felt like a fool. An old lady sitting on one of those stools with that bright light on my face. Feet couldn't even reach the ground. It was mortifying."

"It looks very nice," Mary said.

"I agree," Lance said.

Dressed in a long tunic and leggings, Flora looked like a society lady rather than the woman who had worked as the Mullens' housekeeper for forty years. Brody and Lance had never been able to convince her to spend any money on clothes. Dax seemed to have broken through.

Dax came in then, wiping his hands on a towel. "Hi sweetheart." He folded Mary into an embrace.

"Lance?" Dax held out his hand and they shook. "Good to see you. Come sit, kids. I just put some coffee on."

"We have something we need to talk to you about," Mary said.

"Have a seat in the living room. I'll get us the coffee," Flora said.

Dax and Flora's cottage was a modest fifteen hundred square feet, all on one level. This was meant to be their part-time home, with the residence up in Oregon as their primary one. Flora had told him in confidence she preferred the small cottage they'd had built to her specifications. Like Lance's home, the kitchen and living room were one big space that opened to a patio. Nestled in the trees, they had a peekaboo view of the ocean.

Decorated in tans and greens that mirrored the various trees outside the windows, the room had a comfortable, casual vibe, with hard and soft edges in compatible dichotomy. Exactly like Flora.

"Forget the coffee," Lance said. "We need to get this over with."

"Over with?" Dax rubbed his chin and looked at his daughter. With a thin, angular face, intelligent eyes, and long fingers, he seemed like the poster child for an oral surgeon. Lance could almost see his photograph on a large billboard. *Need oral surgery? Dr. Dax is your man.*

"Please, Dad, just sit," Mary said.

Dax wore khakis, perfectly pressed, and a white sweater that highlighted his almost all white head of hair and closely trimmed beard. Why did he get to have a beard if Lance couldn't?

Dax and Flora sat together on the couch. Mary and Lance took the loveseat opposite them.

"We have exciting news," Lance said. "Two days ago, Mary and I flew to Vegas and got married."

Everything about Dax's demeanor remained calm, including his steady voice. "You did what?"

Flora's already wild curls seemed to stand on end, like she'd just received electric shock. She looked at Lance as if he'd just confessed to a murder. He knew that look. He was in trouble.

"Why in the name of heaven would you deny your mother a wedding?" Flora asked.

That was the first thing out of her mouth? *Interesting.*

"You've been seeing each other?" Dax asked.

"Yes. For a few months now," Mary said, just above a whisper.

"Why hide?" Flora asked. "That's the question here, young man." Again, directed at him. "Was there a reason you had to sneak behind our backs?"

"We weren't sneaking," Lance said. "It's just that our feelings developed rather fast. We've worked closely together for six months now."

"And we became best friends," Mary said.

"One thing led to the other." Lance took Mary's hand. *Clammy palms.* "Before we knew it, we were in love."

"Married? Mary, I'm confused. Just last month you were telling me how you would never get married again," Dax said.

"Lance wore me down," Mary said. "He's very persuasive."

"That doesn't sound like Lance," Flora said. "He's actually quite passive and allows women to walk right over him."

"Flora," Lance said, horrified. This was the problem with having two mothers. Two pains in the rears to deal with instead of one like most people.

Flora sniffed. "I'm just saying the truth."

Mary scooted closer to him. "That's just the surface. Underneath lies the heart of a lion."

He glanced at her, surprised. Did she mean that?

"He decided he wanted me and came after me hard. A girl can only resist Lance Mullen for so long before she wakes up from her stupor to realize the finest man she's ever met loves her and she can't ever let him go."

A lump in his throat made it impossible to respond. *Please, God. Let her truly believe that one day.*

"I'm enormously pleased," Dax said. "We were already family, but this seals the deal in a whole new fashion."

"I was hoping you'd see it that way, sir," Lance said.

"And Mary, I guess this means you like the Mullens after all," Dax said.

"Dad, don't tease. I'm embarrassed by how I acted. Brody hates me."

"Does your mother know?" Flora asked.

"We told her and Doc last night," Lance said. "And Brody, who acted like a complete ass."

"Don't mind him," Flora said to Mary. "He hates change. Always has."

"I have fences to mend," Mary said.

Flora's eyes fixed on him like two shiny buttons sewn into a scary doll. "Honestly, Lance, how could you deny your mother a wedding? There's only you two boys."

How could he deny Flora a wedding? He hid a smile behind his hand.

"It's not funny, young man," Flora said.

Mary sat forward slightly. "We needed to get married faster than we would've planned."

Flora's penetrating glare was enough to cut the couch in half. "You're pregnant?"

"Mary? Is it true?" Dax's calm expression changed to one of deep concern.

"Yes, and given my health issues, Lance and I thought it best to forget an engagement and a wedding."

"For health insurance," Dax said.

"Right," Mary said. "He wants me to have the best."

Dax nodded, stroking his chin again. "Very practical. But are you both sure? This is a big commitment. And a baby right away? It's a lot to handle."

"Dad, it's fine. We're in love."

Dax looked over at Lance. "You're aware, then, of Mary's past."

"Yes, sir."

"She's been through enough in one lifetime. If you hurt her, I'm not sure I can control what befalls you."

Lance smiled. He liked Dax Hansen enormously in that moment. "I understand, sir. I would never hurt her."

"Losing a child isn't something you can understand, Lance," Flora said. "But the rest of us in this room know only too well. This is not a game."

Lance, irritated now, turned to the woman who had once changed his diapers. "Flora, I'm not sure what your point is, but I'm quite aware of the seriousness of her situation, which is why I insisted we get married right away. I'm not a child."

"I know that." Flora raised one eyebrow. "But you've not always made the best choices."

"As in?"

"The girl in New York, for example," Flora said.

"In the past, I've not had the best taste in women." Why did she have to bring that up in front of Dax? "But I've married the finest one there is."

"I just want what's best for you," Flora said.

You're not acting like it. Soon she would pull out naked baby pictures just to complete his humiliation.

"Dax, I promise to take care of Mary and our baby. I have the means to do so. And the heart to do so. There's nothing for you to worry about in that arena."

"Lance is a good boy," Flora said. "A responsible boy. He's very kind and caring to his mother. They say to look at the way a man treats his mother to know how he'll treat his wife. Not the natural leader his brother is, of course, but he has other good qualities."

"Flora, seriously?" Lance shook his head, amused and embarrassed at the same time.

"And, if she can forgive you for depriving her of a wedding by gaining such a beautiful daughter-in-law, then what can I say?"

Dax laughed. "Flora, dearest, I think you've said enough." He reached across the table and offered him his hand, which Lance shook for the second time that morning. "Welcome to my family, son. I'm very happy for you both. Mary's precious to me. For her to have found a young man of integrity and kindness is a dream come true."

Finally. Someone on his side.

"And a baby." Flora fluffed her curls. "It's about time."

There were about to be more babies than even Flora could handle at one time.

"When's the due date?" Dax asked.

"Third week of September," Mary said. "We shouldn't be telling anyone, but we were forced into it last night."

"Brody kept pushing," Lance said. "Why so sudden? Why so soon? Until Mary had to tell him."

"That sounds like him," Flora said. "Brody's overprotective of his younger brother. And, he's a bull in a china shop if there ever was one."

"But he's still your favorite." Lance said.

"Why would you say that?" Flora's tone was one of great injury. How could he dare question her love of him? "I love you both equally."

"I'm just teasing you," Lance said. "I know I'm your favorite."

"You're most certainly not my favorite. Especially today."

Flora blessed him with one of her signature glares of disapproval.

"When will you see a doctor?" Dax asked.

"Doc recommended we find a specialist in the city," Mary said. "We'll know more about what the plan is after that."

Flora nodded. "We'll go with you to the appointment. It's best to have more than one person there to ask questions. You know how doctors can be."

"Go with us?" Mary gripped his knee.

"The kids might rather do this solo," Dax said. "They don't need us."

"Well, you better call me the minute you know anything," Flora said.

"You'll be our first call," Lance said.

"Terrific. Now, who wants a muffin?" Flora asked. "I made my special wheat germ and carrots recipe."

"I thought that was Kara's recipe?" He *knew* it was Kara's recipe. She'd made it the first morning she worked for the Mullens.

"Kara's recipe? That's rich. As competent as she is, she doesn't make up recipes. That's my department."

Lance smiled. "I'll take two."

"That's my boy," Flora said.

In the evening, Lance joined his friends for their weekly poker game, which had morphed into more like a monthly game. With everyone busy with wives and family, Lance was the only one still available for their weekly game. As usual, they met in Brody's game room. They sat around the poker table in their usual spots. Clockwise, with Brody at twelve, then Zane, Kyle, Lance, and Jackson. Besides Kyle, who always wore designer jeans and trendy sweaters or shirts, the rest of them wore faded jeans and sweatshirts. Minnie, the tuxedo cat who acted like a dog, snoozed on the bar's counter, only occasionally opening her eyes to make sure Brody remained at his place at the table.

He loved these guys. Kyle had named them the Dogs when they'd first started playing poker together back in their college days. What had started as a cheesy joke had become sacred. The men around this table were as close as brothers.

College life at USC seemed far away now. What days those were. They'd all shared an off-campus house and lived on pizza and cheap beer. Kyle and Brody had brought home a different girl every week. Zane had preferred monogamy, if changing girls every six months counted as such. Jackson hadn't dated, his heart still broken by the girl he thought he'd lost to a highway in Kansas.

And Lance? Well, his troubles with women were the same as they'd been in high school. *Our sweet, reliable friend Lance.*

Meanwhile, Kyle had entertained twins in his bedroom.

"You remember the twins?" Lance asked now.

"Kyle's twins?" Zane asked.

"Trish and Trash," Brody said.

"Not Trash," Kyle said. "Tracie. Trish and Tracie. You're just jealous, Mullen, because you never had twins sharing your room."

"I could have," Brody said. "Quarterback of the football team gets triplets if he wants."

Lance shook his head, pretending to be appalled. "You guys were all man whores back then."

"Except for me," Jackson said.

"And me," Lance said.

"We know your excuse," Kyle said to Jackson. "But Lance here should've been enjoying himself like the rest of us."

"I never got past the friend zone," Lance said. "You know that."

"We tried to teach you, grasshopper," Kyle said. "But you were a slow learner."

"I know," Lance said.

"If by slow you mean respectful to women, then yes," Jackson said. "Unlike the rest of you clowns."

Zane laughed. "If I recall, the girls threw themselves at *us*, not the other way around."

"Those were good times," Brody said. "So many girls."

Lance set his cards aside in disgust. "I'm out."

Zane put his cards face down on the table. "I fold too."

Kyle tossed two more chips into the center of the table. "I'll raise you."

The other two still in the game met his bet and they all turned over their cards. Kyle fanned four kings on the table. He'd won. Again.

"What the hell, Hicks?" Zane asked. "I didn't think you were smart enough to count cards."

"It's pure luck, baby." Kyle grinned as he scooped the pile of chips into his stack.

"Why was I such a disaster with girls?" Lance asked. "Why did girls treat me like the house mascot instead of a conquest like the rest of you?"

"Well, you were younger," Kyle said. "Brody's little brother."

"No, that wasn't it," Lance said.

Zane watched him from across the table. "You're actually serious. What's bugging you?"

"Is this about the blond I saw you with the other night?" Kyle asked. "Because she looked into you."

"I'm not seeing her again," Lance said.

"You going to tell them why?" Brody asked.

Lance shot him a dirty look.

"Honor said she has a friend she wants to set you up with," Zane said.

"Nah, I'm good," Lance said.

Kyle dealt the second hand of the night. Lance had a lousy pair of twos. He asked for three new cards when it was time and was given three fours. A full house. Maybe it was a sign? They played the rest of the hand in silence. Amazingly, Lance won.

"So, guys, I have a bit of news." Lance pulled his bounty into his stack of chips.

"Understatement of the century," Brody said under his breath. He thrust his cards across the table and headed to the bar.

"Dude, what's up?" Kyle's head was cocked to one side, observing him, as he shuffled the deck of cards. "Everything all right?"

"Sure, yeah." Lance chugged from his beer to buy time. He had to tell them, but suddenly he wished he was anywhere but here. "It's been an interesting couple of days."

"Did something happen?" Zane asked.

"Kind of, yeah. I got married in Vegas a few days ago. To Mary."

Kyle dropped the card deck. Zane jerked backward with such force he almost knocked over his chair. Jackson stared at him with a blank expression. At the bar, Brody tossed a beer cap at the wall.

"She's pregnant," Lance said.

"What the hell are you talking about?" Kyle asked.

"Pregnant?" Jackson asked. "You've been sleeping with Mary?"

"I'm in love with her." He was careful not to say she was in love with him. The fewer lies the better. "She's pregnant and needs insurance, so we just went for it."

Zane's eyes had reduced to slits. "You're in love with Mary Hansen?"

"Mary? Bookstore Mary?" Kyle asked.

Lance threw up his hands in exasperation. "Right. Dax Hansen's Mary. Who else would I be talking about?"

"I don't really know," Zane said. "Because you've *not* been dating Mary Hansen."

"We've spent every day together for months."

"I thought you guys were just friends," Kyle said.

"We were, but things changed," Lance said.

"Something doesn't add up here," Zane said.

"I concur," Jackson said. "What's really going on?"

Brody strode across to the table and gripped the back of his chair with his long fingers. "He had a one-night thing with her and now she's trapped him into marrying her."

"Shut up." Lance stood hard and fast, knocking his chair over. Minnie leapt from the counter and ran under the couch. "Just shut your big fat mouth."

"What's the point of lying to the people closest to you?" Brody asked.

"Hey, take it easy." Jackson stood, holding his hands out like a kindergarten teacher with angry boys on the playground.

"Dude, you were *not* in a relationship with Mary without telling us," Kyle said. "That's not how you roll."

"I didn't tell you about the girl back east," Lance said.

"Good point. Maybe you're a habitual liar," Brody said.

Lance lunged for him. Kyle was too quick, jumping up from the table and pulling Lance back. "Calm down, buddy."

"Brody, you need to check yourself," Zane said.

"You guys are delusional," Brody said.

"Let's take this over to the couch," Jackson said. "And talk through everything." Jackson wrapped his fingers around Lance's shoulders and guided him over to the L-shaped couch. Zane went to the bar and came back with a bottle of scotch and five tumblers.

"Fess up." Zane poured them all a drink as everyone took a seat. Other than Brody, who lurked behind the couch.

"Tell us what's really going on," Zane said.

"We're not going to judge you," Jackson said. "We're here to help."

"Fine. On New Year's Eve, after we left your place, Zane, she was restless and sad. You know how birthdays and New Year's Eve can do that."

Zane and Kyle nodded.

"She asked if we could go back to my place and have some

drinks. After a few tequila and lemonades, one thing led to another." He tossed back a portion of his drink. "The morning after, she told me she's incapable of being in a relationship. She thinks all men are cheaters."

"Why is that?" Kyle asked.

He shared briefly about her past, including the cheating husband and the loss of her baby. "So, I kept my distance. Then, a few nights ago she told me she's pregnant. I had to do the right thing. She needs insurance, for one."

"So, you're just married for the insurance?" Kyle asked. "Nothing wrong with that."

"Why would you lie to us about it?" Zane asked. "I mean, other than it's none of our business."

"We're the Dogs. You know that doesn't hold up as a valid argument," Kyle said.

Lance grimaced. How true that was. "We didn't want her dad to worry about how this would all fall out after the baby comes. Or, Flora and Mom, for that matter. She was embarrassed about the whole one-night stand thing."

"I feel for her on that." Kyle spoke with surprising tenderness. "Apparently getting a girl pregnant after a one-night stand is yet another thing you and I have in common. I'm proud of you for doing the right thing."

"What if she just wants to get her greedy hands on his money?" Brody asked. "You guys are naïve to think that isn't a possibility."

"That doesn't seem like Mary," Jackson said. "She's lonely, but not conniving."

"None of us know her," Brody said. "What would make you say that?"

"*I* know her," Lance said.

"Do you?" Brody wiped his mouth with the back of his hand. "Is it even your baby?"

"We have no reason to believe she's a liar," Kyle said.

Lance gripped his knees and leaned forward. "I'm in love

with her." He turned to address his brother. "Everything I told you last night is true, except she doesn't love me."

"You're in love with Mary for real?" Kyle asked.

Lance nodded, miserable. "Head over heels."

"Well, crap," Zane said. "I did *not* see that coming."

"She's been hurt," Lance said. "She has no intention of letting herself get hurt again. She thinks all men eventually cheat. So, I'm once again in the friend zone."

"Until she downs a fifth of tequila," Brody said.

"Watch it," Lance said.

The muscles in Jackson's face scrunched up in one of his notorious worried grimaces. "To clarify, you're in love with her and you've entered a marriage based on a business arrangement."

"That's right," Lance said.

"You're secretly hoping you can get her to fall in love with you despite her declarations never to get involved again. Is that right?" Jackson ran his hand over his closely cropped blond hair.

"I have nine months to get her to realize I'm the man for her. Then we can live happily ever after with our baby."

"This is the worst idea you've ever had," Kyle said.

Lance grinned. Telling the truth had freed him. "It's epically bad."

"I agree there are a few flaws in the plan," Zane said. "However, he's not the only one in this room to venture into what seemed like a hopeless love story."

"Violet fell in love with me even though she hated my guts for ruining the planet," Kyle said.

"And the town," Zane said. "Don't forget that part."

"You didn't ruin the town. You brought hundreds of jobs," Jackson said.

"Even Violet admits that now," Kyle said. "Mostly because of my superior skills in bed."

"What is wrong with you?" Jackson asked.

Kyle wriggled his fingers. "Not a thing."

"Honor fell in love with me even though I'm a stalker," Zane said.

"You're not a stalker," Jackson said. "I don't like it when you say that. It sounds tawdry and really cheapens a beautiful love story. Anyway, I have the best example."

Kyle laughed. "Yeah, no question. Maggie coming back from the dead wins."

"So, what you guys are saying here is that I shouldn't give up?" Lance asked.

Brody guffawed, like an old man. Lance would love to punch him in his arrogant face and be done with it.

"Dude, not cool," Kyle said to Brody. "What's the matter with you? This is Lance. Best guy we know. Why are you being such an ass?"

Brody shook his head in obvious disgust. "May I remind you that this is Mary Hansen we're talking about? Self-centered, petty, overly reliant on her daddy."

"Let's back up for a moment," Kyle said. "Think about what Mary's been through. I know from personal experience that pain can cause self-destructive behavior. I'm a primary example of that."

"When did you turn into a chick?" Brody asked, but with less venom than before.

"You need to think of things from her point of view," Zane said.

Brody scratched his neck. "That's what Kara said to me last night. Who, by the way, isn't speaking to me."

"Good girl," Zane said.

"Here's what you're going to do about Mary," Kyle said to Lance. "You're going to love her so hard she has absolutely no reason to believe you'd ever want another woman like you want her."

"I agree," Jackson said. "Pull out all the stops. I'm talking romance, not just sex. Woo her. Let her see that you'd do anything to have her."

"Keep showing up every day without expecting anything in return," Zane said.

"Make a grand gesture," Brody said.

"Grand gesture?" Lance asked.

Brody nodded. "In all great love stories, a man makes a grand gesture—a sacrifice that leaves no doubt in her mind how much you love her."

"I think he did that when he married her," Jackson said.

Lance nodded, more disheartened than ever. "I've already made my grand gesture and it didn't work."

"You could read one of those romance novels she loves. Get some tips on how to win her trust," Kyle said.

Lance stared at his friend. "That's a heck of an idea."

"There's a reason why women love them, right?" Kyle pointed at the others. "These knuckleheads could use some tips too. Myself, I'm good."

Brody tossed a beer cap at him. "I'm better than good."

Kyle flicked the cap back at Brody. "Women like romance."

"Like you know anything about that," Zane said. "Jackson here, maybe."

Jackson flashed his gentle smile. "It's easy to be romantic when you're married to an angel."

Kyle clutched his throat. "I think I just threw up in my mouth."

"It's a shame I can't give her tequila. That worked last time," Lance said.

Zane looked over at Kyle before answering, like alpha dogs in collusion. "You don't need it. Be the tequila."

"Yep. Be the tequila," Kyle said. "Wear down her defenses until there's no way she can say no."

"If you love her, fight for her." Brody looked over at him with soft eyes. "And for what it's worth, Kara thinks she loves you. She said there's no way she's that good of an actress. You can't fake the way she looks at you."

Lance closed his eyes for a moment. "God, I hope she's right."

"Me too," Brody said. "If that's what you want." Brody shrugged in a gesture of apology like he used to do when they were kids and had fought over a toy. He couldn't come right out and say the words, but Lance knew he was sorry. "I'll support you."

Lance mumbled a thank you, embarrassed. Then, he grimaced and looked at the others. "Listen, is there any way in hell you could keep this from your wives?"

"Why?" Brody asked.

"It would be nice for Mary if they thought our marriage was real. She needs their support," Lance said.

"Impossible. Honor will kick my ass if she thinks I've kept something like this from her," Zane said.

"I tell Maggie everything," Jackson said.

"Even if I wanted to, it's impossible," Kyle said. "Violet has ways of pulling things out of me."

"Same. When it comes to Kara, resistance is futile," Brody said.

An hour later, they took a break from their game to have slices of pizza. Jackson excused himself to make a phone call but returned a few minutes later to join them back at the table.

"I called one of my med school friends," Jackson said to Lance. "Winifred Block. Freddie. Doctor Block now. She has a practice in the city—specializes in high risk pregnancies. I called her, and she said she can squeeze you guys in tomorrow afternoon."

"Wow, thanks," Lance said.

"Given how far you live from the city, she suggested the two of us work together. I'll see Mary weekly and alert Freddie to any changes. I can do ultrasounds and such between visits, but she would be your primary doctor."

Lance knew that Jackson and his father had completed special OB training knowing they would work in a small-town practice in a remote area.

"If anything goes wrong, we'll get her airlifted into the city. Dad's here for backup too. As you get closer to the due date, you may want to think about staying at Brody's condo in the city."

"I'll let Mary know." Lance helped himself to another piece of pizza. "How's Maggie feeling these days?"

"Pretty good. A little nauseous in the mornings, but so far so good. Her album releases soon, so she's been pretty caught up in that, which doesn't keep her from worrying. Between her and Violet, my ultrasound machine's been busy."

"How *is* Violet?" Lance asked. He was a heel, not having asked after either of their pregnant wives earlier.

Kyle grinned. "Speaking of twins."

"Were we?" Zane asked.

"Trish and Trash," Jackson said.

"What about them?" Brody asked.

"We're having fraternal twins. Boys." Kyle folded a slice of pizza in half like a sandwich.

"No," Zane said.

"Yes. Apparently, I have super sperm." Kyle took a triumphant bite of his pizza.

"It has nothing to do with that," Jackson said, laughing and rolling his eyes. "It's a medical fluke. And technically Violet's the one who released two eggs."

Kyle wiped his mouth with a napkin. "I'll choose to believe what I want to believe."

"Is Violet freaking out?" Zane asked.

"She cried for two days." Kyle said.

"Happy tears?" Brody asked.

Kyle winced. "No, I wouldn't exactly describe them that way. After Jackson broke it to us, she didn't speak all the way home.

Then, she locked herself in the bathroom for like an hour. After the initial shock wore off, she wandered around the house crying and mumbling about four kids under four, which is incorrect, by the way. Dakota will be five by the time the babies come. When the crying stopped, she stood in front of the mirror looking at her expanding tummy—totally cute, by the way—talking about how she couldn't possibly wear a wedding dress or any kind of form-fitting dress ever again, or a bathing suit, or yoga pants. The list went on and on. The only way I could console her was to promise to keep ice cream out of the house. Pregnancy's given her a sweet tooth."

"Seriously, Kyle. She's right. What're you guys going to do?" Brody asked.

"That's a lot of babies," Zane said.

"We're fine. We'll hire help," Kyle said. "I'm totally psyched. Not to mention, she's insatiable when it comes to yours truly. It's like turbo sex lately."

"So tacky," Jackson said. "She'd be mortified to know you're talking about her that way."

"You jealous?" Kyle asked.

"I have nothing to be jealous over." Jackson grabbed another piece of pizza. "Things are dandy at my house too."

"No complaints here either," Zane said. "Married life rocks."

"You guys have to keep the twins under wraps for a few more weeks. Violet wants to tell the ladies herself. She will seriously kill me if she knows I told you guys."

They all agreed. Apparently, twins could be kept a secret better than fake marriages.

Lance glanced at Brody, curious if he would share Kara's news. He didn't have to wait long. Brody cleared his throat.

"Kara's pregnant too—due at the end of September," Brody said. "New Year's Eve was a happening scene here on the Mullen compound."

As everyone congratulated him, Zane got up from the table and tossed his paper plate in the trash. The rest quieted. All these babies, but none for Honor and Zane. Lance exchanged a helpless look with Jackson. There was nothing any of them could do. Honor would never be able to have a baby of her own.

Zane came back to the table with a new beer. "Not gonna lie. It sucks."

Jackson patted his shoulder. "We're all so sorry."

"I'm happy for you guys, but man, it's a hard pill to swallow. Mostly because I wish I could give Honor what she wants."

"What about Sophie's offer?" Kyle asked.

"Her offer remains on the table. I'm still not convinced it's a good idea," Zane said.

Sophie, Zane's half-sister, had offered to carry a donor egg impregnated with Zane's sperm. Personally, Lance thought it was a great solution, but Zane wasn't sure it was a line that should be crossed.

"What's Honor say?" Jackson asked.

"She doesn't talk about it—pretends she's too busy with work and Jubie to worry about it right now. But with Kara and Mary both pregnant, it might break her."

"Man, you know what the answer here is," Kyle said.

"I suppose you're going to tell me," Zane said.

"You bet I am. Take Sophie up on her offer. It's selfish not to," Kyle said.

"There's so few times we can actually fix something for the women we love," Lance said. "I wish I could heal Mary's broken heart. You can actually give Honor the very thing she wants."

"My sperm in my sister's body? Am I the only one who thinks that's weird?" Zane asked.

Jackson cleared his throat. "That's not how it works at all. The embryo would be conceived in the laboratory, so to speak, then implanted in Sophie's womb."

"When you put it that way, it sounds perfectly clinical," Zane said.

"Just think about it," Brody said. "For Honor."

Lance paced between the fish tank and the windows of the OB-GYN waiting room while Mary saw the doctor. No men allowed for these visits, the nurse had informed him with a condescending cluck of her tongue, as she swept Mary behind closed doors. He had no idea what went on in the exam room, but he wished they'd hurry up about it.

Mary had been quiet on the hour and a half drive into San Francisco. He didn't push her to talk. She was worried, quite naturally. Instead, he played Maggie's soon-to-be released album on the car stereo. Her songs of love, loss and redemption were so clearly about Jackson it was almost like peeking into someone's diary. The album was a true work of art. He had a feeling their Maggie was about to be a star.

Tired of pacing and worried his fretful footsteps bothered other people, he sat in one of the uncomfortable chairs next to the fish tank. They should think about investing in more comfortable seats, given their clientele. Women in various stages of pregnancy populated the lobby. Some of the ladies' bellies were so round and large he didn't know how they walked around without falling forward. He assumed they were due soon. Others, as he learned from the woman with an infant sitting next to him, were here for their postpartum visit. What would their postpartum experience be? Would Mary want to leave him as soon as the baby arrived?

After a few more agonizing minutes, the nurse called his name. "They're ready for you, Mr. Mullen," she said.

He followed her down a hallway of what appeared to be many examination rooms. After turning a corner, the nurse held the door open for him. Mary was inside, sitting on an examination table wearing nothing but a hospital gown. She had her arms wrapped around her middle. They should turn on the heat in here. Pregnant ladies shouldn't be cold. Especially not this one who didn't have enough meat on her bones to warm her.

"I'm Doctor Winifred Block, but all my patients call me Doctor Freddie." They shook hands. Doctor Freddie was of Asian descent, with creamy skin and brown eyes in a round face.

"Have a seat," she said, pointing to a chair in the corner as she settled onto a rolling stool.

He smiled over at Mary, hoping to assure her and disguise his own nervousness. She returned his smile with a tight one of her own.

He pulled out the small notebook he'd stashed in the inside of his jacket and waited for Doctor Freddie to fill him in on the plan.

"Taking notes? Good idea," Doctor Freddie said. He couldn't tell if she was making fun of him or praising him. Either way made no difference to him.

"Everything looks good at this point," Doctor Freddie said. "The heartbeat was strong." She handed him a small slip of paper from the shelf behind her. "This is the first ultrasound picture of your baby." She pointed at a dot in the middle of a black and white image. "There is your son or daughter."

"That's a baby?" Lance asked.

"Yes, she or he is only a few centimeters at seven weeks." Doctor Freddie crossed her legs. She wore scrubs and Birkenstocks with red socks. "I'm recommending a progesterone supplement as a precautionary method. This has proven helpful for women who've miscarried or had premature births."

"Helpful?" he asked.

"Meaning, it prevents them," Doctor Freddie said.

"Oh, okay. Well, that's good. Right?" Could he get his voice under control? He sounded like a pubescent boy.

"Yes, that's good. As far as her cervix goes, right now all is well. However, I'll want her to visit Jackson—I mean, Doctor Waller—once a week. He'll keep a close watch. Because of her previous premature birth, I'd like to perform a cervical cerclage at fourteen weeks, regardless of whether we see any softening."

She then explained the possibility of late term bedrest and further information about the use of progesterone shots.

Lance scribbled notes. When he got home he might have to look up some of what she was saying on the internet.

"Finally, Mary's going to need a lot of emotional support, even more so than other expectant mothers, given the trauma of her first pregnancy."

"I'm on it." Lance glanced at Mary. She stared into her lap and twisted a tissue around her index finger. "Is there anything in particular I should do?"

"Listen mostly. Reassure her when she's feeling nervous."

"Okay, of course, yes."

"That's how he is all the time," Mary said, looking up from the task of wrapping the tissue around her finger.

"You're a lucky lady, then," Doctor Freddie said.

"I am," Mary said.

"Lance, would you like to hear the heartbeat?" Doctor Freddie asked.

"Can I?" Lance asked.

Doctor Freddie smiled. "I'll do one better. Because you're a good friend of Jackson's, I'll even do another ultrasound, so you can see the flutter of the heartbeat." She moved a plastic contraption with a screen closer to the examination table.

Mary lay back. "Come closer," she said. "And hold my hand."

He leapt from his chair and did as instructed. Mary's hand was cold and clammy. "You okay?" he asked softly.

"Yes, but I'm glad you're here."

Doctor Freddie pulled on a pair of gloves. To his horror, she lifted a phallic shaped wand from the machine and told Mary to push her feet against the stirrups. "Scooch down a bit. That's right," Doctor Freddie said.

She placed the wand between Mary's legs, and presumably, up into the place where plastic should never go. Good God, he hoped it didn't hurt.

He was distracted from his thoughts when a black and white image appeared on the screen.

"Do you see there? That little flutter? That's his or her heart beating," Doctor Freddie said.

Yes, he saw it. His baby's heartbeat, strong and furious. He squeezed Mary's hand. "Look at that."

"Isn't it something?" Mary asked.

He nodded, unable to speak because of the ache in the back of his throat.

"All right, then. Let's get you two out of here. Go have a healthy lunch. I can't emphasize enough, Mary, how important nutrition is. You're at a healthy weight, but it's important to eat food packed with nutrients, take your prenatal every day, and drink plenty of water."

"I will," Mary said.

"How much water exactly? And is there a cookbook I should get?" Lance fetched his notebook from his pocket, ready to add this latest bit of information to his list.

Mary smiled up at him. "I doubt there's a cookbook just for pregnant ladies."

"Don't worry," Doctor Freddie said. "You're going to be a great partner to Mary."

"I'll do my best," he said.

Mary was quiet as they walked out of the office and down to the garage. She declined his offer of a nice lunch, opting for a sandwich instead. When they were on the freeway headed home, she slouched against the car door with her jacket pulled tight around her waist and stared out the front window. Rain drizzled from a gray, dreary sky. His windshield wipers, set to low, made an intermittent whoosh.

Since she'd told him that the physical relationship between them was over, she'd slept in the guestroom. She was usually gone by the time he woke in the morning and slinked off to her room shortly after returning home in the evenings.

"You want to talk about it?" he asked.

"Not really."

The car ahead of them changed lanes without using a blinker. Lance hated that. It was bad enough to drive like a maniac on slippery roads. The least one could do was tell the car behind you what idiot move you were about to make.

"People should use their signals," she said.

He chuckled. "I was just thinking the same thing."

The drizzle cleared. His wipers squeaked across the window.

"I'm afraid to get attached to the baby," she said.

"The heartbeat was strong. Doctor Freddie knows what to do."

She let out a long sigh.

"I'm scared too," he said. "But seeing the flutter of her little heart made me feel a lot better."

"Meme had that too." She pulled her jacked tighter. "Until it stopped."

"We know this time. Doctor Freddie is a specialist. And we have Jackson practically in our backyard."

She nodded and closed her eyes. "I guess."

"You tired?"

"Exhausted."

"Take a nap. We'll be home soon enough."

"I need to go into work. We can't keep the store closed all day."

"About that. I think we should hire some help. Just until you're feeling better."

Surprisingly, she didn't argue. "You're the boss," she said, sleepily.

"I could make you soup for dinner. And a big salad with all kinds of nasty greens that are supposedly good for you."

"You know how to make soup?" she asked.

"I know how to buy it from the grocery store."

She smiled. "Maybe you better get it from The Oar instead."

"Does this mean you'll agree to have dinner with me instead of hiding in your room?"

"I'm not hiding."

"Seems like it to me," he said.

"I'll have dinner with you tonight, okay?"

"But like sex, it's just dinner. Doesn't mean anything, right?"

She turned in the seat to glare at him, her arms crossed over her chest. "Has it ever occurred to you that it's hard for me to be around you without wanting to end up in the bedroom?"

He tightened his grip on the steering wheel. What did he say to that? For that matter, what did it mean?

"Don't you see how this is going?" Mary asked. "I'm already hurting you. I should never have allowed it to get this far."

"Allowed it? What does that mean?"

"It means you're too charming. You make me feel things I don't want to feel."

"I do?"

"Yes. And it makes me mad."

"Wanting me to take you into my bed makes you mad?" he asked. "I don't get it."

"I'm not talking about sex. God, Lance, I'm just saying…I don't know what I'm saying." She turned away in a huff and slumped against the door once again.

He wanted to smile but held back. She could tell him all day long she didn't have feelings for him—that it was just sex for her, but it was a lie. He must continue to be good to her. Eventually he would break down her resolve to remain single. Slow and steady wins the race. *Be the tequila.*

They drove in silence for a few miles until Mary turned to look at him. "Doctor Freddie reminds me of no character from any book I've ever read." She leaned closer to the dash and fiddled with her air vent. "It bothers me. I can always place people. Not her. Does that worry you at all?"

"Should it?"

"Yes, everyone should be able to be described as a character in a book," she said.

"Why?"

"You love your spreadsheets, right? It's the same for me. I like to classify people—put them in a category, so to speak."

"Are you admitting to being as weird as me?"

"Isn't it obvious?" she asked.

"So, what we've got here is a confession. Excellent." Cheered by the sparkle that had returned to her eyes and hoping to distract her, he proposed a game. "I'll throw someone out and you tell me who they remind you of."

"You're just trying to distract me."

He grinned. "True. Okay, Brody."

"It's a tossup between Snape and Darcy."

"Oh my God, Snape? No way. He's totally Darcy. Intense, somewhat brooding, but the heart of a hero. That's the real Brody. Misunderstood, just like Darcy."

"Is this what it's like when you defend me to them?"

"You're misunderstood, yes."

"I'm sorry you have to do that. Defend me, I mean."

"Don't be. Anyway, Brody's a hero to so many. Including me."

"You weren't ever jealous of him? All the attention? All the women?"

"I *was* jealous of the women. Now I'm jealous of his relationship with Kara."

She turned away and looked out the window. "I'm jealous of that too."

"You could have that. With me."

She visibly stiffened. He slowed for a curve in the road. It wasn't until another straight section of road that she spoke.

"Give me another one," she said.

"Kyle."

"That's easy. Pip."

"Wow, yes. That's perfect." The seeker of fortune after a stark childhood. "Zane?"

She appeared to ponder this for a moment, before snapping her finger and thumb. "Got it. Almanzo Wilder. Can't you see him driving into a snowstorm to bring back wheat for the starving town?" Mary asked.

"You lost me."

"The Little House books." She waggled her finger at him in mock judgement. "Lance, you've got to commit to the stack."

"It's a big stack."

"So you say."

"What about Jackson?" *Keep her talking about books.*

"Jackson's so obvious," she said. "Atticus Finch."

He smacked the steering wheel, happy with himself. "I've read that one."

"Thank God I'm not married to a complete illiterate."

That afternoon, Lance was at the desk in the office above the shop when he heard Mary calling to him. He went quickly to the stairway. "Are you all right?"

She waved her hand dismissively. "Yes, yes. I'm fine. However, we have a problem. You need to come down here."

He trotted down the stairs. Immediately, he understood. A ragged dog with gray fur and black, floppy ears lay on the floor next to Mary's desk. When Lance approached, the dog raised his head, smiled, and wagged his tail. His face was spotted with black, especially his nose, which gave the impression of freckles.

"This guy followed that mean preschool teacher in—you know, the one Violet got in a fight with because she was late to pick Dakota up?"

He nodded, as if he followed, which he most certainly did not. "Go on."

"I figured he was with her, but when she came forward to buy a book, she was quite clear the dog did *not* belong to her. In fact, she hates dogs. Too needy. Her words. She prefers cats if she had to choose, which she has no interest in doing because animals do nothing but ruin furniture and stink up a person's house. No wonder Violet hates her."

Was this story going somewhere?

"Anyway, this guy just flopped on the floor and refused to leave. And, he keeps smiling at me," Mary said. "Which is very disconcerting."

Lance held back laughter as he knelt to examine the mangy mutt. No tags or collar. "Let's see your paws, old guy." As if he understood, the dog raised his right front paw. The pads of his feet were worn, like he'd come a long way to arrive at their store. He scratched behind the dog's ears. "Where'd you come from, buddy? Did someone drop you off and leave you?"

"He smells terrible." Mary smiled indulgently at the dog, despite her words to the contrary.

He *did* smell awful. Now that he looked closer, Lance realized the dog's fur was closer to white than gray.

"What do we do?" Mary asked. "He can't stay here. He'll drive customers away."

"In his current state, yes. But after a bath and some grooming, he might actually bring them in."

"Dogs and books *do* go together," Mary said. "Everyone knows that."

They did?

"I'll take him over to Rosie's. She'll get him fixed up."

"I presume Rosie is a seventy-year-old groomer who works out of her house?" Mary asked.

"That's right. How'd you know?"

"Because that describes half the people in this town."

"You say that like it's a bad thing." Lance got to his feet. "I'll go out and get a leash and some food."

"Wait a minute, we're not keeping him, are we?"

"What else would we do?" Lance asked. "He needs a home. We have one."

"Because it's crazy. We just met him. How do we know he's not dangerous?"

"Does he look dangerous?" Lance asked. As if he understood his cue to look adorable, the dog wagged his tail and smiled wider.

"He has the sweetest face," Mary said. "But I don't know anything about dogs."

"And I don't know anything about babies or books, but you don't see that stopping me, do you?"

"Do *you* know anything about dogs? This is perhaps the more relevant question."

"We always had dogs growing up. My dad loved them," he said.

"Do you love them?"

"I do. I've wanted one for a long time. And old freckle face here seems just right."

"What if he's lost and his owners want him back? What if we get attached to him and they snatch him away?"

"Given his state, he hasn't had a home for a long time."

Mary clasped her hands together and stared at the dog. "We don't even know his name."

"Freckles."

She burst out laughing. "There's something the matter with you."

"What do you mean?"

"No one says yes to everything. Not normal people."

"Normal people are so boring." He winked at her before turning his attention to the dog. "Come on, Freckles. Let's get you some chow."

Freckles rose to his feet, spry as could be. This was a young dog, he felt certain. On impulse, he grabbed Mary and kissed her cheek. "We'll be back in a few."

He strode across the shop and out the door, Freckles at his heels. Out on the sidewalk, he leaned over to speak closely with his new friend. "Now listen, buddy, you've got to do your part and convince her what a great guy I am, okay? And you've got to be super lovable, so she forgets to worry so much about the baby. Can you do that?"

A short bark and spirited wag of his tail gave Lance the answer he was looking for. "All right then. Let's go make you pretty."

8

Mary

FOR MARY, the weeks after her first doctor's appointment passed without incidence, other than the arrival and subsequent takeover of the house by one spoiled dog. That first night, Freckles came home from the groomers sporting a fresher scent, trimmed fur, and a San Francisco Sharks dog collar around his neck. He wasted no time making himself right at home, snarfing his meal of kibble before snuggling into his new doggy bed with a happy grin.

Lance hung a bell on the front door, hoping to teach him to ring it when he was ready for a bathroom break. There was no need. Apparently, before abandoning him, Freckles' previous owners had taught him the finer points of bell ringing. The first morning in his new home, he trotted to the door and rang the bell with an elegant push of his paw, then sat on his haunches with that silly smile and waited for a gloating Lance to take him outside.

What was it about Lance Mullen that made everything look easy?

Now, Mary stood at her bathroom sink brushing her teeth. When had mint toothpaste become disgusting or was there something wrong with this tube? Did toothpaste expire? A wave of nausea rumbled through her stomach. She set aside her toothbrush and stood for a moment, hoping for the queasiness to subside. No such luck. She stumbled to the toilet and heaved into the porcelain goddess.

Sweating and lightheaded, she washed out her mouth with water and tried again to brush her teeth using the horrible toothpaste. No go. Nine weeks pregnant and morning sickness had descended with a vengeance. She needed Lance.

He was at the kitchen table, staring at the screen of his open laptop. Steam rose from his mug of coffee. Damp hair and the scent of his aftershave told her he'd already been out for his run and had showered. Freckles lay near his chair, sleeping with his head on his paws. They both startled to their feet at the sight of her. "You don't look so great," Lance said.

"Morning sickness has arrived."

"What do I do?" Lance asked.

"I need different toothpaste. One without a hint of mint." Freckles jogged over to her and stared up at her with a concerned expression.

She patted the top of his head. "Don't worry, Freckles. It's just the baby causing trouble." He cocked his head to the side and whined.

Lance peered at her, like he was trying to translate a foreign language. "You're the same color as the white walls."

"I feel awful. Ironically, the only thing that will make me feel better is food."

"You rest. I'll make you something. Eggs?"

An image of runny yolks oozing over a piece of toast brought a new wave of nausea. She brought her fingers to her mouth. "No, just dry toast, please."

He escorted her to the couch and insisted she curl up with a pillow and a blanket. "You want cartoons?"

"Huh?"

"When Brody and I were sick, Flora always let us watch cartoons."

"That would be adorable if I weren't so sick," she said feebly.

Another sympathetic whine erupted from Freckles as he curled into a ball under her feet. He wasn't allowed on the couch. Lance had trained him, somehow, that he was not to jump on the furniture. His devotion to Freckles' education boded well for his skills as a father.

Lance tucked a blanket around her legs. "Just rest. I'll be right back."

She obeyed, closing her eyes. They were tired and scratchy, despite having slept close to eleven hours. Sounds of Lance moving around the kitchen soothed her, despite the nausea. She drifted off for a few minutes. Next thing she knew Lance was next to her with a plate of dry toast and a mug of what appeared to be weak tea. She sat up and took a tentative nibble of the toast. "I swear I can taste every one of these eleven grains."

"Twelve, according to the package," he said.

She finished one piece of toast and waited to see if it stayed where it belonged. "I feel a little better."

He encouraged her to sip from the cup of tea.

"How did you know this is what I needed?" she asked.

"I texted my mom," Lance said. "She told me weak tea was the only thing she could stomach when she was pregnant. That and ginger ale."

"I didn't have any of this with Meme. I felt great the whole time." What a fool she'd been. She'd nested and daydreamed about the three of them living together as a happy family. Meanwhile, Chad had been sneaking his barista girlfriend into his office. In truth, she didn't know if they'd met in his office for their trysts. She'd never asked him. After he'd left, she'd never spoken to him again. Instead, for months afterward, she'd spent sleepless nights wondering and imagining how such a clandestine affair happened right under her daydreaming nose.

Lance jumped up from his spot on the coffee table. "I'm going to the store for toothpaste and ginger ale."

Kara called shortly after he left. Mary didn't want to answer. She didn't have the energy for a stilted, awkward conversation. She did it anyway.

"Hi Kara."

They exchanged pleasantries, then moved on to how they were feeling. Kara was pleased to say she felt completely normal, like she wasn't even pregnant. Mary shared about her onset of morning sickness.

"I'm sorry to hear that," Kara said, sounding sympathetic. "The girls and I were talking and thought it might be nice to have a little wedding-shower-after-the-wedding-type of get together. But only if you're up for it."

She wasn't. However, Lance wanted her to forge friendships with the wives. She had to try. "I'd love nothing more. Let's have it here at the house. Lance is dying to show it off." Was that even true? How easy it was to lie once one started.

They agreed on a date for the following week. Before they hung up, Mary asked for one favor. "I don't suppose it can just be us and not Janet or Flora?"

Kara chuckled. "I think that can be arranged. But you know, they're going to be all over a baby shower."

"Right. I suppose they will."

"Don't worry. I'm here for you. I've got Flora's number, so you let me deal with her. I have stories about her that'll make you laugh. You remember I was initially hired to work as her replacement when Flora had her surgery. Remind me to tell you about the time I made wheat germ and carrot muffins. Now when she comes over, I pretend I don't know how to cook certain dishes, so she still feels like the boys need her. That's what she calls them. The Boys. I always think of it with a capital B. I know she can be annoying but try and remember that until she found Dax and Cameron, they were all she had. She feels like Brody and Lance are her biggest accomplishments. She's invested in everything they do. Too invested."

Mary could understand the motives of a lonely woman, especially one who'd lost their own child. Guilt crowded out her ill-feelings. "I'll try and remember. Thanks."

"Keep in mind, though, if you ever need to vent, I'm here for you."

After they hung up, Mary finished her toast and tea. Freckles grinned and wagged his tail, like he approved. She petted him and thanked him for his concern. "I'm just fine, Freckles. Nothing to worry about. Feeling sick is good when it comes to pregnancy."

Freckles sighed and placed his chin on her thigh. She could almost hear him promising to take care of the baby once she or he came.

"You're just like your master." She scratched under his chin. "Sweet as can be."

As promised, the ladies who called themselves the Wags showed up at the house a little over a week later. The gifts had been opened and now they were on to the tea and tiny sandwiches portion of the afternoon, with Maggie's album playing in the background. Honor's gift was an embarrassing set of lingerie, completely inappropriate given that soon Mary wouldn't be able to fit into her current granny underwear, let alone these filmy, miniscule pieces of lace sewn together. Maggie and Violet had both gifted her with art—a hand-blown glass vase and a watercolor landscape of the ocean, respectively. Kara's gift had surprised her. It was a silver bracelet with four charms: the letter "L", a baby rattle, a heart with the word "sister," and a wine glass.

"To represent Lance, the baby, and new friendships. Someday

we'll be able to drink wine again, so that's a promise of fun times to come. And the heart is us. Sisters."

Oddly moved, Mary fought back tears. "Thank you. I love it. Thanks, all of you. This wasn't necessary."

"I almost forgot, I brought cake," Violet said. "Since we can't have wine, we'll have the next best thing."

They all gathered around the kitchen table. Outside the picture windows, the fog had disappeared. Afternoon sun peeked through the clouds and flooded the room with light. Mary pulled the shades down a smidge to combat the brightness and joined the rest of them at the table.

Mary listened as the other ladies chatted about one thing or the other. She was an outsider. Words never came easily when she was in a big group. These women intimidated her more than most. *Make an effort. Think of something to say.*

She should have had Lance leave Freckles instead of taking him out for a day with the human Dogs. His reassuring grin would really help right now.

"How are you all feeling?" Honor asked. "As the only one here not pregnant, I feel the need to wait on you all hand and foot."

"I'm excited, but nothing compared to Brody. He can't talk about anything except, 'when the baby comes'," Kara said. "He already hired Trey Mattson to decorate the nursery, even though we won't know the sex of the baby until he or she comes."

"You're waiting to find out?" Maggie asked.

"Yes, aren't you?" Kara asked.

"No way. I had to know," Maggie said.

"Past tense?" Honor asked. "Are you holding out on us?"

"Yes, we just found out. We're having a girl." Maggie patted her tummy with a dreamy smile. "Won't Jackson be cute with a little girl?"

Everyone nodded.

"There's something about men and their little girls. Jubie has

Zane wrapped around her little finger," Honor said. "It's ridiculous."

"No one is as ridiculous as Kyle is about Mollie Blue," Violet said. "If it weren't for me, the child would grow up spoiled rotten."

"All these babies," Honor said with a mournful sigh. "We'll never get another girls' night out ever again."

"Fortunately, there's Flora," Maggie said. "She's already making the rounds with baby advice."

"Violet, are you holding out on us? Did you find out the sex of your baby yet?" Honor asked. Violet and Maggie were both due the middle of August. She would have had her twenty-week appointment already.

Violet pushed her hair away from her eyes and buried her face in her hands. "Kara already knows. I'm having twins." The words came out muffled, but there was no doubt what she said. "Jackson could see it right away in the first ultrasound. Two placentas. Two babies."

"No way," Maggie said.

"It can't be," Honor said.

Violet looked up, her mascara smudged. "It is. Four children under five. Kyle keeps reminding me that Dakota will be five by the time the babies come. As if that helps."

"Two placentas? That means they're not identical?" Honor asked.

"Right." She held up her hand before anyone had the chance to speak. "It gets worse. Boys." Violet burst into the ugly cry. "Two wild boys. Two Kyles."

Maggie scooted her chair closer to Violet and put her arm around her friend's shoulder. "It'll be just fine. Two Kyles will be wonderful."

"No, it won't. Between him and Dakota, I'm barely surviving as it is. You should see how they roughhouse. Last night they broke a lamp at the rental house. Our new house won't be ready until summer, probably right around the time I'm supposed to give birth to *twins*." She started to wail.

"You poor thing." Maggie patted her back with a helpless glance at the others. "A big family's a blessing though."

"Is it?" Violet snuffled. Mary handed her a wad of napkins.

"I think so," Mary said. "I always wanted a big family."

"Me too," Honor said softly.

Violet lifted her head and hiccupped. "I'm sorry, Honor. I'm such a bad friend."

"No, no, don't be sorry," Honor said. "I'm going to get my big family. Just not as quickly as you're getting yours."

"Oh, God." Violet wiped her eyes and picked up her fork. "I need more cake."

"So, Mary, we have something we want to talk to you about." Kara looked over at Maggie as if for help.

Mary swallowed the butterflies that leapt from her stomach to her throat.

"You know how the Dogs can't keep their mouths shut or out of one another's business?" Maggie asked.

Mary nodded. They knew. Lance had told them. She would bludgeon him with the heaviest book in the house the moment he returned home.

"Lance told them, and they told us," Honor said.

"Told you what?" Mary asked, quietly, as she waited for the hammer.

"We know you guys married for the insurance," Kara said.

"Yes." What else could she say? "I suppose it makes you hate me all the more."

"We don't hate you," Honor said. "Don't be silly. I'm glad Lance was able to offer you insurance. It makes perfect sense, especially given your health concerns."

"I understand why you didn't want your parents to know," Violet said. "One of the worst days of my life was when I told my parents I was pregnant with Dakota."

"My dad wouldn't understand why we did what we did,"

Mary said. "Not just a marriage for business reasons, but casual sex."

"Is that all it was?" Honor asked with her eyes on her plate.

"We agreed it would be a one-night thing," Mary said. "But then, you know, the baby made it more complicated. The moment the baby comes, we'll file for divorce and commit to co-parenting as best friends. Lance deserves to marry the love of his life, not be stuck with me."

"You're best friends?" Maggie asked. "That part's real, right?

Mary nodded. "Lance gets me, which is more than a person like me should expect."

"Don't say that," Violet said with her mouth full of cake. A piece of frosting stuck to the end of her nose. "You deserve the best, just like the rest of us."

Maggie used a tissue to wipe Violet's nose.

"Anyway, it'll make it that much sweeter when you fall in love for real," Honor said.

"What?" Mary asked.

"I don't mean to brag or anything, but I called it on Kara and Brody long before it happened. And I knew Violet and Kyle had the hots for each other even when they were sworn enemies."

"*I* knew you and Zane were in love," Maggie said. "From the first time I saw you two together."

"You and Lance. Meant to be," Honor said. "I knew it when I saw him kiss you on New Year's Eve."

"No, you have it wrong. I don't feel that way about Lance."

"He feels that way about you," Honor said.

Mary looked at her piece of untouched cake. What could she say to that? Honor, as usual, had it right. "I'm not in a place where I can be in a relationship."

"Lance is a great man," Kara said. "He's nothing like your first husband."

"It's hard to recover from betrayal. I totally get it, but Lance isn't the cheating kind," Honor said.

"None of our husbands are going to cheat on us," Maggie said.

Mary scraped a bit of frosting from the corner of her plate. This is the conversation she wanted to avoid. They didn't need to hear her opinion on their marriages.

"I'd kill Zane and he knows it," Honor said.

Was she serious? Did she really think Zane wouldn't eventually wander? He was surrounded by sexy women throwing themselves at him.

"Jackson was loyal to me for twelve years and he thought I was dead," Maggie said.

"I trust Kyle with my life," Violet said. "He would never cheat on me."

"What about the nanny? That Mel girl." Why had she blurted that out?

"Perfect example of why I trust him," Violet said. "Before we were even together, she made a pass at him and he rejected her because he was in love with me."

"Before Violet, Kyle would've been all over it," Honor said.

"Thank goodness you saved him from himself," Kara said.

"Are we talking about the woman who worked for Kyle as a night nanny?" Maggie asked. "Super young? Fake boobs?"

"Yeah, the one who reminds Kyle of a cat," Honor said.

"She's a terrible person," Violet said. "Seriously creepy. I half expected to wake up with her over my bed with a knife aimed at my heart."

Mary thought about how she'd come into the bookstore asking for billionaire and nanny romances. Should she mention it? Instinct told her to keep quiet. There was no reason to scare Violet. The girl was sad but probably harmless.

"God, this is good cake," Violet said.

Honor passed her uneaten piece down to Violet. "You better have mine."

"I'm going to get fat." Violet grabbed the plate and stabbed her fork into the deepest part of the frosting. She pulled it out and looked at it lovingly before popping it into her mouth.

"You're eating for three," Kara said. "But you should be careful. I say that as a medical professional, not as your friend."

"I hate you right now," Violet said.

Honor turned to Mary. "I'm bossy, so forgive me, but I've known the Mullen brothers for a long time. I knew their father before he died. Those men, like the rest of the Dogs, don't have a cheating bone in their gorgeous bodies. They were raised right, as were Zane and Jackson."

Violet waved her fork. "Kyle wasn't raised right. His mother left his family, which broke his heart. I know he would never break up our family for meaningless sex. Even if I get really fat."

"You're not going to get fat." Honor returned her focus to Mary. "You're afraid to get hurt. But you say Lance is your best friend and clearly there's an attraction between you—that right there is love. Just think about it before you walk away from someone who could make you happier than you ever thought possible."

"You *are* bossy," Maggie said.

"I've learned to accept it about myself," Honor said.

"It's called leadership," Violet said.

An idea struck Mary out of nowhere. *Little Women*. God knew changing the subject was a great idea. "You ladies remind me of the characters from *Little Women*."

"Wait, which one am I?" Honor asked.

"Amy," Mary said.

"The young vain one?" Honor asked, laughing.

"The extra pretty one," Maggie said. "And talented."

"You're definitely Beth," Mary said to Maggie.

"Great. She dies young," Maggie said.

"That was before antibiotics," Kara said.

"And Kara, you're definitely Meg," Mary said.

"Of course, I am," Kara said. "She's the oldest and most sensible. And, the first to get married."

"That leaves only Jo. There's no way I'm Jo," Violet said. "She was the smartest one. That's definitely not me."

"You're very smart," Maggie said. "Plus, she was feisty like you."

"No, Mary is Jo," Kara said. "And Violet you're Marmee."

They all collapsed in laugher at the sight of Violet's appalled expression.

"Oh my God, you're right. I'm even going to have the four kids to prove it." She held up her empty fork. "And a huge mama stomach."

Kara gasped as her face twisted in pain.

"What is it?" Honor asked.

"I don't feel well." Kara got to her feet. "I need the bathroom." She scurried across the floor to the bathroom just off the front entrance of the house.

"She didn't look good," Maggie said.

"What could be wrong?" Honor asked, her brown eyes wide with fear.

A cry like that of a wounded animal came from the bathroom. Maggie leapt to her feet and ran like a gazelle to the door. Mary and the other two followed closely behind. "Kara, what is it?" Maggie asked.

No answer, other than a muffled yowl, this time like a kitten in search of its mother.

Not this. Not Kara. Mary knew that sound. She'd miscarried.

Maggie, obviously panicked, tried to open the door. It was locked. She fell to the floor. "Kara, open the door. Please."

"Do you want us to call 911?" Mary found her voice.

The crying behind the door stopped. "It's too late."

"Are you bleeding?" Mary asked.

"Yes. It's too much. I know. I'm a nurse. It's happened."

The ladies all exchanged looks, frozen with uncertainty.

Honor stepped forward and tapped on the door. "Kara, it's me. What do we do?"

"Get Brody."

While Honor called Brody, Violet and Maggie managed to get Kara out of her bloody clothes and into a warm bath. Mary, needing something to do with her idle hands, dumped the clothes into the washer. When she passed by the bathroom, she saw that Honor and Maggie knelt by the tub, taking turns dripping water down Kara's back as she wept into her hands.

Mary went out to the front room to wait with Violet. They huddled together on the couch. "What's taking so long?" Mary asked. "They're only up the road."

"We called only five minutes ago," Violet said.

"Seems like an hour."

"Yes."

Mary strained, hoping to hear a car barreling down the driveway. Only the sound of waves below the cliff greeted her.

"Did you get to hold her? Meme?" Violet asked.

"I did. We gave her a proper burial too."

"I can't imagine how awful that was," Violet said.

"Thank you." She patted her friend's hand.

"Are you scared about the new baby?" Violet asked.

"I wish the answer was no." If she lost this baby, there would be no more. This one was her only chance.

"The first thing I thought of when they told me I was carrying twins was the risk that I could lose one. It terrified me."

"I don't wish it on anyone," Mary said.

"What should we do for Kara?"

"Just be there for her when she's ready to talk. I wasn't ready before my mother died. After I lost her, it was double grief, knowing that she was the only one in the world that grieved for Meme like I did."

"I'm here if you ever want to talk now." Violet took her hand and they sat there like little girls.

"It may take Kara a while to bounce back," Mary said.

"And with all of us pregnant. It'll just make it worse," Violet said. "I feel like such an idiot about crying over the twins."

Mary squeezed her hand. "Women spend way too much time apologizing for their feelings, worried over how we might hurt someone else just by expressing our own worries or grief. You have every right to be scared."

They grew quiet, still holding hands.

From the stereo, came the sound of Maggie's singing, clear and resonant. The last track of the album was a cover of *Amazing Grace*. It had been Jackson's mother's favorite hymn.

Mary's eyes stung.

No, please, don't think of her. Not now. You must to stay strong for Kara. There's no room for your own grief.

Mary drifted back to the day they'd buried Meme.

It was early spring in a graveyard outside of Boston. The air smelled of freshly cut grass. The sun was high and bright in a cloudless sky. A day made for children to play in the park, or for new mothers to push their babies in strollers. The beauty hurt her, ripped her skin from her body. She wanted to scream at God. *How could you make a beautiful day like this and take my Meme?*

Her parents, a few friends from Mary's work, and Chad and his mother gathered around the tiny white coffin. It was covered with pink roses, so many Mary wondered briefly if her father had ordered the wrong amount. She listened to the pastor read from a passage in the Bible, but the words did not penetrate her foggy mind. She fixated on the pink rose right in the middle of the small coffin. It was the smallest bud she'd ever seen, not yet ready to bloom. Why had they picked it when the rose should've been given the chance to bloom? Damn them all. Why would they do such a thing? It was unconscionable.

Chad and her mother each took one of her arms as the pastor's wife, Carol, began to sing the first notes of "Amazing Grace." Her voice, sweet and high, cleared Mary's mind. She heard the words and music for the first time, really heard them.

For a thousand years.

Was blind but now I see. Was Meme in heaven now with the angels? Would they hold her if she was scared or hungry? Who would take care of her now that her mother had been left on earth?

Once was lost but now I'm found.

She wished the song would never end. If the sweet sound continued, she could stay with Meme. She could hear the voices of the angels welcoming her baby. She could believe they would see each other again.

When we've been there ten thousand years.

She prayed silently. *Please God don't take me further in my life than this moment. Just let the hymn go on and on with this song in an endless loop so I don't have to walk out of here and leave my baby in the dark, cold ground.*

Carol held the last note as if she knew Mary's prayer. But it ended after all. Her beautiful voice was not that of an angel but of a human like Mary, stuck on earth. The leaves of the maple tree next to them shuddered with the last note.

Mary fell to her knees and howled. The pain gobbled pride and gutted her, split her open and left her sprawled on the ground begging God to take her too. Her mother knelt beside her. She wrapped her arms around her grown daughter and rocked her like a baby as the tiny coffin was lowered into the ground.

Now, beside her, Violet's arms encircled her, held her close, as her mother had. Mary touched the side of her face, surprised to find it wet. When had she started crying? Maggie's voice faded away with the last note of the hymn.

"I'm sorry." Mary wiped her face with her free hand.

"Don't be," Violet said. "Don't ever be sorry for your grief."

"That hymn. It was sung at Meme's funeral."

"Oh, sweetie."

"Like Brody and Kara, I had the nursery all decorated too," she whispered. "For a baby that never came home."

"What was the nursery like?"

Mary was surprised by the question. People never asked questions like this. Discussions of death were to be avoided.

"I spent weeks and weeks on every detail," Mary said.

"Tell me."

She'd painted the walls pink and yellow and had used a stencil to paint Meme's initials. On the wall across from the crib she'd arranged framed vintage covers of her favorite children's stories.: *The Velveteen Rabbit, Goodnight Moon, Corduroy, Ferdinand, The House at Pooh Corner*, and *Are You My Mother?*

The first night after the funeral, she'd sat in the rocker her father had lovingly refurbished from her own nursery and stared at that cover. *Are You My Mother?* What if Meme was searching for her? Where was her daughter? Was she wandering the afterlife looking for her? Mary had rocked and wept, holding the stuffed bear her mother had brought over when she first told her parents about her pregnancy.

Finally, exhausted, she'd taken the cover of *Are You My Mother* from the wall and fallen to the floor. She'd cradled both the stuffed bear and the picture to her chest and begged God to take her. *Please, take me to Meme. I have to find her. She has to find me.*

In the morning, she'd awakened in the same position. Chad stood in the doorway, his face, twisted and ugly, full of contempt for her.

"It's not like we knew her," he said.

She'd raged at him, digging her nails into the flesh of his arms and chest. "I knew her. I knew her, you son of a bitch."

"He said my grief wasn't warranted because I didn't know her," Mary said, softly, to Violet. "But I did. The moment I saw her face, I knew her exactly."

Violet rested her head against Mary's shoulder. "I know. Dakota too."

"Even before, we know. Kara knew."

"Yes," Violet said.

Brody and Lance burst into the room, with Freckles on their heels. "Where is she?" Brody asked.

"In the bathroom getting cleaned up." Violet ambled to her feet, encumbered by her belly. "Wait here. I'll get her."

Freckles ran to Mary and licked her hand before sitting on his haunches like he waited for her command. If only there were something a sweet dog could do for her friend. She looked up at Lance, who stood frozen in the middle of the room.

Mary reached for him, like it was pure instinct. He took her in his arms. She clung to him until she could breathe again. They turned just as Kara came into the room, wearing the pajamas Mary had set out for her. Escorted on each side by Maggie and Honor, Kara hobbled, her face bleached of color. When she saw Brody, the wounded animal cry from earlier unleashed from her chest.

"I'm here." He ran to her and scooped her into his arms. She looked like a ragdoll against his large, muscular frame as she buried her face into his chest.

"I'm here," he repeated.

Without another word, he strode across the room and out the door. Mary moved from Lance to the other women.

Lance knelt on the floor and put his arm around his dog. "What do we do?"

"Pray," Mary said.

The other women nodded as they moved together in an unspoken dance—a dance without words or music other than the notes of motherhood. The melody swelled and coursed with the flow of their blood, the beat of which were their children's thumping hearts, whether on earth, heaven, or growing in their wombs.

They held hands and bowed their heads. Honor whispered a prayer. The words did not matter because they knew every word, as did God.

We are not alone when others grieve with us. Mary had not known this until she felt Violet's arms around her, their tears intermingled in the fabric of their blouses. Now she understood. When one mother weeps, we all weep.

Are you my mother?

I'm your mother. I'll always be your mother.

The weeks rambled by with work, evenings with Lance and Freckles, morning sickness, and nights where she slept long and soundly. She and Lance had established a routine. Unable to hide, as he put it, she found herself in the same place every night. By his side. They made dinner and hung out together, either reading or watching television. Lance had found a reality show on television about three obstetricians and their patients. Lance was especially obsessed, with Mary not far behind. They were fascinated by the tales of the couples and the births of their babies. The filming of the actual deliveries left little to the imagination. Even Lance had become accustomed to watching the details of each birth.

He seemed careful around her, sure to keep his distance physically. It broke her heart, but she knew it was best. She could not tell him the truth. If he knew how she'd tricked him, they would no longer be friends, let alone lovers. Keeping his friendship was vital to their baby's eventual happiness and security.

At the beginning of her fourteenth week of pregnancy, she had her weekly appointment with Jackson. The young Doctor Waller performed an ultrasound and assured her the baby showed the right amount of growth and a strong heartbeat. Her cervix was behaving as it should, but he agreed with Doctor Freddie that she should have a cerclage put into place at the end of the week.

After the examination, Mary asked Jackson for news of Kara.

"She hasn't come to work since it happened," Jackson said. "My dad's been filling in for her."

"Lance stopped by their house the other day. The housekeeper said they weren't accepting visitors," Mary said.

"If space is what they need, then we have to give it to them, even though it's hard," Jackson said. "As a man, I just want to fix it for them."

"Lance too." Just that morning Lance had told her how helpless he felt. Brody wasn't the type to talk through his feelings. Between the miscarriage and his forced retirement, Lance knew Brody was hurting. There wasn't a thing any of them could do.

"Is Maggie feeling well?" she asked.

"Yes. She's rehearsing with her band in the city right now. But she's plagued with guilt."

"About Kara?"

"Yes, and about her friends from New York. Lisa and Pepper. Did you meet them at the wedding?"

Mary nodded. They were hard to miss. Gorgeous and glamorous, they'd glittered like diamonds.

"The three of them went to NYU together and were all struggling actresses for years in New York," he said. "Now that Maggie's having success and they're not, she feels strange."

"It would be awkward," Mary said. "Female friendships are tricky, especially between women with so much in common."

"Maggie said that too. Men are lucky, I guess. We just mock one another and get into occasional fist fights and all's well."

After he left, she dressed and confirmed her next appointment with the receptionist. She'd left Freckles tied to a post outside the doctor's office. By the time she got back to him, an anonymous donor had given him a bowl of water and a chew toy. She looked up and down the street, but the culprit was nowhere to be seen. This town—they loved dogs and babies.

She untied his leash from the post. Freckles gave a hopeful wag of his tail. A walk would do them both good. She had an hour before she had to open the shop. Temperatures were in the mid-sixties with sunny skies and no wind, a promise that spring would indeed arrive by the end of the month. "Come on, then. But afterward, straight to work."

He wagged his tail and jumped into the air.

"Crazy dog."

Mary stopped at the car to change into a pair of tennis shoes she kept in the trunk. She put on her sunglasses and followed Freckles down the sidewalk toward the ocean. He walked at the perfect pace with his head held high as if to demonstrate what a superior creature he was to ill-mannered dogs. They soon reached the end of town where a long stretch of public beach sprawled in a lazy arc along the coastline. She and Freckles stood by the wooden bench and looked out over the water. Initials of lovers were carved in various places on the bench. *Decades of sweethearts canonized forever. How many have stayed together?*

Gentle waves crested and broke over the sand. Seagulls squawked overhead. "Nuisances," she said to Freckles.

He barked in agreement and pointed to the beach with his nose.

"Down to the sand?" she asked.

Another bark.

"Fine, come along."

Dressed in jeans and a light cotton blouse, the sun warmed her back as they trudged over the sand. The beach was empty other than a few walkers and hungry seagulls. She decided to let Freckles loose. He deserved a chance to run after seagulls. When they reached the wet sand, she knelt to unlatch the leash from his collar. Instead of running, he looked up at her for permission. "Go ahead. Run."

He barked and jumped at least two feet in the air, floppy ears like the sails of a boat, before taking off down the shore. As she turned to watch him, she noticed a woman with a long stride just up ahead. Long brown hair swept in a ponytail swung as she walked. Kara.

Should she say something or just let her be? Since the night of the miscarriage, they hadn't talked. Mary had sent a card and a book up to the house, but as Jackson said, they needed privacy.

She shouted out to Kara, almost hoping her voice would get lost on the breeze. Kara turned and put her hand over her eyes to shield the sun. Mary waved. Kara returned the gesture and started toward her. A wave crashed near Mary's feet. She scampered away.

Kara's tall, muscular frame looked small next to the ocean. *Nothing like the Pacific to remind us of our fragility.* Dark smudges under her eyes hinted at sleepless nights. Still, she looked better than the last time Mary had seen her, with cheeks pink from exercise and the brisk air.

"I'm sorry I haven't been in touch." Kara dug a hole into the damp sand with her foot and pushed stray hairs away from her face.

"It's nothing to worry over. I understand."

Kara squinted as she turned her gaze to the water. "Today's the first day I've left the house."

"I'm not surprised." She could imagine all too well what the past few weeks had been like for Kara—all day in her pajamas, unwashed hair, intermittent crying, unable to keep any food down.

Kara stuffed her hands into the pockets of her sweatshirt. "Brody's worried about me, so I had to pretend I felt like a walk."

"It's a nice day." Mary took off her sunglasses and cleaned them with a corner of her blouse to hide her discomfort. "The sun always cheers me."

"Does it?" Kara asked in a tone that mimicked a sigh.

"No, that's a lie. The day of Meme's funeral was a day like this. The sun made me mad."

Kara turned toward her and smiled. "Really?"

"Furious. At God mostly."

"Me too," Kara said. "Not about the weather."

"The beauty of the world seemed an affront that day," Mary said. "Like the colors were too bright, almost mocking."

Kara waved her hand toward the ocean. "Like this. When I first moved here I couldn't stop marveling at the beauty. But today it makes me cold."

"I understand."

The women stood together as the waves crashed to shore inches from their feet and sprayed mist. Seagulls flew and screeched overhead. Miles out to sea, a cargo ship looked no bigger than a toy.

"I appreciated your kind note," Kara said. "And the book was perfect. I haven't been able to read, but maybe today I will."

"It's what I would've wanted. An old friend to comfort me." She'd sent a copy of *Little Women*. "I'm sorry. I can't tell you how much. Especially because I know only too well what it feels like," Mary said.

"I wish you didn't."

"Me too. I wish that for both of us," Mary said. "I'm here if you need to talk. After Meme died no one would talk about her. Friends and people at work seemed to think mentioning her death would remind me of it and make me feel worse. When the truth was, her death was always with me. Every second of every day. Acknowledging it would have been a relief. Maybe they thought death was something contagious."

Kara pointed up the coastline. "Want to walk?"

"Sure, I have some time before I have to open the shop."

They headed north, walking briskly without talking.

After a few minutes, Kara broke the silence. "Brody wants to try again right away."

"Is that what you want?"

"I guess. I'm a nurse, so I know it wasn't a viable pregnancy. There's a reason it happened, some abnormality, but for some reason that doesn't help. I wanted *that* baby. Not a substitute. Men don't understand."

"Most don't." Chad hadn't, but he was a pig, so there was that.

"How'd you get through it?" Kara asked.

"Books. Time. I'll never get over it, but eventually I started to want to live again. I believe it took me longer than most. I'm stubborn that way." She smiled to take the bitter edge from her voice.

Freckles circled back around to them, barking a hello.

"Who's this?" Kara asked, clutching Mary's arm. "Friend or foe?"

"This is Freckles. Our new dog," Mary said. "Definitely a friend. Not much of a foe to anyone, I'm afraid."

After assurances that they were fine, Freckles leapt ahead, ears plastered to the side of his head as he sprinted down the beach.

"Where did he come from?" Kara asked.

She explained how Freckles showed up at the shop and Lance immediately suggested they adopt him.

"Lance can't resist a dog or a child," Kara said. "And they can't resist him."

"They say dogs and children can always tell the best people."

They continued to walk, arms linked, as they followed the grinning dog.

"He came to us just when we needed him," Mary said. "A distraction from my worries."

"Someone to love," Kara said.

"That too."

"Walking feels better than I thought it would," Kara said.

"My mother always said any problem could be solved during a brisk walk on a beach."

"It's not true."

"I know," Mary said. Freckles barked at a wave that broke too near him. "Some hurts are too big even for the ocean."

"I came here today looking for God. I've always been able to find him by the ocean," Kara said. "But again, all I feel is cold."

"My mother used to say something else, which I *do* think is true. God shows up in other people. He sends the right person to you when you most need them. Even if you didn't know you did."

Kara pressed Mary's arm to her side. "I believe we have proof of that today."

"After Meme, I went to a grief support group for parents who'd lost a child. One of the women in the group was an actress. She'd lost her little girl to cancer. In previous meetings she'd shared with us about her little girl—how unselfish and generous she was—how she believed our purpose was to help others. One night she told us she'd been offered a part in a play about a mother who lost a child. Her initial reaction was to turn down the part, sure it would be too painful. But then, on the way to our meeting, her child's favorite song came on the radio. It was like a sign, a reminder, of her daughter's belief in service to others, and she thought of all the parents who had lost a child. Perhaps the play would mean something to them, remind them they're not alone, or break open a taboo topic, maybe even soothe a broken heart with her courageous performance. She said, if she could help someone with her work, then her incredible loss might mean something. Not that she wouldn't continue to wish for a different outcome, but that there was a kernel of beauty in her pain. I've thought about that a lot over the years. All the books, the hearts of the writers spilled onto those pages, how they've helped me, how they used their pain to write stories and poetry that entertain and heal and remind us of our humanity. Other than recommending books to people in various kinds of pain, I've never thought I had much to offer. I've used my pain as a shield instead of for good."

"Lance says the opposite about you. He says you help people every day at the shop."

"He sees me as better than I am."

"You helped me today," Kara said softly.

"If that's true, then I'm grateful."

"We could come again tomorrow," Kara said. "Walk some more. Find God in each other."

She swallowed the lump in her throat. "I'd like that. We should go back. I've books to match with their perfect owner."

She called for Freckles to follow them. He hesitated for a moment before tearing down the sand toward them. "Let's go, boy. Back to town."

Freckles took the lead as they headed back, until a fat seagull taunted him by squatting in the sand and staring at him with a beady eye. What was a dog to do but chase her?

"Get her," Kara shouted.

"This dog."

"Impossible not to love," Kara said.

"Kind of like his owner."

Kara glanced at her but didn't comment.

Life continued. We lost and found, gave and received. Sometimes dogs showed up at your shop and grinned their way into your heart. Friendships developed out of shared pain. God showed up at the beach. The circle of life? Not really. More of a circuitous path of mistakes and triumphs and tragedy and joy and everything in between.

When they reached the path to the parking lot, Kara took one last glance at the sea. "I'm going home to get cleaned up. Then, I'm going into the office. Jackson needs me."

And, so it went. Women kept on. After the weeping and the bargaining, there was only one choice. Keep going.

9

Lance

A FEW DAYS later, Lance drove Mary into the city to have the cerclage put in. Doctor Freddie was doing the procedure herself. She'd assured Lance that it was a routine procedure and that Mary would not be put under, merely numbed with an epidural. He had to hold onto a back of a chair when the doctor described how *that* was done.

He waited, pacing around the lobby of the office until he received a dirty look from a cranky pregnant lady. He sat, crossing and uncrossing his legs. Next, he tried to read a book on his e-reader, but nothing captured his attention. Finally, Doctor Freddie came out to get him. Everything went well, she assured him as they walked down the hallway toward Mary's room.

Mary looked remarkably well, given the fact that Doctor Freddie had been up in her with a needle and thread. He shuddered but put on a smile for Mary. Doctor Freddie advised them that Mary should take it easy for the next few days and to expect cramping and a little bleeding. "Please call if you're concerned. I'll send a note to Jackson this afternoon to fill him in."

They thanked her as Lance helped her off the table and out to the car. She looked pale and a little shaky. He suggested a shake or ice cream, but she declined. "I just want to go home."

Home? Was she starting to think of his home as her home? *Please God.*

"Do you want to find out if we're having a boy or a girl?" he asked.

"Definitely."

"I guess I do too. It will help with the nursery."

The next afternoon, Lance and Freckles headed into the shop after spending the early morning working on Mary's portfolio. He hadn't shared it with her yet, but he'd taken a little of his own play money and put it into her account. In case his plan to get her to fall in love with him was a flop, she'd have money to buy a house. He'd spent the rest of the morning reading *Anne of Green Gables*. He'd only meant to read a chapter, but Anne with an "e" had sucked him into the story. He'd been thoroughly enjoying the book until he came to the chapter with Matthew's death. *Matthew dead? Working the fields, he just dies right there? No, this is wrong.* He'd wanted to throw the book across the room.

Instead, he'd thought about his dad. Denial had come swift that morning the doctor had told them he'd died on the operating table. He listened in disbelief. His dad had been healthy, an athlete all his life. This had been a routine operation.

He turned onto the main street of town. The sun disappeared behind an angry purple cloud. He sighed. Stupid rain. He was sick of it. As if he sensed his master's discomfort, Freckles raised his head from where he napped in the back seat and let out a sympathetic yawn.

He parked behind the shop and let Freckles to do his business before they went inside. If he could just remember the last words his father had said to him, he could have peace. All he could remember of that day was sitting in the waiting room of the hospital and the taste of the coffee from the machine. A bitter, metallic taste that would forever be tied to the day his father died.

From a few feet away, Freckles barked and tilted his head as if to ask him what his troubles were. "I'm just feeling a little sad." The dog's ears pitched forward. "I miss my dad." He bounded over to him and licked Lance's hand. "Thanks, buddy."

They walked in through the backdoor. School was out for the day. He could see at least half a dozen high school kids having sodas in the café. Mary was at the desk working at the computer. She wore a knit maternity dress that showed her round bump and tall black boots. Her hair fell across her face and she had a pencil between her teeth. Always, when she worked at the computer, she had a pen or pencil between her teeth. This amused him. Why would she need a pen when at the computer?

Freckles nudged her leg with his nose. She pushed back her hair and removed the pencil from between her lips before petting Freckles. "Hey guys. What're you doing here?"

"I was restless. So, Freckles suggested we come into town and take you to lunch."

"Restless?" She tapped her pencil against her chin.

"Kind of sad." He pulled *Anne of Green Gables* out of his bag. "This, young lady, has caused a grown man to cry and made me think of my dad."

"Matthew?"

"Precisely." He sat in the chair next to the desk.

She gave Freckles another pat before resting her hands on her stomach. Her fingers were long and slender. She kept her nails trimmed close and never wore polish. He liked that.

Lance's phone rang with his brother's ringtone, startling them both. "Hey Brody, what's up? What? Gone? Like someone took them?"

He dropped his phone into his lap. "Mollie and Dakota are gone. Someone took them."

"Took them? As in, kidnapped?"

"Kyle and Violet woke up this morning and they weren't in their beds."

"Who would do such a thing?"

"Violet thinks it's her dad. He threatened to take Dakota last Thanksgiving. He didn't think Violet was doing a good job with him."

"Why would he take Mollie?"

"To punish them? Kyle said it got ugly between them. He had to throw the old man out of the house."

"How would he get in, though? The house was locked, right?"

"Brody said Kyle's keys went missing shortly after Thanksgiving. They think he might've snatched them, planning this."

"Are the police looking for him?"

"Yes. Both her parents are missing. Their car is gone, and the house is closed up, like they're gone for a long time."

Lance's phone rang again. Brody. "Any news?" He nodded. "Yeah. Okay, I'll be right there." He hung up and turned to Mary. "Brody wants us to come out to the house. Everyone's there."

10

Mary

MINUTES LATER, they drove past the turnoff for town and up the road that led to the Mullens' property. Rafael was at the security gate this afternoon. Instead of waving them through, he came out of the booth. Lance stopped the car and rolled down his window.

"Brody told me what happened," Rafael said. "I wanted to let you know I'm here if you guys need me. I was in special operations in the military. I have experience searching for the devil."

Mary had heard somewhere that Rafael had aided in the capture of several high-level al-Qaeda operatives. She studied him now, curious if she could see that disciplined, tough military man in his even features. He wasn't particularly tall, with lean sinewy muscles. More like a soccer player than a football player, if she had to put him in a category. With his dark skin and almost black eyes, she guessed he was of Mexican or Puerto Rican descent. However, he reminded her of Victor Hugo's very French character, Jean Valjean, from Les Misérables. Tortured and righteous, his eyes portrayed a man who had witnessed great evil and sorrow as well as done things he was not necessarily proud of but were necessary to protect those he loved.

"I'll let him know," Lance said. "Thanks."

Rafael pushed the button for the gate and they passed through.

"You like him?" Lance asked.

She looked over at him, disconcerted. "I don't know him. He seems...complicated."

"Do you like men like that?"

"Why would you ask?"

"You were staring at him," Lance said.

"Was I? I'm curious about him, I guess."

Lance's fingers had turned white from gripping the steering wheel. Her stomach turned over. He was jealous.

"I'm not interested in a relationship with a man of any kind," she said. "If that's what you're asking."

"But you think he's hot?" The muscles in Lance's neck twitched.

She tugged the sleeve of her dress, suddenly warm. "He's handsome, yes."

Lance pulled into Brody's circular driveway. He turned to her. "The thought of you with someone else makes me physically ill." His blue eyes bored through her like intense lasers meant to open her soul for inspection.

"Lance, I'm pregnant. I'm hardly in the running for bachelorette of the year." She smoothed her hands over her round belly. "Hello, I don't think anyone's interested when I lead with this."

He rested his forehead on the steering wheel.

She put her hand on his shoulder. "I'm not interested in anyone." *But you.*

They were interrupted when Kara came out of the house. Kara embraced them both before filling them in on the latest.

"Kyle and Violet are inside. The police are trying to track down her parents. Cell phones aren't working, or they've been thrown out."

They went inside. Violet and Kyle were huddled together on one end of the couch. Kyle's usually dark skin was a shade of gray. Violet held a box of tissues, her face streaked with tears.

Kyle's phone rang. He grabbed it from the coffee table. "It's the detective." His hands shook as he swiped hello. "What? Really? For weeks now? All verified. Okay. So, we're back to no leads?" He nodded and rocked back and forth. "Yes. Yes. Of course. Anything we can think of, yes."

Kyle hung up the phone. His eyes glazed over in panic as he turned to his wife. "It's not your parents. They're in South America. They've been there for weeks. All verified by police."

"Then who could it be? Who would do this?" Violet's voice was two octaves higher than usual. Mary ached for her.

"The detective said to try and think of anyone we know who might do this," Kyle said. "Anyone who knows us well enough to have a key."

"No one but the Dogs," Violet said.

"Not even them. We haven't given out keys to anyone," Kyle said. "Not even the house cleaners."

That was when it hit her. Mel the nanny. The books she'd asked for. The hints about lovers with obstacles that prevented them from being together.

"I think I know who took the kids," Mary said, blurting it out before thinking.

"What did you say?" Kyle asked.

"Mel. Your former nanny. She came into the store asking weird questions about romance books about a nanny and single dad." Mary relayed as much of the conversation as she could remember.

"But she's not even living here anymore," Violet said. "I saw her a few weeks ago and she said she was moving to San Diego."

"She could've been lying," Lance said.

"We know she was a liar," Kara said. "Right?"

"And she had access to your house at one point, right?" Mary asked.

"Not the rental house, no," Kyle said.

"When did you notice the set of keys missing?" Mary asked Violet.

Violet looked over at Kyle. "I'm not sure. Sometime around Thanksgiving. We figured they'd been lost during the move."

"Was this before or after you fired Mel?" Mary asked.

Kyle paced back and forth between the couch and Violet. "It was around the same time. I think anyway."

Violet lurched to her feet. "Kyle, do you remember how she used the bathroom off the kitchen?"

He shook his head, no.

"I do," Violet said. "We waited for her in the foyer while she ran back to use it. She could've grabbed the keys then."

"But why would she do this?" Violet asked. "Revenge?"

"Money, probably," Lance said. "Most things come back to money."

"Or love," Mary said. "In this case, unrequited."

"She did hit on me pretty hard," Kyle said.

"That's an understatement." Violet crossed over to Kyle and slipped under his arm, visibly shaking like the leaves on the trees outside the windows.

"I think she's obsessed with Kyle," Mary said. "This is a way to get his attention. I don't think it's about money."

"What do we do? Where do we find her?" Violet asked.

"I have a feeling she's going to reach out to Kyle. One way or the other," Mary said. "And I don't think she'll harm the children. This is a fantasy in her mind that she and Kyle are supposed to be together. Wherever she is, she's imagining that Kyle's going to meet her there and run away with her and the kids."

"It seems so farfetched," Kyle said. "I mean, Violet and I are married now. We're pregnant. How is that not a big red flag that I'm not interested?"

"She's delusional," Lance said with a hint of sadness in his voice.

"If anything happens to them, I'll kill her with my own hands." Kyle's voice broke.

"I just read a novel about something similar," Mary said. "Same thing. The nanny was obsessed with the husband. She had this fantasy life built up in her mind that the two of them were going to run away together. When she took the baby, she went to the place where she thought the husband would want to be with her. In this case, it was his office. I know it sounds weird, but she thought she would just show up there and they would leave together. Is it possible she's thinking something like that?"

"I can't think of anywhere that would be," he said. "I never went anywhere with her."

"Did you ever tell her anything about what you liked to do?" Lance asked. "She could've taken it as a signal that you wanted her to meet you there."

"I did tell her about my property," Kyle said. "One day I caught her looking at the plans. It's the only thing I ever shared with her that was personal."

Kara and Brody came into the room with coffee and sandwiches. "Honor and Zane are on their way over. Jackson called too and said that he and Maggie are flying home from L.A. this evening and will be here as soon as they can."

They filled them in on Mary's theory. "If she's right, we need to get the police over here to help us figure out what to do," Brody said.

Kyle had already punched some numbers into his phone and walked out of the room.

While he was gone, they tried to get Violet to eat a sandwich, but she couldn't. "There's no way I can keep anything down." She began to cry. Mary led her over to the couch and helped her sit. Her stomach made her unsteady. She and Kara sat on either side of Violet.

Kyle returned. "Detective Ryan's on his way. He says they can track her phone, figure out where she is. If we're right that it's her."

A few minutes later, the doorbell rang. "I'll get it," Brody said.

Brody came in with a stout man in a suit, introducing him as Detective Ryan.

"Good to meet you." Detective Ryan wore round glasses that mimicked his round face. Neatly combed hair slicked back with gel made him appear as if he'd just gotten out of the shower.

Detective Ryan wasted no time with pleasantries. "You have this girl's number?"

Kyle nodded. "Yes."

"Here's what we're going to do. You're going to call her, feel her out. Real nice like. If you're right and she's done this in some bizarre attempt to get your attention, play nice. Lead her on a bit."

"And if it's not her?" Kyle asked.

"Then we move onto the next plan," Detective Ryan said.

Kyle sucked in a deep breath. Violet shuddered.

"Put your phone on speaker," Ryan said.

Kyle did as asked. The phone rang three times before she answered.

"Is it really you?" Mel sounded victorious, like a woman who'd just won what she wanted. Mary's stomach curdled with anger.

"Hey Mel. Listen, this is going to sound kind of weird."

Before he could continue, she jumped in. "I did something crazy. For you. Please don't be mad."

"What did you do?"

"I missed the kids so much. Since *she* pushed me out of their lives. I just had to see them, so I took them for a little joy ride. That's all. Just up the road from Cliffside Bay."

"Are they all right?" Kyle's voice stretched to the brink of panic as he clearly tried to keep up the act.

"They're fine. I took Dakota to McDonalds. He said his mother never allowed him to have junk food."

Kyle looked over at Violet, his eyes wild.

"You should've asked if you could visit with them," Kyle said.

"Are you mad?"

"Not mad. A little disappointed you didn't feel you could just come talk to me."

"It's her. She keeps you in a cage, hidden from me."

"How about if I come see you guys? We could talk without Violet there."

"I would love that."

Violet had compared Mel to a cat many times. She was right. Mel purred instead of talked. Mary hugged her bump and shivered. *Please God, don't let her hurt the children.*

"Where are you?" Kyle asked.

"I'm up north. By a lake. That's how I always imagine us. With a house by the lake."

"Can you send me the coordinates? I could come see you right away."

"Yes, please. Come. I'll wait for you."

Kyle's phone beeped with a text.

"Did you get it?" Mel asked.

"Yes, I can see where you are," Kyle said. "I'll come for you."

"There's only one thing. I didn't keep Dakota. He doesn't fit with us. It's just you and me and Mollie. Not the other two."

Violet pressed her hands to her mouth as if to keep from screaming.

"What did you do with him?" Kyle fell to his knees, holding the phone out in front of him and staring at it in disbelief. "Are you there?"

"Yes, I'm here."

"Where's Dakota? Tell me right now," Kyle said.

"I left him at the McDonalds."

"When? When was that?"

"About an hour ago."

"Where was it? Which McDonalds?"

"Do you know where Stowaway is?"

Stowaway? Cameron lived there. A town slightly bigger than Cliffside Bay but not by much. It was about an hour north.

"I left him in a booth," Mel said. "He's fine."

Detective Ryan typed furiously into his phone, then ran out of the room, most likely to put out an Amber Alert.

"Listen to me carefully," Kyle said. "You stay where you are. I'll be right there. We'll be together. Stay put. Okay?"

"I'll be here."

A deputy stormed into the living room. "We've got local police in Stowaway headed to the McDonalds."

Detective Ryan returned, along with two deputies. He explained the plan, which was to make it appear as if Kyle were alone. In reality, the police would be right behind them. "We'll park and run in," Ryan said. "Surprise her."

"I'll go with him," Lance said. "I can stay hidden in the car, but he shouldn't go in there alone. We don't know what kind of weapons she has."

"I can send one of my guys," Ryan said.

"No, I want to do it," Lance said. "Please."

"It should be me. I don't want you in danger," Brody said.

"No, Brody. I have to do this," Lance said. He was Kyle's best friend. This was his job.

"You sure?" Brody asked.

"Yes. It has to be me," Lance said to Brody before turning to the detective. "Please, sir. Let me go with him."

"I don't know if I can do it without him," Kyle said.

Detective Ryan relented. "You're to keep your cell phone on."

"Yes sir," Lance said.

Ryan talked through the rest of the plan, quickly. While they made their way up to Mel, two deputies would take Violet to

Stowaway. "By the time we arrive, I'm sure they'll have found your son safe and sound. Stowaway's a quiet little town. We'll find him."

"Can my friend come with me?" Violet asked.

"Yes, of course. Let's get moving," Detective Ryan said.

Minutes later, Mary and Violet were in an unmarked police car with two deputies, Snow and Moore. Snow communicated via cell phone with the police in Stowaway as they raced north. After a few minutes, Snow relayed that the local police had stormed the McDonalds. There were no little boys matching Dakota's description currently there. However, one of the employees remembered seeing him leave with an elderly lady. They'd assumed she was his grandmother. A description of both Dakota and the old lady had been dispatched to police stations all over the state of California.

Mary and Violet held onto each other in the back seat. Mary prayed silently.

After another fifteen minutes, Snow took another call. "Great news. Yes, we're thirty minutes out." He turned back to Violet. "They found him. The old lady took him to the police station. Apparently, he was quite articulate about what had happened and that his mother and father would be worried sick."

Violet crumpled against Mary in obvious relief and started to cry. "That sounds like him."

They pulled into the parking lot of the police station forty-five minutes later. The deputies advised them to stay outside while they went into get Dakota. "You ladies don't need to see what's inside," Snow said.

Violet leaned against the car without taking her eyes from the door. Mary looked up and down the main street of the small beach town. With its quaint, old-fashioned storefronts, including a candy and a hardware store, it was like falling back in time. She remembered Cameron telling her they had a city ordinance to protect the aesthetic.

Dakota came running out. "Mama." He ran into Violet's

arms. She fell to her knees, rocking him against her chest. "Thank God you're all right." She held him away from her for a moment and peered at him. To Mary, he looked the same sturdy, sweet blond boy he'd always been.

An elderly lady came out from the doors, clutching a light blue purse to her chest. Violet stood, thanking her.

"This poor child. Just awful what happened. My, my, isn't he a smart one though. He spotted me in the booth across the restaurant and came right over and told me the whole story. We knew just what to do then, didn't we, young man?"

"Go to the police," Dakota said.

"Again, thank you," Violet said. "I was so scared."

Dakota tugged on his mother's arm. "We have to go get Mollie Blue. That weird lady took her."

"That was Mel. Did you remember her?" Violet asked.

"No, Mama."

"She came to take care of Mollie when you were sleeping at night," Violet said, almost to herself. "Of course, you wouldn't remember her."

"She came in my room and before I could scream, she put a towel over my face and it made me go to sleep. I woke up when we were driving. She didn't even know that Mollie was supposed to be in her car seat. She was on the backseat with me, no seatbelt over her. I patted her, though, like you told me to when she cries and you're fixing her bottle."

"That's my brave boy."

"I was scared, Mama." Plump tears rolled down his cheeks. "Will she hurt Mollie?"

"No, she won't. She's just very mixed up right now." Violet looked over at the deputies. "Have you heard from your men who are with Kyle? Is he there yet?"

Deputy Snow stepped forward and patted Dakota's head. "Few minutes out. She's down some dirt road. But she's stayed there. We'll get her."

"Do we wait here or go there?" Mary asked.

"You ladies go across the street and get a coffee." He pointed to a Starbucks. "We'll keep you posted on everything."

They crossed the street with Dakota holding on to his mother's hand. Mary felt such relief that Dakota was safe, her legs felt weak. When they were settled on a soft couch in front of a fireplace, Dakota crawled onto his mother's lap and fell asleep. The women waited anxiously for news from the dirt road where baby Mollie's fate could be decided by a disturbed young woman.

11

Lance

BECAUSE KYLE WAS too shaken to drive, Lance drove them to their destination. When they reached the beginning of the dirt road just outside of Stowaway, they changed places. The car bounced in the potholes of the dirt road that led to the cabin. The cops followed closely behind until they reached the last bend in the road, where they stopped. If Mel's car was there, Kyle was to call and alert them and they would proceed on foot to ambush her.

They took one last sharp turn. Lance crouched low in the passenger seat. A cabin stood at the edge of a muddy pond. The front porch and patchy roof sagged in decay. A toy wagon and tricycle, abandoned long ago, rusted at the bottom of the stairs. What must be Mel's old Nissan was parked under the branches of an old cherry tree. Pink blossoms fell like snow onto her car, covering the hood.

"She's been here for hours," Lance said. "Look at the hood of the car."

Kyle spoke into his phone to the detective. "She's here."

The detective gave him final directions. "Keep her there. Make her think her plan worked. We'll come from behind. Lance, keep a close watch on him, but from a distance. Keep us informed of what's happening."

"Yes, sir," Lance said. He had his cell phone programmed with Ryan's number. He was also wired. The detective and his team would hear every move they made. *Please God.*

Kyle pushed open his door and ran toward the house. Lance followed but stayed hidden behind the trunk of the cherry tree. Kyle ran up the steps to the front porch and tried the door. Locked.

Lance scanned the yard. No one. He stepped from behind the tree and pointed toward the back of the house. Kyle nodded and disappeared around the corner of the house.

Lance followed, making sure to keep some distance between them. Tall grasses dampened his shoes and the bottom of his jeans. At the corner of the house, he stopped and peered out to the yard.

Kyle stood about ten feet from a figure in a blue coat who stood near a pond. Her back was to them. Before she could turn and see him, Lance darted behind an overgrown rhododendron not far from the pond.

Kyle shouted to her. Mel turned. She had Mollie in her arms. Her raven black hair looked almost purple in the bright light of the afternoon. Mollie's pink blanket flapped in the breeze. Sheer joy spread over Mel's face.

"I knew you'd come."

"I'm here." From the bush, Lance watched Kyle move toward her until he was close enough to reach out and grab her.

"Give me Mollie," Kyle said.

Mel shook her head and stepped closer to the water's edge.

"No. She's fine." From what Lance could see, Mollie slept peacefully in Mel's arms.

Kyle moved nearer to her, his voice steadier. "What're you doing, Mel? This isn't the way to get my attention."

"I had to get you away from her, so we could talk," Mel said.

"You scared me when you took the kids. You could've talked to me about this, not involved the babies."

Mel's eyes and hair were wild, like she'd stuck a fork into an outlet. "Do you know how she's played you? She's wormed her way into your life because she wants your money. But I love you for real. I would never fake it with you."

"I'm sorry about that. But now we can talk freely. We can make a plan. Wherever you'd like to go. But first, can I hold the baby?"

"No. First you tell me the plan." She clutched Mollie close to her chest. The blanket lifted in the breeze. Something shiny in Mel's hand glinted in the sunlight. A pistol, no bigger than a flask. She had a gun next to the baby. Did Kyle see it?

"I knew you felt the same way. You've hidden your feelings because of her. But we can be together now."

"That's right. We can escape. Maybe buy a little piece of property near the ocean."

"Off the grid where we can be together," Mel said.

Lance spoke to him silently.

Play her game. Keep her on the hook.

"But I need to hold Mollie," Kyle said.

Mel tightened her grip around the baby. "I told you she's fine with me."

"Let me take her. She gets heavy. You've done enough."

"What's that noise? I hear something." Still cradling the baby in one arm, she raised the pistol with her left hand and pointed it straight at the bush where Lance was huddled. "Come out with your hands up. I can see you."

Lance did as she asked. Hands in the air, he walked closer.

"What the hell? Where did you get a gun?" Kyle asked.

"I've had it," she said. "From before."

Before what?

"Take it easy," Kyle said. "It's just my buddy Lance. He's on our side."

She waved the gun. "You said it was just you and me. No one else."

"It will be. As soon as you hand the baby over to me, we'll go wherever you want. I'll buy you dinner and we'll talk through everything."

"Up north where no one can find us," Mel said.

"I want my baby." Kyle inched closer to her.

She aimed the gun at Lance. "Don't come any closer or your friend gets it."

Lance took in a deep breath. *Don't panic. Stay still.*

"Mel, not this. Not like this." Kyle's voice sounded like ice hitting cold steel. "You could get into trouble and then how would we be together?"

Just keep her talking. The police would be here soon. They'd take her down.

"Put the gun away," Kyle said.

"You've betrayed me." She turned the gun on Kyle. "If I can't have you, no one will."

A deafening crack of a gunshot sounded in the spring air. Mel crumpled to the ground with the baby in her arms. Blood spilled from her head onto the wet grass. Kyle reached her first, grabbing the baby.

Mollie started to cry. Lance didn't know much about babies, but one who could scream that loudly sounded quite healthy. He was afraid his legs might fall out from under him as he ran toward his friend.

The cops advanced, guns aimed at Mel. But the girl was still. They'd killed her. Lance stumbled backward, away from the dead girl, swallowing hard to keep from vomiting. Kyle shielded Mollie against his chest and took off for the car. How was there so much blood? He stumbled after Kyle.

More cop cars arrived, sirens blaring. Kyle appeared not to notice as he opened the door and rummaged through the diaper bag. He pulled out a bottle of formula and climbed into his car to give Mollie her bottle. Lance leaned against the side of the car.

He shook so hard his teeth chattered. A delayed reaction to a gun being pointed at his head, perhaps? He fell to his knees and bowed his head to pray. *Thank you, God, for keeping us all safe.*

He sat on the grass with his head in his knees. Inside the car, Kyle murmured to his baby daughter. "It's all fine now, Mollie Blue. No one will hurt you."

Violet. He needed to call Violet. He grabbed his cell phone from his jeans and punched in her number.

Violet, with a panicked voice, answered after one ring. "Lance?"

"Mollie's fine. We got her." He'd save the details for later. No need to frighten her further. "The police are taking care of Mel. Kyle's feeding Mollie a bottle. She's unharmed. Completely perfect."

"Thank God. Thank you for going with them," Violet said. Lance sobbed silently at the sound of her voice. The idea of what could have happened overwhelmed him. Sweet Violet. Innocent Mollie. His brave best friend helpless and frightened. The next second, Mary's voice came on the line.

"Lance, are you all right?"

He sobbed harder. His Mary. Their unborn child. How useless he was to protect them.

Lance?" Panic heightened the pitch of her voice. "Are you there?"

"Yes, I'm here. It was awful. So awful."

"When can you come back?"

"It may be a while," he said. "The police will have questions for us. Can you take Violet and Dakota home or are you too shaken?"

"No, I can. I'm fine. I'll call everyone and let them know

everything's all right. Kara and Brody just called to see if we'd heard anything yet."

"I'm glad you're okay," she whispered. "I was worried."

"Me too."

"I'll see you at home. Do you understand? We're all fine."

"Yes," he whispered.

"Just come home."

"As soon as I can."

They hung up.

Lance slid into the driver's side. He patted his best friend's shoulder.

"Jesus, Lance, I could have lost Mollie, or been killed and left Violet alone to raise these kids without me."

"I know, bud. But it's okay. You're all okay now. It's going to be fine."

With a voice as dry as a desert, Kyle dipped his chin to his chest and closed his eyes. "I have no idea how to keep them safe. Not one clue."

"I know." He *did* know. They were no longer boys, but men. To keep their families and loved ones safe from harm was now the primary goal. But they were all at the mercy of evil. It could take them out at any given moment.

He wanted to build a life with Mary, provide for her, protect her. These were old-fashioned ideals, of course. The women they knew and loved would chastise him if he were to express them out loud. Regardless, it was truth. Men wanted to shield their families from harm. He gazed up into the pink blossoms of the cherry tree. They rustled in the breeze and dangled precariously. A heavy rain would toss them from the branches and scatter them across the hard ground.

Lance placed his hand on Mollie's head as she sucked from her bottle and gazed into her daddy's eyes.

Kyle wiped his eyes. "Thanks for being here, man. I swear to God, I don't know what I did to deserve a friend like you, but I'm grateful."

"I'd do anything for you."

"She could've killed you," Kyle said.

He managed a smile. "I'd have died trying to help my friend. There are worse ways to go. But you owe me a beer."

"And a scotch."

Hours later, Lance put on soft music and turned on the fireplace. Mary was in the kitchen, putting together a quick dinner of steak and salad. Freckles lay in his bed, mostly asleep, with an occasional glance at Mary as if to ensure her safety. Outside, the sun had fallen, bringing darkness and a fat full moon that hung low in the sky. Lance went outside to his deck. He leaned over the railing and peered out to the sea that waited like an old friend below the cliff. The moon lit the water and illuminated the waves as they crested and rolled to shore.

The horrific events of earlier almost seemed like a bad dream. They were all safe now. Best to focus on that and not replay the death of a young woman. He turned around to watch Mary. She was methodical, careful even in the way she shredded lettuce, not haphazard but in even chunks. Her movements in the shop and here in his kitchen were precise and succinct, never a wasted moment.

Lance had inwardly flinched when Mary had described Mel as delusional. How was he any better than Mel? He was living under the premise that he would somehow win Mary over. Would he? So far, the evidence pointed to a *no* as fat as the moon. He saw the way she looked at *special ops guy*. Like she wanted to eat him for dinner. Not quite as excited as she'd been about a peanut butter sandwich earlier, but close.

Rafael. Even his name sounded badass. Lance was not badass. He was *nice*.

He went inside. She greeted him with a smile. Steaks sizzled on the stove. The salad was on the table, as were two wine glasses. One with red wine, the other with seltzer.

"Smells great," he said.

At the stovetop, she held a spatula in midair. "What's wrong? Your face is cloudy."

"Cloudy?"

"My mom used to say that. You know, like something's bothering you."

He considered telling her the truth for half a second. Not a good idea.

She came over to him, concern in her eyes. "Seriously, are you feeling unwell? It was an awful day."

He nodded. "Not unwell. Just kind of undone."

Mary placed her hands on his upper arms. "It's understandable. What can I do? Would you like me to make you a drink? Something strong?"

He inhaled her scent, his gaze on her birthmark.

She covered it with her hand but smiled up at him. "Don't look at it."

"I think it looks like a question mark," he said. "Curious, like you."

Her eyes softened. Smoke rose from the pan on the stove.

She yelped and ran to it. "Now they're well done. Darn."

"I like well done."

She lifted the steaks from the pan and turned off the burner. "You do not. I know you like them medium."

"It doesn't matter. I'll like them because you made them."

"You'll lie straight to my face?

"Maybe."

"Ooh." Her hand flew to her stomach. "Baby loves to kick me in the ribs."

"Does it hurt?"

"Just a little. I love it." She gestured toward the table with her chin. "Go sit while I make you a drink. What would you like?"

"Do you know how to make drinks?"

"I have a small repertoire. My dad likes Manhattans and Gin Martinis. So, I know how to make those. And pour wine."

"I'll take a Manhattan."

She moved around the kitchen, mixing the drink before joining him at the table.

"You're looking remarkably good," he said. Her color and glow had returned the past few days.

"It helps that the nausea is gone. I'm starving now." She set the drink in front of him, then grabbed the plate with the steaks.

He took a sip of his drink. "Delicious. Thank you."

She sat next to him at the table, placing her hand on her stomach. "I wish I could enjoy being pregnant without feeling so nervous all the time."

"Me too."

"This will be my last baby, after all."

"You don't know that. You're still young."

"This is my last baby." She put salad in both their bowls. "Tell me what happened today."

He cut his salad into smaller pieces, buying time. Did he want to tell her? Or would it just upset her?

"You can tell me. I'll be fine. I'm strong." She cut into her steak. "Dammit, well done."

He cut into his steak. Blood seeped onto the plate. The images from earlier flashed before his eyes. Mel's head wound had gushed blood. So much blood. Nausea overwhelmed him. He pushed back from the table but stayed in his chair.

"Lance?"

"Not feeling great all of the sudden," he said.

She pushed the drink toward him. "Have some of this."

He did so, then hung his head and squeezed his eyes shut. Would he ever get those images out of his head?

She reached over to him and squeezed his wrist. "It's over now. Everyone's fine."

"Except for Mel. She was so disturbed. I know what she did was wrong, but she's someone's daughter."

"I hadn't thought of it that way. I was only thinking of our friends and that precious baby and how scared I was. But you're right." She touched the side of his face with her fingertips. "I love your heart."

What about the rest of me? Could you ever love all of me?

He let the strong drink run down the back of his throat. "I'm sorry. Please, eat. I know you're starving. The baby needs some iron."

"True."

They ate without further discussion, the clank of knives and forks the only sound. He took several bites of the salad and steak but pushed the rest around on his plate. His mind whirled and jumped from one thought to another.

When their meals were finished, he cleaned the dishes and then joined her in front of the fire. He tucked a blanket around her and sat closer to her than he usually did. The fire threw shadows around the room.

"Are you sure you want to hear about what happened?" he asked.

She nodded.

He told her the details, ending with the police shooting Mel. "The guy was a hell of a shot. She had a baby in her arms."

"Poor Kyle," she said. "And you—you were in danger. If I'd known, I would have been beside myself."

"When she had the gun pointed at my head, I wasn't thinking about her," he said. "I was thinking about you and our baby. It's the first time in my life that my death would affect someone else. You guys need me."

"That's true. We do." She spoke softly, looking at the fire. "But your death would affect a lot of people. I don't think you realize how loved you are."

He shrugged.

"For the first time, it occurred to me how awful it would be without you."

"If I die, you'll be taken care of."

"I wasn't thinking about the money," she said.

He watched her, looking for evidence of her meaning.

"It's hard to imagine my life now, without you in it," she said.

"I can't imagine my life without you either." He drew closer, lifting her chin with his fingers.

12

Mary

IN EARLY APRIL, Mary waited on the examination table for Doctor Freddie to come in for their appointment. Lance sat in the guest chair, his foot shaking as fast as Freckles' tail often did. He got up and went to the window, then came back to the chair.

"Sit down. You're making me nervous."

He jerked at the sound of her voice. "I'm sorry. I'm jumpy as hell."

"I've felt her or him moving around a bunch today. I'm sure everything's fine." She gazed up at the ceiling.

"You're remarkably calm today," he said as he came to stand at her side.

"I'm excited to find out the gender."

They'd decided, after a few discussions, to find out. There were enough variables in their future that knowing the sex seemed like a legitimate thing to do.

Doctor Freddie came in then. She set her laptop aside and

gave them a warm smile. "Shall we take a look and see if we have a Jane or a John?"

They both nodded. Mary glanced at Lance. He bounced on his toes like a kid before Christmas.

Doctor Freddie spread gel over Mary's stomach. Doctor Freddie pulled the monitor closer to them and placed the transducer on her bump. He knew what to expect after spending way too long on the internet. "Let's see what we've got here." Lance held his breath. The baby looked like a baby. A head and limbs were obvious.

The doctor measured the baby. "Perfect growth for this stage." She pointed to a small white dot in between the baby's legs. "And that right there is a little girl. You're having a daughter."

"A little girl?" Lance asked. "Are you sure? I thought for sure it was a boy."

Mary looked up at him. She had an image of him with a little girl sitting on his lap, worshipping his every word. He would be good with a daughter.

"I wanted a girl," Lance said. "But I didn't want to tell you in case it was a boy."

"I just want a healthy baby," Mary said. *A fat, healthy baby like Mollie Blue.*

"Every indication says you're going to get your wish," Doctor Freddie said. "Try not to worry so much. I know it's hard, but the more relaxed you are, the better for the baby."

Afterward, Lance suggested lunch and a little shopping if she wasn't too tired. She agreed. "I'm starving," she said.

They found a French café around the corner from the hospital. She ordered a grilled veggie and cheese sandwich. Nothing had ever tasted as good.

"Good?"

"The best sandwich ever," she said.

"Great. Eat up." Lance said with an approving glance at her half-eaten sandwich.

"It's nice to be past the queasiness." Her diet of crackers and water had not helped her skinniness. She felt like a bag of bones with a watermelon attached. So much for looking luscious like Violet. Even Maggie had filled out slightly. Not Olive Oyl. She took another bite of her sandwich. "I might need one of these for the ride home."

"Now you're talking."

After lunch, she bought a few maternity dresses for warm weather and light cotton leggings and blouses. Lance suggested they look at some things for the baby. "It's time to order furniture, don't you think?" he asked.

She'd been afraid to jinx it before now, but he was right. They could relax and enjoy the journey. Plus, she couldn't disappoint him by saying no. A few blocks up from the café, they found a baby store. "It looks expensive," she said.

"I don't care. I'm buying whatever you want for our daughter." He stopped in the middle of the sidewalk and grabbed her hands. "We're having a *daughter*. A baby girl."

"I had a feeling."

He sobered. "Is it okay? Does it make you sad, thinking of Meme?"

Oh, Lance. She loved how he asked about her, said her name, didn't dismiss her feelings. Most people just pretended like Meme had never existed. Even her dad.

"I'll always be sad about Meme," she said. "But it doesn't mean I'm not excited about this little girl." She patted her stomach. "Who's doing flipflops, by the way. She liked that sandwich."

They spent a leisurely hour looking at furniture for the nursery and chose several items, including a crib and changing table. Lance insisted on buying a teddy bear and a soft pink blanket. She couldn't help but remember how the little dresser in her old home had been stuffed with clothes for Meme. Her mother had started buying them the moment she'd found out Mary was pregnant.

As they walked to the car with their packages, Lance took her hand. "You all right?"

"Yes. Just remembering."

He tightened his grip on her hand. At some point their little girl would have two nurseries. That thought made her knees weaken. *I don't want her to have two homes. I don't want two homes. I want to be with Lance.*

No you don't. You're safer this way. Alone.

As if she knew her thoughts, the baby kicked, hard, just below her left rib cage. "Give me your hand." She placed it on her stomach, hoping the little garbanzo bean would do it again. *Thump.* There it was. "Did you feel that?"

His eyes glittered like they had during the ultrasound. "I sure did." He shook his head. "There's a baby in there."

"Our baby."

"No matter what, I'm going to be here for you both. Don't ever doubt it."

I want to be with Lance.

She could not do it. No, the risk was too great. Stay with the plan.

On the way home from the city, the sun shone brightly. Wildflowers in purples and yellows and pinks dotted the hillsides. Mary closed her eyes, drowsy in the comfortable car with the sun streaming in through the windows. When they reached the highest peak on the highway, she asked Lance if he minded pulling over. She wanted to look at the view. He did so without hesitation, parking in one of the empty spots. Today, they had the lookout all to themselves. Too early in the year for tourists. They walked to the edge where a barrier kept people from falling over the cliff. A breeze rustled Lance's hair and brought the scent of the sea. A barge crossed the water, moving slowly. Further out, a ship seemed anchored in place.

She breathed in the air and looked out as far as she could. When she was a child she thought she could see Japan from the Oregon coast. Back then, she'd tried to imagine the little children across the world. Were they like her? Did they peer across the ocean and wonder if there was anyone on the other side? She'd been lonely then. An only child without many friends, other than the characters in the books she'd read. She'd wanted a playmate. A friend, like Lance.

She moved closer and rested her head against his shoulder. "I'm going to miss you when you go."

"I'm not leaving."

"You will, eventually."

"Not far."

"We have to start making plans for our divorce," she said. "I should figure out where I'm going to live."

"We'll figure it out later. Not now. Right now, my job's to take care of you."

"What about custody? How will we arrange it?"

He turned to look at her. "We'll do whatever's best for our girl. You can have the house if it comes down to that."

"Lance, no."

"I can buy something else if I have to."

She sighed, suddenly tired. "You're impossible."

"I've heard that before."

When Mary was a child, she loved the library, with its cool, clean floors and stacks of books. It was the best place for a shy, skinny girl with buck teeth. Back then, her mother worked in her father's oral surgery office, so Mary was alone in the afternoons after school. When she was old enough, she caught the city bus to her neighborhood library. She was to wait for her mother there, doing homework or reading, which was just fine with Mary. For hours, she would read in the chair by the window, unnoticed by staff or patrons. She was the invisible type. Invisible was preferable to the alternative. Some might be lonely, but not Mary. The books were fine company. Staying unnoticed during school years was a blessing. Just ask any bullied kid and they'd tell you that straight away.

She was reminded of the charm of invisibility when she was summoned to her father's house by his new wife. Mary wanted to politely decline the invitation for coffee, but she knew it was inevitable. Flora was part of her family now. Her father loved Flora. He appeared happier than he'd been since her mother's death. She wished she could be happy for him.

With a purple scarf in her curly salt and pepper hair and dressed in a long tunic over leggings, Flora looked casual yet stylish when she welcomed Mary inside the cottage. The scent of cinnamon permeated the room.

"Come in, come in. Can I get you tea?" Flora asked as she led her into the cozy kitchen.

She declined and commented on the delicious scent.

"My famous coffee cake," Flora said.

Famous?

As if she'd heard her question, Flora clarified. "Famous to my boys anyway."

"Your boys?"

"Brody and Lance."

Right. She thought of them as her children, having helped raise them during her years of employment with the Mullens. "I was there the moment they brought home both the boys. Brody was a monster, even back then. Huge head and those eyes that stared right through a person. He grew into his head later, of course. Lance, on the other hand, was the most precious baby you've ever seen. Affectionate and even-tempered. If he detected sadness or loneliness, he offered a hug. Even to strangers on the street." She pointed to a box on the coffee table. "I pulled out some photographs of Lance when he was small. There were more of Brody, being the first, but I found some good ones of Lance too."

Mary sat on the couch and picked up the stack of photos. The first was of a naked, toothless, and plump baby laughing into the camera. "He was so fat."

"Yes, he was a chubby little guy back then," Flora said from the kitchen.

The second photo was of Lance as a toddler. Wearing red pajamas, he sat by the Christmas tree with wrapping paper piled high around him.

Flora set two pieces of cake on the table. "That was the year he asked for a toy cash register." She chuckled. "He was always interested in money."

"How funny." Mary smiled, imagining Lance punching the keys and pretending to take money.

"We thought so at the time," Flora said. "Looking back, it makes perfect sense. He used to love going to the grocery store with me. When he was a little older, he learned about coupons. He'd cut them all out of the Sunday paper and we'd shop on Mondays. He got the biggest kick out of getting things on discount. It was a riot."

Flora picked up another from the stack. "This is him in high school running cross country."

In the photo, Lance ran along a trail, his young body lithe and lean. "I didn't know he ran cross country," Mary said. He often ran in the mornings. She admired his discipline.

"Did you play any sports?" Flora asked.

"No, I was the bookish kind. P.E. was my worst class."

"When I was young, women weren't allowed to play sports. I would've loved to. Instead, I got pregnant and was sent away to live with the nuns." Flora set the photograph down on the table and looked out the window. "I was so in love with your father back then."

Mary knew the story. Her father was poor and lived with his single mother. Flora's parents were pillars of the community and disapproved. When Flora became pregnant, she was sent away. They took the baby boy from her. She never knew what had happened to the baby. Mary's father was gone by the time she'd returned, with no idea what had happened to his girlfriend. Over forty years later, Flora hired a private detective who found both Mary's father and their baby boy. Cameron Post lived just north in a town called Stowaway. He'd been adopted by a nice couple, both of whom had passed on by the time Flora had found him.

"You know how it is to lose a child," Flora said. "I never got over it. The way they took him from me." She shut her eyes and pursed her lips. "I try not to remember the sounds of his cries when they ripped him from my arms. But they haunt me."

Mary understood all too well. "It's not something you ever get over."

"No, but Brody and Lance helped me to love again. They kept me busy, especially Brody. He was naughty when he was young, always playing pranks and causing mischief."

Mary placed her hand over her belly. Would this child help her love again? Could she love another baby like she'd loved Meme?

A moment from that morning played in front of her eyes. She and Lance were at the breakfast table eating oatmeal and reading, a habit they'd developed over the past few weeks. He read slowly. For every two pages she flipped, he turned one. Every so often, he stopped and stared into space, as if to absorb a passage.

The sun peeked through the clouds and spilled into the room. His hair was damp from a recent shower. Near the base of his neck, a lock curled in the shape of a snail shell. She wished to touch it with her finger and wind the silky strands around her skin.

He laughed at something in the book, and it sounded like water boiling in a pot. Lance, slow and steady. The cross-country runner, pacing himself in anticipation of bumps and hills, maybe even the occasional root or hole. Not quick like her.

Joy filled her. The shadow of grief still lurked in her heart, slowing its beat, but not extinguishing it. There, in the simple pleasure of a good book, a warm breakfast, and the companionship of someone she loved more than anyone in the world, joy crept through the fog and nestled next to the grief, as if to say, we can be here side by side in the same heart.

Flora's voice brought her back to the present. "This one here is Lance on his first day of kindergarten. Wasn't he sweet?" In the photo, Lance grinned, his two front teeth missing. Freckles scattered over his nose. Big blue eyes stared into the camera.

"He was adorable," Mary said.

"Yes indeed. Let me ask you something," Flora said. "Have you fallen for him yet?"

She blinked, startled by the question. "What do you mean?"

"Dear, I know you married because of the baby. Everyone knows this to be true. My question is if you've managed to stay cold to him or if he's wormed his way into your heart."

"It's no one's business but ours." *Interfering bossy old lady had no right to pry.*

"I'm not sure that's quite accurate. Dax loves you and I love Lance. That makes your marriage our business."

"Loving us doesn't give you carte blanche entrance into our relationship."

"Here's my point," Flora said. "Lance's happiness is important to me. I want to feel assured that the woman he's married to appreciates him. This business arrangement you two have is not to my liking."

"All due respect, I don't really care." She stood, unsteady on shaky legs. How dare this woman talk to her this way. Business arrangement?

"Lance deserves the best," Flora said.

"I agree. But right now our focus is on the baby. We'll work out what's between us on our own. You and my father should stay out of it. If you'll excuse me, I have things to do."

She ran into her father on the way out the door. "Whoa there. Where are you going in such a hurry?" he asked.

"Anywhere but here." She pushed past him and headed for her car.

He followed her and grabbed the car door before she slammed it shut. "What happened?"

"Your wife is an interfering old bat, that's what."

"Mary Catherine. Shame on you."

"What's between me and her precious Lance is just that. Between us. You two don't get to dictate what we do."

"I agree."

"Tell *her* that," Mary said. "She called my marriage a business arrangement and said I wasn't good enough for Lance."

"Is that true? Is your marriage just for the baby? For insurance? Because I would've taken care of things for you."

She sighed and placed her hands on the steering wheel. "I know, Dad. Which is why we decided marriage was the best option."

"And there's nothing between you?"

"We're best friends. We'll co-parent well together."

His thick eyebrows lifted as he gazed down at her. "You ever think that's what marriage is? Two best friends."

"We're not in love, Dad." Why couldn't he just let it go?

"You'll divorce, then? Once the baby comes."

"We'll see. I'm not sure. We're not thinking that far ahead."

"Mary, I wanted you to have a real marriage. A family like we had."

"Like we had? You had a son you didn't even know about. Our life was a lie."

"What a ridiculous thing to say. How could it be a lie if I didn't even know about him?"

"You never told me you loved someone before Mom."

"It never occurred to me you'd be interested," he said.

"Did Mom know?"

"Yes. We shared everything. She loved someone before me.

It's unrealistic to think otherwise."

"How could you just forget her?" Mary gripped the steering wheel until her knuckles were white. "And start up with someone you hadn't seen for forty-five years. How do you do that?"

"The feelings came back, honey. It happens."

"What if Mom were still alive? Would you have just run off with her?"

"Of course not. I loved your mother very much."

"How is this supposed to work in heaven?" Mary looked up to the sky through the windshield. Angry clouds hung low. "Are you up there with your two wives?"

His hands fell to his side. "I don't know how it works. All I know is that your mother would want me to be happy while I'm still on earth, with or without her.

"How do you know that?"

"We talked about it many times."

She stared at him, flabbergasted. "You did?"

He smiled. "Sure. We used to joke about who of our friends would be acceptable. She had a soft spot for Ellen Cunningham."

"She *was* nice. Good cookies."

"Great gardener," her father said.

"But she's not widowed."

"Right. So, it's a moot point." He leaned his forehead against the doorframe and looked down at her. "Honey, you're too old to be this upset about me remarrying."

"You don't get to tell me what I feel or don't feel."

"Why can't you be happy for me?"

"I am."

"Not really," he said gently.

"I hate seeing you with her. The way you stare into each other's eyes makes me physically ill."

"I get that you miss your mom, but it was time for me to move forward. There were a lot of lonely years there."

"You had me," she said.

"That's another reason why I needed to move forward."

"What does that mean?"

"As an example for you. It's time you let yourself love again."

She turned away and glared at the dashboard.

"Is there any chance you could love Lance?" her father asked. "Think about the baby."

"It has nothing to do with whether I love him. I can't trust him. I can't trust any man. You're all cheaters. Even you."

He blanched and stepped back from the car.

"I know about your affair. Mom told me. If you could do it, any man could."

Obviously flustered, he raked a hand through his hair. "It was a terrible mistake. One your mother forgave me for."

"Why? Why did you do it when you loved her?"

"Mary, it's impossible for you to understand. But men, *some* men, are broken in ways you can't see on the outside. I hadn't healed from the traumas of my childhood. With that came self-destructive behavior. A need for my ego to be built up by outside sources. You were a little baby and your mother wasn't doing well."

"So, you helped her by screwing another woman?"

"That's the thing. I felt helpless and inadequate, so I did something to try and feel good about myself. It was one time. One stupid mistake. Your mother knew me like she knew her own hand. She understood why I did it. Not to say she forgave me easily, but your mother was wise. She knew our family was more important than holding onto her anger. So, she forgave me. We went into therapy, which was the best thing we ever did as a couple. I learned a lot about myself and when we came out the other side, after the hurt and betrayal eased, we were closer than I ever thought I could be to a person."

Mary rested her head against the steering wheel.

"Honey, you can't let my mistake or Chad's betrayal ruin the rest of your life. Lance Mullen is a man who already knows his worth. He had a family that made sure he knew unconditional love. Don't you see? He won't cheat because he doesn't need to."

"But what if it's me? What if I'm so terrible to be married to that I push him into an affair? Look what I did to Chad."

"Chad was immature. You married too young and you weren't suited, honey. Surely you see that now?"

"Am I suited to Lance, Dad? You said yourself, he's a fine person. I'm not."

"It hurts me to hear you say that. You're your mother's daughter. You know what kind of person she was."

The very best.

"You've said yourself Lance is your best friend and confidant. The way he treats you is everything I've wished for you. Flora's sure he's in love with you."

"Flora thinks a lot of things."

He kept one arm on the car door. "You should give Flora a chance."

"She's bossy and opinionated. Even Lance says so."

"Both true. But Lance loves her, right?"

"Very much."

"Can you promise me you'll try harder to forge a relationship with her?" he asked. "For me?"

"I'll try. But not today. Today I need to go home." *I need to see Lance. Talk to him. Have him put his arms around me and assure me everything's going to be all right.*

When she started the car and drove out of her father's driveway, the song she and Chad had chosen for their first dance at their wedding came on the radio. She quickly changed the channel. Memories of her first husband seemed to have great power today. They were everywhere, even on the radio.

A month after her mother had died, three months after they'd buried Meme, she'd found texts on his phone. A nude photograph of the barista and a series of exchanges that were not meant to be seen by his wife. When he'd come out of the bathroom after showering, she'd thrown the phone at him.

She remembered the beginning of that horrible exchange in vivid detail, only it was in black and white like in a dream.

"Who is she?" Mary wore a flannel nightgown, the material thin at the elbows. Some days she didn't get dressed. This was one of them.

Chad picked up the phone, his face puckered like a rotting apple. "She's someone I met. Since you've been so…"

"So what?"

"Depressed."

"I'm not depressed. I'm sad. There's a difference."

"Okay. Since you've been sad."

"Are you in love with her?"

"Yes."

Prickles of pain, like the moment after you realize your arm's fallen asleep and you shake or rub it to waken it, spread through her. "When were you planning on telling me? When did it start? Before Mom died? After?"

"Before we got pregnant. I wanted to tell you. But then we found out you were pregnant."

A brick tore through her chest. She stared at him, her mouth hanging open like in a cartoon. "This started before? Before Meme?"

"I'm sorry. I didn't mean for it to happen. I tried to break it off, but it's impossible. I have to have her."

"You have to have her? Are you five?"

"Mary, you've been a zombie."

"This started before I was a zombie. You were sleeping with another woman when your wife was pregnant."

The rest of the night was a blur. She remembered throwing a lot of household items, including a lamp, the television remote, a vase his mother had given her, and their framed marriage certificate. While she threw things, he packed a suitcase, dodging flying objects. Then, he left. The door slammed. His tires squealed as he pulled out of the driveway. He couldn't wait to get away. She stood in the middle of the living room of her empty house. The hum of the refrigerator was loud in her ears. She sank to the floor and crawled to the couch. For the third time in her life, she wished it would end.

Now, she pulled into Lance's garage and breathed a sigh of relief when she saw his car. Freckles greeted her when she walked inside, wagging his tail and licking her hand. "Hey buddy. Where's Lance?" Freckles barked and pointed toward Lance's office with his chin.

He followed her as she set her purse and keys on the kitchen table and walked over to Lance's office. Normally, she didn't bother him while he worked, but she needed to see his face. The tightness in her chest made it hard to breathe. She needed Lance.

She and Freckles stopped when they came to the open doorway of his office. Lance's simple wood desk faced the sea, so his back was to them. He was dressed in what she knew were his favorite faded jeans and an old t-shirt he'd bought at a music festival with Kyle one summer. No shoes. He preferred bare feet during the warm months and socks during the winter. Details she'd learned over the last few months as his roommate.

He clicked away at his computer, seemingly engrossed. One computer screen displayed a spreadsheet, the other a live feed of the stock market. Opaque shades over the large window were drawn to dim the bright sun. Only a blue streak of sea was visible from the bottom of the window. His desk was always tidy. She'd noticed it before, amazed that he moved large amounts of money around with a click of his mouse. Like Lance, his office was deceptively simple at first view.

Freckles, tired of postponing their visit, trotted over to Lance. He sat and wagged his tail, secure that his master would stop what he was doing and pat his head. He didn't have to wait long. "Hey boy, did you give up waiting for Mary?"

Mary rapped on the door frame. "I'm home." He turned, his chair sliding easily across the wood floor. "I should've known you were back. This crazy dog's been waiting by the door since you left."

She smiled as she crossed over to him. Her fingers twitched with a sudden urge to place her hands in his glossy hair. She perched on the edge of his desk instead.

Still seated, he rolled a few inches back and looked up at her. *All his attention on me, like I'm the only thing in the world that matters.*

"How did it go with Flora?" he asked.

"Not great."

"What happened?"

She thought for a moment about how much to share with him. It was impossible not to tell him the story without telling him about Flora's question. *Have you fallen for him yet?*

"She knows our marriage was because of the baby," Mary said. "She said they all know."

"Really?"

"Then she asked if I'd fallen for you yet."

"That sounds like something she would ask." His smoky blue-eyed gaze moved away from her face. He got up from his chair and pulled the shade all the way down. "What did you say?"

"I told her it was none of her business."

"I'm sure that went over well." He crossed to the other side of the office and sat in the dark leather loveseat.

"She wants you to be happy," Mary said. "Which apparently is the justification for getting in my business."

"She's not exactly good with boundaries," Lance said with a grimace.

"I left abruptly and ran into my dad on the way out." She crossed the room and sat on the coffee table next to the loveseat. "We talked about his affair. He told me he did it because he felt bad about himself—that's why some men cheat. Do you agree with that?"

He tilted his head to the ceiling and rested his neck on the back of the loveseat. "I don't know. If I loved a woman enough to marry her, I would rather die than hurt her."

"That's what he said about you."

"Your dad?"

"Yes, he said you're too secure to cheat. He said something else too. Something I wonder about."

They were interrupted by the sound of his phone buzzing on the coffee table. Lance glanced at the screen. His breath caught. The tips of his ears reddened.

Before she could stop herself, she looked at the screen. *Tori Hawthorne.*

Tori Hawthorne had called twice, according to the number next to her name. Who was Tori Hawthorne? A twist of dread ran up the back of her spine. Trouble.

He stood and shoved his hands into his pants pockets. His eyes had turned a hard blue. "What should we have for dinner?"

"Who is Tori Hawthorne?" she asked.

He shrugged. "Not someone I expected to hear from again." His voice had an edge she'd never heard before. Who was this woman?

"Old girlfriend?" she asked.

"*The* old girlfriend. The one who cost me my job," he said.

The girlfriend. The *married* girlfriend from New York.

"What does she want?" Mary asked. As if he would know. Stupid question.

"I can't imagine."

He picked up his phone and stared at it, the muscles in his cheeks flexing. "I'll call her back. Just out of curiosity."

Freckles whined and looked up at Lance with a worried expression. *You and me both, Freckles.*

"I'll take it into my bedroom." Without a backward glance, he was off. Freckles stayed behind, turning his attention on Mary.

"Come on, bud. Let's go." She snapped her fingers and he followed her into the living room. Using the remote, she turned on the stereo. Her tablet was on the end table. She picked it up and turned it on, hoping to focus on the latest romance she'd downloaded. But the words swam in front of her eyes. She couldn't focus. Not with Lance in the other room talking with a woman he'd once loved and possibly still did. What if she called with the intention of winning him back? Maybe she'd split from her husband.

I wish my mom were here. What would she say to her mother if she were here? *I did something terrible to the man I love and now I can't have him.*

What would her mother say to that?

She'd had a gentle voice and the softest hands.

Mary imagined her sitting across the room, knitting, her small, soft hands moving faster than it seemed possible. They reminded Mary of a hummingbird's wings, so fast they seemed almost still.

Mom would encourage her to tell him the truth. *Give him a chance to forgive you.*

Lance came back into the room before she could delve any further into her mother's suggestion. His hair was askew. Two blotches of pink smeared his neck, like overly applied blush. He went to the liquor cabinet and grabbed a bottle of vodka. He leaned against the open cabinet, breathing heavily.

Lance undone? She didn't know what to do.

She waited. Finally, he turned around to look at her.

"You won't believe it," he said.

"What?"

"She's here. In town. She had the nerve to come here. She's staying at the lodge."

"To see you?"

"That's what she said. Her marriage blew up, not surprisingly, after I left. She's divorced. She wants me back. Can you believe the audacity to come here without calling or emailing or texting? *Something.* You don't just show up in a person's sanctuary with your dirty laundry and expect him to welcome you with open arms."

"What did you tell her?"

"I told her I'm married."

"Oh."

"And that I'm very much in love with my wife. And to go home." He rocked back on his heels and shoved his hands in his pockets.

"You loved her. Didn't you?" Mary asked.

His gaze settled on the floor before looking back at her. "I thought I did. But I realize now I had no idea what love was. I wanted her, physically. But love? I didn't even know her." He downed his shot, then came to sit on the easy chair's ottoman with his hands on his knees. "There's part of the story I didn't tell you. She wasn't married when I first met her. The first time I laid eyes on her was at a party for the firm. She was there with her dad, dressed in this thin white dress, no bigger than a handkerchief. The dress, not her. She caught my eye and kind of gave me a signal like she wanted me to ask her to dance. I'm shy with women, you know, but dancing is always good because then I wouldn't have to talk much. We danced and afterward we went out for food and talked. She told me she was *almost* engaged."

"Almost?"

"He'd asked her, but she was thinking about it. Then, one thing led to another and I took her back to my crummy apartment. We had sex. By the next morning she was gone. I called her. She said the whole thing was a mistake and that she'd decided to marry Nigel. She said she could never marry a guy who lived in a hovel in Brooklyn."

Mary's hands flew to her mouth. "She said that for real?"

He smiled. "She was the type of girl who could insult you and still make it sound sexy as hell."

"Charming."

"She's complicated. So, I let it go. I'm not the type to chase another man's wife. Or, I wasn't then. A whole year passed before I saw her again. In that time, I'd made some good decisions about investments and had made a ton of money, which she didn't know, of course. But it gives a man a different feeling about himself when he has money. I'm ashamed to admit it, but it's the truth."

"Did you see her at work functions?" Mary asked.

"No. I was thankful for that at the time. We ran into each other in a bar one night after I'd been working late. She'd been crying and drinking. Nigel, she said, was mean to her, verbally abusive. She confessed she hadn't wanted to marry Nigel but felt pressured by her father. Nigel's old money. Howard, her father, always had a thing for that, like it was some elite club he wanted to get into. I took her out for food to counteract all the booze. And here's the kicker. She played right into my vanity. 'I can't stop thinking about the night we spent together.' That's what she said—and it did the trick. Boom, I took her back to my apartment. I don't fully understand it myself, but soon I was having a full-fledged affair with her. She told me she was going to leave Nigel, which I was stupid enough to believe. Finally, I got tired of the runaround and broke it off. That's when she told her father."

"And he fired you."

"Yes. Which, as it turns out, is the best thing that ever happened to me. Because I came here, where I belong."

"Do you think that's why Tori's here? Because you're rich now?"

He placed both hands into his hair and dropped his head. "I don't know how she would know that."

"Would she have married you if she'd known back then how successful you'd be?"

"I have no way of knowing. Anyway, it doesn't matter now. She's on her broom headed home."

Mary wasn't so sure. Tori Hawthorne didn't sound like a woman who disappeared gently into the good night.

She looked up see Lance watching her. "What?" she asked.

"What your dad said to you about having an affair because he felt badly about himself?"

"Yes?"

"That's why I was with Tori. If I could get her, then it would prove that I was good enough. I wouldn't just be Brody Mullen's little brother."

"How would she prove your worth?"

"Because, finally, a woman loved me. I've never had any luck with women. I'm the friend, the guy you call when you have a problem. I thought she was different. The one for me. The same was true for my job. I was good at it and it had nothing to do with football or my dad or brother. It was mine. My time in New York was my attempt to prove I was worthy. And then I blew it all up. I don't know if insecure men cheat, but I know they chase after women they can't have." Abruptly, he rose to his feet, his features twisted in a way that made her think of a tornado. "I need to take a walk. Get out of this house for a while." He snapped for Freckles, who obediently followed him.

She jumped when the door slammed hard enough to shake the windows. Trembling, she hugged herself. What had she done to anger him? Or was it Tori? Had she stirred him up? Would he go to her? Was her memory one he couldn't let go of, even though he said he didn't love her?

Mary curled into a ball on the couch with her hands on her basketball stomach. How was it possible that a man like Lance felt the need to prove himself? There was nothing wrong with him. That he hadn't found the right woman had nothing to do with him and everything to do with the women he chose. Was that the crux of it then? He chose unwisely and then turned on himself when it didn't work out? Was that what she'd done with Chad? Chosen the wrong man and then blamed herself when he'd cheated? Who was she hurting with her fear of betrayal? Not Chad. Not her father.

Her mother's voice came to her loud and clear. *You're hurting yourself. And Lance. He loves you. You're the woman he thinks he can't have. The question is, what are you going to do about it?*

13

Lance

LANCE SQUINTED INTO the sunlight and wished he'd brought his sunglasses. Freckles, undaunted by the bright afternoon sun, trotted ahead. They walked down his driveway and headed toward Brody's. The vodka shots had relaxed him, but the phone call with Tori still ate away at him. What nerve the woman had to show up in his town. His town. Far away from the madness of her world.

All the feelings of inadequacy had risen in him the moment he talked with Tori. Here he was in the same situation. He'd been fooling himself into thinking his plan to win Mary was working. He had to face facts. Once again, he'd doomed himself to a broken heart. Hope was for idiots. Did he really think by sheer force of will he could get her to let go of her fears and love him?

When he reached Brody's, he rang the doorbell. Kara answered and immediately drew him into a hug. She knelt to give Freckles some love and was rewarded with a wet kiss on her neck.

"Come on in, Freckles. I have one of those bones you like."

"How did you know he likes those?" Lance asked.

"I bring them to him when Mary and I walk. That's how I won him over. Same with Brody. All males respond positively to being fed."

She led them into the kitchen. Brody was there, on the phone, but he waved at Lance.

"Do you want a drink?" Kara asked as she tossed an excited Freckles a chewy bone.

"Beer sounds great." Lance felt the vodka but not enough to blunt the pain. For the first time in a long time, he wanted to check out for a while. Forget Mary for an afternoon. Impossible, of course, but he could try.

Kara grabbed a beer for him and a water for her. They ambled out to the backyard. Freckles ran here and there, sniffing and rolling around in the grass. With the onslaught of warm weather, the pool's cover had been removed and the outdoor furniture had been cleaned and arranged around the patio. Flowers and shrubs bloomed under the spring sun. They strolled around the yard looking at the flowers. His attempt to seem interested in Kara's Teacup Dogwood must have been obvious, because she steered him over to the alfresco kitchen to sit in the shade.

Brody joined them then, beer in hand. Freckles came running up to give Brody a friendly lick on his arm.

"Freckles, it's been too long." Brody scratched behind Freckles' ear before grabbing another chair to come sit with them.

Kara excused herself, leaving them alone.

"You want to throw some darts?" Brody asked.

"Not really. I'd rather drink." He told him about Tori's arrival in town.

Brody took a long look at him. "Women like that always show back up in our lives. It's inevitable."

"Trust me, I want nothing to do with her. All I want is Mary."

Brody strode over to the cabinets under the outdoor grill and grabbed a handful of darts. Lance reluctantly got to his feet. His brother couldn't have a conversation unless he was simultaneously playing a game. It annoyed the crap out of him. Especially since his big brother always kicked his butt no matter the game.

Brody handed Lance four darts and took the first shot. Bullseye. Of course.

Lance's landed a little right of center. Brody's next shot mirrored his first.

"Flora came by earlier. Mad as a hornet," Brody said. "Run in with Mary."

"Yeah?"

"Says Mary's trouble."

"I'm aware of Flora's opinion."

"But you don't care?" Brody asked.

"Not really, no. I care about *Mary's* feelings. Flora needs to mind her own business."

"That's not her strong suit." Brody tossed another dart into the bullseye.

"Flora's not great at seeing anything outside her own point of view."

Lance tossed a dart at the board. Left of center.

Brody gathered the darts from the board and handed a few to Lance. "What did Dad always say? Slow and steady wins the race. You'll get her yet."

"Not in this case."

"I never thought I'd say this, but you and Mary seem right together. She's soft with you, all the hard edges blurred. I don't know what's going on with her, but something doesn't add up. The way she looks at you, I'd bet a lot of money she's in love with you."

"No, man. I wish it was true, but I've been kidding myself."

"You want some advice?" Brody asked.

"Can I stop you?"

Brody threw another dart into the middle of the board. "I say call her bluff. Tell her you think you should part ways, other than being there for the baby. It's basically what Kara did with me. The minute I thought I'd lost her for good, I got my act together really fast."

He thought about this as he tossed another dart. Bullseye. Finally.

"Nice one," Brody said.

"What made you change your mind about Mary?" Lance asked.

"My wife's very persuasive. She and Mary have shared a lot during their walks. I see her differently now. You know, not everyone's like you. I'm not great at digging through people's defense layers to see the real person. You and Kara do that like it's as easy as breathing."

Lance tossed another dart. Bottom of center. "That's a nice thing to say," he said gruffly.

"I'm jealous of that quality, to tell you the truth."

"When everyone in the world's paying attention to your older brother, it's easy."

"What's that mean?" Brody held a dart to his chest.

"All the focus was on you, which left me a lot of time to observe others." At his brother's crestfallen expression, he put a hand on his shoulder. "It didn't bother me. Not really."

"It did, though. I can see it in your face."

Lance hurled another dart at the board. It landed at the far-left bottom of the board. "This is America. Football is king of everything, which made you royalty. It's hard not to feel invisible every so often."

"With Mom and Dad? Or Flora?"

"No, not them. Just at school and college and everywhere else. I couldn't take a woman on a date without her starting the conversation with you." He walked to the board and pulled out the darts. He stood there for a moment, poking the points into the palm of his hand. "Tori never did that. She didn't know anything about football. Maybe that's why I fell for her."

"The first time Kara and I met Mary, she didn't know who I was, then she made some crack about how people should read instead of spending all their time watching some barbaric game."

Lance smiled despite his misery. "That sounds like her."

"It didn't go over well with my pretty football fan or her quarterback. That said, you have to add her to the list of women who couldn't give two nickels about me."

"No wonder I love her." Lance handed Brody a few of the darts.

Brody looked off into the distance, arms at his sides. "Our house was always all about football. I never thought that fact bothered you."

"I used to stand upstairs and watch you and Dad toss the football back and forth in the backyard. It was a private club I couldn't hope to get into. So, I focused on academics, which isn't the worst outcome in the world."

"Dad was always bragging about how smart you were. If you want to know the truth, I was jealous sometimes too. The only thing I've ever been any good at was football."

"I'd say we did pretty well when we combined our talents," Lance said. "Your body. My brain."

Brody nodded with a sad smile. "Your brain will never be forced into retirement, unlike my body."

"You still missing it?"

"I always will. Football was never a job to me. I loved every second of it. If not for my very real human fallibility, I would've played forever. It felt like a death when I had to retire. Everything I thought about myself suddenly disappeared. It was like, who am I if I'm not a football player? Kara was really understanding—put up with me moping around for six months. After the miscarriage, I had to step up for Kara. I had to go deep and realize my purpose in this life was to take care of her, be there for her, like she had been for me." His voice lowered, tight with emotion. "The hardest thing about being a husband is not being able to fix it. I can't take away the grief about her mother or her disgusting human being of a father. I couldn't fix it when we lost the baby."

"I know. If I could erase Mary's pain, I would in a minute. However, we have to accept our limitations."

"Which kind of sucks."

"Still, I'll give it one heck of a shot," Brody said.

"This is a new season. New purpose," Lance said.

"That's right. And no matter how you slice it, I've been one lucky man."

"I'd give anything to have what you have with Kara."

His big brother turned to him and looked him squarely in the eye. "You remember this—you're a Mullen. We're tough. No one can break us. Not even a woman."

He pretended to agree even though he knew it was the absolute opposite. Mullen men set themselves up for absolute brokenness when they loved a woman. Brody had forgotten because his bride was inside the house fixing his dinner.

Lance and Freckles spent the next morning at the shop with Mary. While she helped customers, Lance worked at the desk on the financials. Freckles napped at his feet.

The bell on front door rang out, indicating a new customer. Lance looked up to see a woman in a hooded red coat enter the shop. A gust of wind blew the pages of a discarded newspaper from a side table onto the floor before the door shut behind her. The woman pushed back her hood. Tori Hawthorne smiled at him. "Hi Lance."

Despite the wind and rain, she looked as polished as ever. Her white blond hair was pulled into a neat ponytail. She wore slim black pants and a pink blouse with a large bow at the collar. Puffy sleeves at the wrists reminded him of a groomed poodle.

Like an idiot, he sat there gaping at her, unable to utter a word. She sailed across the shop, her black pumps barely making a sound on the wood floor. When she reached him, he managed to stand and come around the desk.

She kissed his cheek. "They told me at the lodge I might find you here."

"What're you still doing in town?" The familiar scent of her perfume curled the hairs inside his nostrils. What did she do? Bathe in the stuff? He coughed and stepped backward, smacking into the edge of the desk.

Freckles, on his feet now, growled.

"It's okay, boy." Lance steadied him with a command to sit. Freckles obeyed but kept his focus on this new enemy.

"I couldn't break the promise I'd made to my father," Tori said. "I couldn't leave town without seeing you."

Mary appeared at his side and held out her hand to Tori. "I'm Mary Mullen. Lance's wife."

"It's a pleasure." Tori's cool blue eyes settled on Mary's stomach. "A baby on the way. How delightful."

Had she always sounded so pretentious?

"Lance was surprised to get your phone call," Mary said, her voice ice cold.

The corners of Tori's mouth twitched into one of her half smiles he remembered well. "I'm here as an ambassador for my father. He'd like to offer you a position. I didn't have a chance to tell you during our brief phone call."

His old job?

"He's prepared to give you a partnership," Tori said. "Your former clients left in droves. The guy who took your place is a mess."

A partnership?

He didn't need the money. *Remember that.*

"A partnership. What you always wanted," Tori said.

"Things have changed," he said.

Tori's gaze flickered around the shop. "Yes, so it seems. What a quaint little store. Well done." This last part was directed at Mary.

"We like it," Mary said.

"Hear me out, at least," Tori said to Lance. "I'm on my way out of town in a few hours. Let me take you to lunch. Like I said, I promised my father I'd talk to you about his offer."

He looked over at Mary to gauge her reaction. She gave him a quick nod. "Why not?" she asked. "After what they did to you, it's certainly worth a good laugh."

Damn. Mary had a sharp tongue when she wanted to. He draped his arm around her shoulders. "Would you like to join us?"

"No, Freckles and I have work to do." Mary placed her hand over her round tummy and held up her cheek for a kiss. She was quite the actress. He loved her for it. She knew how important it was that Tori think they were happily married. *Success is the sweetest revenge.*

"Let's head up to The Oar," Lance said to Tori. "It's our stomping ground."

"Stomping ground? What connotations that evokes." She nodded at Mary. "Again, such a pleasure. Good luck with the shop. These old brick and mortar shops are an endangered species."

Lance waved at Zane when they entered The Oar. Zane brought over menus after they'd slipped into a booth near the front window.

Lance introduced them. "This is Tori Hawthorne," Lance said.

"Right. Tori from New York. Lance mentioned you once," Zane said. *Once. Nice one.*

"Only once?" Tori lifted an eyebrow and spoke without inflection. "We meant a lot to each other at one time."

"I think he mentioned you cost him his job. Yes, that was the reference point, if I remember correctly." Zane said all this with his surfer boy smile as he set a menu in front of her.

She smiled stiffly. "And you're Zane. A Dog and the bar owner. The reverent way he used to speak of your little gang made me wonder if you all were actually a secret society with initiation rituals."

"The five of us go way back," Zane said. "We've seen one another through thick and thin."

"Our weekly poker game is a ritual of sorts," Lance said.

"Yes, well worth leaving a lucrative career in New York to play poker once a week with the guys." Tori pointed to the surfboards that hung on the wall. "I've never seen boards as art work."

"Really? Well, you're welcome then. Drinks?"

"White wine, please," Tori said. "Unless it's from Oregon."

"You have something against Oregon wine?" Zane asked.

"Doesn't everyone?" she asked with a sharp pitched laugh.

"Careful," Lance said.

"Not everyone, no," Zane said. "But I'll be sure to get you a nice oaky Chardonnay from California."

"I'll have an IPA," Lance said. "Preferably one from Oregon."

Zane shot him a look before heading back to the bar.

"He's not how I pictured him," Tori said.

"How so?"

"I imagined a rather dull surfer dude."

"Dull? You mean, dumb?"

She shrugged one skinny shoulder. "Maybe a little. He's snarkier than I imagined. You always said he was such a…what did you call him? A standup guy. I believe that was the phrase."

"My friends don't like you. What can I say?" Lance asked. "They know the full story about what went down."

With her napkin, she scrubbed a spot on the plastic menu.

"Rather unforgiving, isn't it? I thought Californians were about peace and love." Same cool, unflappable girl he'd once loved. She never cared what anyone thought of her. That was the thing with rich girls. They assumed rules didn't apply to them.

"It's not 1965," he said.

She tapped the table near his left hand. "Where's your wedding ring?"

"I don't have it yet."

"Why's that?"

"None of your business."

"Touché."

Zane came with the drinks and asked for their lunch orders.

"What do you recommend that isn't fried?" Tori asked Zane.

"You'll like the Brody Salad," Lance said.

"Oh, yes, the famous Brody Salad," Tori said. "No dressing, please."

Lance ordered one as well. "I'll have mine with the dressing." Zane left without a word.

"You're making a mistake on the dressing," he said to Tori. "It's a secret recipe."

"I'll take my chances." Tori lifted her glass. "To old times."

He drank from his beer without acknowledging the toast. "Did your father really send you out here with a job offer?"

"I asked if I could come. I had no idea you were married."

He followed her gaze to the window. What did she see when she looked at his town? Did she notice the way the flowers were displayed outside the grocery store? Had she admired the signage over his shop? Was she as taken as he by apple blossoms or the blue of the sky? What about the scent of the sea that drifted up from the beach?

It didn't matter what she thought, but still, a need for her to see Cliffside Bay as he did tugged at him. This was his community. Everyone and everything he loved was here.

"I have no intention of coming back to New York," he said.

"Mary's having our baby in September. I want to raise the baby here surrounded by my friends and family."

She smiled, moving her glass in a circle in the way he'd once found intriguing. "Is that why the rushed marriage?"

"Nothing rushed about it. We've known each other for a while."

Tori lifted her eyebrows. "Really?"

"Really."

"She's pretty."

"I didn't ask for your opinion."

"Daddy's offering a full partnership. He says it was a huge mistake to fire you."

"Not interested." *Huge mistake.*

She drank from her glass, eyeing him. "I find that hard to believe. You were always so ambitious."

"Things change."

"I suppose they do."

"Are you happier now?" Lance asked.

"Now?"

"Divorced," he said.

"I suppose. He was vicious when he drank. I didn't know that until it was too late. I wish I'd chosen the right man."

He scoffed and crossed his arms over his chest. "What did you think? You could just come out here and get me to move back to New York and now that I'm a partner, we'd just pick up where we left off, only this time I'm on the 'appropriate to marry list'?"

She twisted her tennis bracelet around her wrist. He'd forgotten that habitual gesture. "I didn't expect that, no. I *did* think you'd be interested in my father's offer. Over time, I thought you might forgive me and we could start over."

"You ruined my life."

"That's an exaggeration, don't you think?" She pulled a travel sized sanitizer from her handbag and squirted her hands, then rubbed them together. "You don't belong here." She pointed at the surfboards on the walls. "This is what they think of as art work? Think of the life you would have back in New York. You could have everything you ever wanted."

"You're right, it is an overstatement. If it weren't for you, I wouldn't have found the life I'm truly meant to live. The one here."

"A partnership in the firm. Do you know how much money we're talking?" she asked.

The old ambition floated in front of him like a ghost. He imagined puckering his mouth into a siphon and sucking the old familiar apparition up, bringing it back to life. But no. This life Tori offered was no longer what he wanted or needed. He silently saluted the ghost of ambition as it floated by him, no longer a friend or foe.

"I don't need money," Lance said. "I've done well enough."

"Father says it's never enough."

"And that right there is why I'm here and he's there," Lance said.

Zane brought their lunches and left them alone without a word. He didn't need to say anything out loud, Lance knew what the glitter in his friend's eyes meant. *Get the hell out. Run away as fast as you can.*

Tori picked at her food. He'd forgotten that too. She never ate much, with no regard to the cost of the meal. He made a mental note to tell Mary. She would enjoy hearing that detail.

"Mary's a librarian?" Tori asked. "Turned bookstore manager?"

"I told you that last night."

"And you really bought the bookstore?"

"What's your point?"

"I had no idea you were interested in books," Tori said. "I recall your interests were money and me."

He stabbed a piece of chicken with his fork.

Tori reached across the table and clapped her cold fingers around his wrist. "Can you honestly look me in the eyes and tell me this is enough for you? A librarian? A bookstore? In a one stoplight town?"

"Your description is inaccurate. Mary is a complicated, intelligent, totally fascinating woman. I worship her. Our bookstore was an institution in this town. When I heard it was in trouble, I knew I had to buy it and make it profitable. Because, as you say, I'm interested in money and I know how to make it grow, but it's more than that. Every town needs a bookstore—a place where people of all ages can come and ask the local shopkeeper to help them find the perfect book. When all is said and done, the stories in those pages help us make sense out of chaos. This one stoplight town is a community, which I know you wouldn't understand because you've never been part of something that isn't comprised of a gaggle of backstabbing, catty social climbers. The people here care about their town and one another. This town is my home. Everyone I love is here. No amount of money or esteem will ever change that. Please, Tori, go home. Give your father my best but tell him to find some other schmuck willing to work eighty-hour workweeks. I'm home where I belong." He stood, throwing some bills on the table. "Good luck, Tori."

Zane winked at him on his way out the door. "Well done."

"You can find me at my bookstore." Lance grinned at him. "With my wife."

When he returned to the shop, the young woman they'd hired for the early evening shift told him Mary and Freckles had left for the day. "She said to tell you to meet her at home."

Two minutes later, he was on the road to his house. It wasn't like Mary to leave the shop before 5 p.m. She was upset. He cursed Tori under his breath.

When he walked into the house through the garage door, Freckles bounded out to meet him. Wagging his tail, he led Lance through the living room to the patio. The angle of the late afternoon sun hovered between the awning and horizon, showering the patio with light and warmth. Mary sat in a shaded area with her feet resting on an ottoman. His copy of *Anne of Green Gables* rested on her lap. Dark sunglasses covered her eyes.

"Hey." He sat next to her and placed a hand on her leg.

She took off her sunglasses. Her eyes were red and puffy. She'd been crying.

"You okay?" He cleared his throat. What was he supposed to do now?

"You came back."

"Was that ever a question?"

"She looks like Grace Kelly."

"Not really."

"Beautiful and sophisticated." Mary's words sounded like one long sigh.

"I used to think so. But now I see her through a new filter."

"The moment I set eyes on her, I saw what attracted you to her. She's the symbol of everything you ever wanted."

He nodded. "I suppose she *was*."

"Elitist, rich. She's art gallery openings and opera seats and the Hamptons. That life you pursued with such ambition. I can't compete with that." She put her hand over her stomach. "And a partnership? It's all you ever wanted."

"Wanted. Past tense."

"Did she bring up the bookstore, how it was beneath you?"

"She did."

"And me? An uptight librarian?"

He smiled and wrapped his hand around one of her feet. "She didn't say uptight."

"She asked if you married me because I was pregnant, didn't she?"

"Something like that, yes."

"And called our town boring and unsophisticated."

"I believe she described it as a one stoplight town. Which is inaccurate, as were her other observations. I set her straight about everything. Every town needs a bookstore because books make sense out of chaos. Cliffside Bay is a community of people who know that family and friendship matter more than who you are or what you do for a living. I may have said something about her inability to understand why or how I could feel the way I do because she runs with a gaggle of backstabbing, catty social climbers."

"Oh."

"Then I told her how you were the love of my life, everything I've ever wanted, and that I worship you."

Mary sucked in her bottom lip and looked up at him. Unshed tears glistened in her eyes. "You said all that?"

"I did. It was quite the rant. You can ask Zane about it sometime. Then I told her to go home."

"You weren't at the lodge having sex with her?" She smiled as a teardrop ran down her cheek.

"Um, no." He shook his head. "Is that what you were thinking?"

"Maybe." She looked down at her lap.

"Why would you care?" he asked. "You've already said you don't want this…me."

"It's more complicated than that."

"How's it more complicated? You know how much I love you. You know the man I am. Either you love me or you don't."

She wiped at her swollen eyes with a rumpled tissue.

Should he take his brother's advice and throw the gauntlet? Her tears told a different story from her mouth.

"I think I should move out. Brody says I can move in with them," he said. "You can stay here until the baby comes and then we'll find another house for you."

14

Mary

MARY STARED AT him as panic rose from her gut to the back of her throat. She clasped her hands together. "I don't want you to leave."

"It's not fair to me. You know that. I'll make sure you have everything you need."

"I need you here."

"Why?"

"I just do." She started crying harder.

"Why were you crying when I was with Tori? Did you really think I was with her?"

"It's like a spinning top I can't control. The thoughts came faster and faster until I could practically see it play out before my eyes."

"And why do you care?" He lifted her chin, forcing her to look into his eyes. His voice was low, but resolute. "Tell me the truth. Tell me or I have to leave this house. I can't live like this any longer."

Her face reddened. "You really want to know? The thought of your hands on her made me feel like I was dying."

"And what does that mean exactly?"

She looked away, gathering her thoughts. If they were to have a chance she had to tell him her secrets. The lie between them would invade like an angry weed. "I'm in love with you. I have been since our first night together. Before that, even."

"I don't understand. Why wouldn't you just tell me?" A myriad of expressions passed over his face, going from mournful to confused to hopeful.

"I've been trying to drive you away."

"Why? Because you're afraid?"

"No, that's not it. Not with you." She jumped when Freckles bounded out to the patio and barked, then lay next to the chair with his chin on Mary's feet.

"Why then? Knowing how I feel about you?" Lance brushed her cheekbone with his fingertips. The dog at her feet, the man at her side, the baby in her womb. This was her life. The way it was meant to be. This was her family.

She closed her eyes for a split second, enjoying the sensation of his skin on hers, knowing it might be the last time she ever felt his touch. When she opened them, she ran her knuckles across the spiky stubble on his chin. "Because I did something horrible. Something unforgiveable."

"What could you possibly do that I wouldn't forgive?"

"I lied. I wasn't on the pill and I'm not allergic to latex."

"What?" Lance drew in a sharp breath, like someone had sucker punched him. "Why would you lie about that?"

"I wanted to get pregnant."

He stared at her like he'd never seen her before. "You had sex with me for a baby?"

His words ripped through her, left her limp with self-hatred. "It wasn't calculated beforehand. I don't know what got into me. It was that stupid party. I spent the night seething with jealousy.

Everyone was so obviously in love and pregnant. And there I was, just this dried up shell of a person. Then, you kissed me and something awakened in me. Suddenly, I wanted to feel something besides pain. I wanted to be with you, my favorite person, and just forget everything for a few hours. I got drunk and in some part of my intoxicated brain I decided I wanted your baby. I had it all worked out after that third drink. You were the perfect sperm donor. Handsome and smart and so kind. It was like this loop in my brain. I want Lance's baby."

"Sperm donor?" He continued to stare at her with the same blank look in his eyes.

"Let me finish. Please. I swear on my life it wasn't precalculated. The tequila did something to my brain." She choked on her tears. "The next morning, I woke up, horrified at what I'd done, praying nothing would come of it."

"But it did."

"Yes, and then you did the decent thing, like you always do, and there was no way I could argue with the logic of a fake marriage. And by then I knew without a doubt how much I loved you, but I'd ruined it, like I do everything. The one decent man in my life and I managed to do something so heinous it can't ever be forgiven. Please, just know how sorry I am. I know you won't be able to forgive me, but I had to tell you the truth. You deserve that. I'm begging you, please don't let this effect how you feel about the baby. She'll still need you to love her even though you hate her mother."

"Let me get this straight. All this time you've loved me, but you thought I'd never be able to forgive you, no matter how much I love you."

"Yes."

"And, that night was the first time you thought of using me as a sperm donor?" The corners of his eyes crinkled. Was he on the verge of smiling?

"Yes. I was in love with you, but I was in denial. I was scared to let myself go there with you because I didn't think you'd ever feel the same way and I'd be heartbroken all over again. But clearly my subconscious wanted this because my drunken brain came up with the baby idea. I had it all worked out that I'd leave with the baby and live in the woods."

"The woods?" He laughed.

He's laughing?

"Or *somewhere* by myself. I swear, it was the tequila. I'd never thought of anything like that in my life."

"You in the woods? That's hilarious."

"It's not funny." Why was he smiling?

"You were in love with me all this time?" His gaze searched her eyes for clues, like an archeologist with an ancient map. "Even before New Year's?"

"Yes, on some level anyway. But then all my baggage ruined everything. What kind of person does that? Takes something so great and makes it ugly?"

He cupped her face with his hands. "If you think I could hate you for some drunken decision that was probably an unconscious choice to bring us closer, then you have no idea the depth of my love for you."

Her vision blurred from the tears that swarmed her eyes. "It's such a giant lie."

"Everyone makes mistakes. The difference between those who move forward from them is only this—forgiveness. I forgive you. Can you forgive yourself for a mistake that's going to bring us so much joy? A mistake that brought us together?" He caught her falling tears with his thumbs and brushed them away as smoothly as the words flowed from his mouth to her heart.

"When you put it that way—it doesn't seem like such a big thing." She hiccupped.

"I'm not totally innocent either. I knew all along I wanted to make you fall in love with me. When you told me you were pregnant, I took it as a sign that we're meant to be." He grinned as he reached behind them to pull tissues from the box on the table. "Can we agree it doesn't matter what motivated us to do what we did that night? Those choices led us to right where we belong. Together."

She accepted the tissues and wiped her eyes. "That's the thing, though. The tequila was the delivery mechanism. What really drove me was my heartbreak and loss. Instead of compassion, my losses have made me bitter and jealous. Hateful. How can you love a person like that?"

"Sweetheart, you're not Jesus."

"What?"

"I mean, you're human. Other than one rash decision in a moment of extreme weakness, a very honest human." He smiled gently and caressed her trembling bottom lip. "Yes, that night you looked around the room and felt empty. I did too, and I haven't gone through half the losses you have."

"You did?"

"Heck yeah. I was so in love with you. I thought you'd never return my feelings. Meanwhile, my best friends are living their dreams with their soulmates by their sides. There I was with hardly the courage to kiss you."

"You did, though."

"Yes, I did. I told myself I *had* to kiss you. Not just any kiss. It had to be epic. I needed to be more than I'd ever been before to make you see that we're soulmates."

He picked up the copy of *Anne of Green Gables* from her lap. "You want to know who I am? I'm Gilbert. I'm Gilbert to your Anne. He waited and waited for her, steady and loyal, even when he thought there was no hope of her ever loving him. That's me."

Gilbert Blythe. It was obvious now that he said it. He wasn't Lancelot to her Genevieve. He was Gilbert to her Anne. Steady, generous Gilbert who sacrificed his own desires so that Anne's dreams could come true.

"Anne with a 'e'. Mary with a 'y'." He scooted closer and stroked her cheek clean of tears. "I'll always come back to you. Don't ever worry about that."

She collapsed against him with her arms wrapped around his neck. "I thought I was going to lose you."

"Yet you risked telling me the truth."

"I knew a lie like that was too big. It would come between us somehow."

"It'll take more than that to shake me. As long as you want me, I'll never be anywhere but right by your side."

"Will you marry me for real?" She peeped up at him through her damp lashes.

"Baby, I already did."

That night, Mary dreamt. She stood in the doorway of Meme's nursery. Her mother sat in the rocking chair with a little girl on her lap. She read to her from *Are You My Mother?* The little girl was about six with dark pigtails and light blues eyes. Maggie's *Amazing Grace* played from the speakers. The little girl looked up from the book. She smiled, and her face lit with the light of a thousand suns.

"Hi, Mama."

"Meme, is it you?"

The little girl smiled wide. Her two front teeth were missing. "I love the room you made me. Nana reads me all the books."

"Were you looking for me?" Mary sobbed and wiped her eyes. "I thought you might be afraid. I've been so worried."

"I knew where you were the whole time. I knew you before I was even born," Meme said.

"You did?"

"I was never afraid. I'm here with Jesus and my Nana, so don't worry."

Her mother looked up from the book. She was without wrinkles. Her hair, brown and shiny, hung in waves around her face. "Hello, darling. We're having such a lovely time."

"You look so pretty, Mom."

"The air is wonderful here. Plumps the skin right up."

"I love you both so much," Mary said. "I miss you."

"We know, Mama," Meme said.

"It goes both ways, darling. But you mustn't cry. We'll be here for ten thousand years and for ten more after that. Don't be sad any longer. You'll see us when it's time. Right now, Lance and the new baby need you. I'm terribly proud of you. You've been strong and brave."

She woke. Tears dampened her pillow.

Beside her, Lance stirred and pulled her into him. "Are you all right?" he asked.

"Yes. Just a dream." She nestled into the curve of his body. "About my mom and Meme."

"A good dream?"

"The best."

"Try to sleep, my love." He kissed her shoulder.

Lance and the new baby need you.

The shades were open. She could see from the top of the window a sliver of a moon and billions of stars scattered over the inky night. Her mother and Meme were up there amongst the stars. She smiled and closed her eyes. She slept.

On a night in early June, the entire gang met in San Francisco for Maggie's concert. The album had been out for several months. Two singles had been released and were nestled near the top of the charts for the singer/songwriter category. Tonight, she would open for a popular folk-rock band, *The Spangles*. An all-female band, their audience was mostly women. Other than the Dogs, Doc, her father, and Kyle's brother, Stone, there were only a handful of men.

Maggie had gotten them seats in a private box above the main floor. The venue held two thousand and was packed. While they waited for the curtain to rise, Jackson poured champagne and sparkling cider.

"I'm glad you guys are all here," Jackson said. "I'm a nervous wreck."

"She's going to kill it," Zane said.

"I predict she gains a bunch of new fans tonight," Honor said.

"But none of them even know who she is," Jackson said. "What if they talk all the way through her set?"

"No way," Kyle said. "She'll have them eating out of the palm of her hand."

Violet, with her hand on her very pregnant belly, agreed. "They won't be able to resist her."

While they waited, everyone mingled and sipped their drinks. Mary, tired, decided to take a seat and just watch the scene unfold. The Dogs were busy babysitting a very nervous Jackson by sneaking him sips from a flask. Her father and Flora hung with Doc and Janet in the far corner. Violet, looking very pregnant, was also seated with Kara by her side.

Sophie arrived a few minutes later. Honor clinked her glass and asked if everyone could listen up. She nestled in the crook of Zane's arm. "Now that Sophie's here, we have something we want to share."

Sophie beamed.

"We went through with the surrogacy plan," Honor said. "Sophie's pregnant. We're due around Christmas day."

Everyone congratulated them.

"What made you change your mind?" Kyle asked Zane when it quieted.

"You guys convinced me. It was suddenly obvious I was being totally selfish," Zane said.

"We're beyond excited." Honor clapped her hands together. "Jubie is too. She wants a girl, of course."

"Not to steal your thunder or anything," Brody said. "But speaking of pregnant."

"We are too," Kara said. "And, you won't believe it. We're due around Christmastime too."

"You guys are such copy cats," Honor said.

She and Kara hugged. "I'm beyond happy for you," Kara said.

"Maybe Pepper's right. There must be a baby making magic potion in the water here in Cliffside Bay." Kyle placed his hand on Violet's belly. "Some of us make doubles."

"They're not a latte," Violet said.

"You ladies complained there weren't enough citizens under seventy here in town, so we decided to do something about it," Brody said.

"I don't think it had to be entirely up to us," Lance said.

"If not us, who?" Honor asked.

Sophie glowed like only a twenty-one-year-old in her first trimester of pregnancy could. She slipped into the seat next to Mary.

"How are you feeling?" Mary asked.

"Like a rock star." Sophie giggled. "But that's my sister. Isn't it so exciting?" Her aqua eyes, so like Zane's, sparkled.

"No morning sickness?"

"Not a bit. I'm past twelve weeks already, so I'm hopeful I've dodged the bullet." Sophie lifted her long blond hair off her neck. "My biggest complaint is how hot I am all the time." Mary couldn't help but smile. Sophie was easy to match with a character. Always positive, with a zest for life and a heart for others, there was no better choice than Heidi.

"We'll be through the hot months by your third trimester," Mary said. "Me, on the other hand, will enjoy my third trimester during the hottest months of the year. Not that I'm complaining. Whatever it takes to keep my little girl inside for a long as possible, I'll endure."

Sophie sobered. "Everything's all right, though?"

"So far so good. I haven't had a chance to tell you yet, but I think it's amazing what you're doing for Honor and Zane."

Sophie flushed as she put her hair into a ponytail. "It's completely selfish, if you want to know the truth."

"I don't think that's the definition of selfish," Mary said, smiling.

"Doing this makes me feel so good. When do we ever get the chance to give something really meaningful to the people we love?"

"Not often."

"I have two half siblings I never knew about, and that we managed to find one another is a miracle, but to be able to honor my dad this way, is truly a blessing."

Two young women joined them in the box. It took Mary a moment to place them. Pepper and Lisa. Maggie's best friends from New York. They'd all gone to college together at NYU and had spent another eight years trying to break into the Broadway scene. From what Mary could remember from the wedding, Lisa had left New York around the same time as Maggie. Pepper was still there, as far as she knew.

Goodness, they were unfathomably pretty. Lisa was fair and blond, with a face that could only be described as classically beautiful. Honestly, she was so beautiful Mary had no idea how the woman wasn't a famous actress. Of average height with an hourglass figure, she was all grace and elegance, with an innocence that reflected from her light green eyes. Her creamy skin, obviously untouched by the sun, appeared flawless.

Pepper, on the other hand, was small with dark hair cut in a short bob with bangs that would look terrible on most people but were perfect to frame her large, ash-gray eyes. Mary thought she was suited for her name, as she was fiery with a quick laugh and sarcastic wit. Mary's mother would have described her as too thin, but Mary found her glamorous.

The crowd hushed as Maggie entered the stage. Carrying her guitar and dressed all in black, she greeted the audience a hearty welcome as the drummer, lead guitarist and bass player took their places. Her red hair shone under the lights. From their seats, it was hard to make out the features of her face, but in the overhead screen her fair skin looked luminous. She strummed the first chords of the title track of her album and began to sing. As her voice rang out into the hall, Mary's arms covered with goosebumps.

Between songs, Maggie told short, mostly humorous stories of the origin of the songs and of her life in New York. Any time Mary looked over at Jackson, he was in the same position with his hands on his knees, pitched slightly forward, and a proud smile directed at Maggie.

Before the last song of the night, Maggie spoke into the microphone. "When we put my first album together, my producer and I approached it like a story. This is the journey of a long and circuitous road away from and back to the love of my life, Jackson Waller. I've loved him since I was six years old when he roughed up a mean boy harassing me on the playground. We lost each other for twelve years. During that time, I poured the ache of that loss into my songs. I'm happy to say, he's here tonight, looking out for me once more, which I suppose means I'll never write a decent song again. They'll be nothing but sappy love songs about my husband." She slipped her guitar strap over her head and set the instrument in its stand, then turned sideways with her hands pressed against her belly. "As you may have noticed, we're having a baby in August. This is my last concert for a while. Thanks for being such a wonderful audience." The crowd cheered. She went to the piano and spoke into the microphone. "Every song on this album is for Jackson, but this last one is the one I wrote for our wedding. I hope you'll enjoy it."

She went to the piano and began to sing. Mary's eyes filled as she listened to the ballad, thinking of her own love story with Lance.

When the song ended, Maggie thanked the crowd for being there and making her feel so welcome. Claps and whistles filled the room. They all leapt to their feet, shouting and screaming for their Maggie. She looked up at them and blew a kiss. "And thanks to my friends for coming out tonight and my brilliant, gorgeous husband. Goodnight."

She left the stage, but the crowd kept cheering. Would she go back out? They clearly wanted her.

Maggie appeared without the band, holding her guitar. "Well, if you insist, I'll play you one more. This is brand new one called "Song for Lily." I wrote it last week for our baby girl."

She strummed the guitar and sang into the microphone. This was a mellow ballad with hints of a lullaby in the melody. When she sang the first stanza of the chorus, tears sprang from Mary's eyes. "Wherever you are, there I'll be."

After Maggie left the stage for the last time, Jackson buried his face in his hands. "I was worried, but she did very well, don't you all agree?"

"We agree." Zane punched him playfully on the shoulder. "As usual, you were the only one worried."

The next day, Mary and Lance attended a party at Violet and Kyle's new home to celebrate the end of Maggie's first concert tour. Upon their arrival, Lance joined the men around the pool while Violet gave Mary a tour of the house. They started on the first floor, an open concept with the kitchen, dining room and living room meshed into one large space. The house was decorated in a traditional style but with hints of the contemporary tossed in for texture. Cream cabinets contrasted with a massive kitchen island in cobalt blue. Light granite counters speckled in gray shone under the light of tall windows. Dark furniture and walnut flooring hinted that this was a family house. "Less likely for little grubby hands and feet to do their damage," Violet said.

The scent of fresh paint and the vases of lilacs displayed on the dining room and coffee tables accompanied them as they strolled over to the stairs. The second floor consisted of five bedrooms and a playroom. They stepped inside the playroom. "This was supposed to be Kyle's office." Violet patted her large bump. "But since we're about to become a family of six, we decided it was better to have a place for the children to play. Kyle's office is now where the pool house was supposed to be. He'd imagined nights of debauchery with the Dogs, but instead he'll have a place to work without the sounds of screaming children."

Tall shelves ran the length of one wall. Bins of toys and books were neatly displayed. Several child sized tables and chairs were in the middle of the room. A train set occupied one end of the room. "Kyle's train. He lets Dakota play with it sometimes." Violet laughed. "I'm kidding."

They went to the window that overlooked the back yard and looked down at the party. Warm and sunny, the early June day was made for an outdoor summer party. The older couples played cards at a round bistro table under the shade of the awning. Sophie worked the grill and talked with Kara and Maggie, who sat at the long, rectangular dining table. The Mullen brothers and Zane were in the deep end of the pool, treading water and tossing a ball back and forth. Kyle sat on the side of the pool with his feet in the water with baby Mollie, dressed in a pink sunhat and polka dotted bathing suit, on his lap. Jubie and Dakota took turns on the slide in a competition for who could make the craziest arm gestures on the way down. Honor stood on the side of the pool wearing a red bikini no bigger than a few tissues. She was apparently the judge of the slide game. After each child came up from their plunge into the water, she held up fingers to indicate their score. So far, they'd each only received five fingers. "This game may be rigged," Mary said.

"Yes, I'm afraid so."

"How wonderful for the kids to have a place to swim."

"I was a nervous wreck about the pool," Violet said. "But Kyle took Dakota to swimming lessons all last winter."

"He's clearly a natural," Mary said. "There's nothing better than a slide when you're a kid."

"Whose idea do you think that was? Kyle pretended it was for Dakota, but we all know that's not true. I swear, my husband's an oversized kid." Her voice softened. "Given his childhood, I don't have the heart to deny him any fun."

"Have you been all right?" Mary asked. "I haven't seen you much since that awful day."

"I can't say it hasn't affected us. We're even more cautious with the kids now. We're nervous to hire another nanny."

"You'll find someone you can trust. Mel was an anomaly."

"Has Lance talked about it?" Violet asked. "Kyle said he was shaken. I mean, who wouldn't be."

"He hasn't said much."

"Men."

"Yes." Mary stroked the soft curtains. "I have to tell you something. It's about Lance and me. We're in love for real. I'm so happy." She turned to look at her friend.

Violet smiled and pulled her into a hug. They started to laugh as their baby bumps bumped. "And everything's good between you?"

"Better than I could ever have imagined," Mary said. "I was foolish before."

"Fear will do that to you."

The arrival of several more guests distracted them. They watched Maggie greet Pepper and Lisa, who were dressed in sundresses that barely covered their perky bottoms, and high-heeled sandals. Lisa's fair hair was swept into a low ponytail and her dewy skin flushed pink from the warmth of the afternoon. *Or a really good blush.* Pepper's hair was the same color as her name and hung just below her ears in perfect waves. Dark sunglasses covered half of her heart-shaped face. An aura of glamour floated about them like golden-era actresses.

Mary smoothed the front of her maternity dress and wished

she'd made more of an effort with her hair instead of simply putting it into a braid.

Beside her, Violet sighed. "Do you see their flat stomachs?"

"Yeah."

"God, they're both so pretty. Like movie stars," Violet said.

"I kind of hate them."

"Me too." Violet sighed again. "Do you think I'll ever have a flat stomach again?"

"I don't know. We might both be a mess after this."

"We're not inviting them next summer," Violet said with a dry laugh.

Mary wrapped her arm around Violet's shoulder. "But think of the beautiful babies we'll have next summer."

"Right. And all they'll have is their perfect little bodies and their gorgeous faces."

"I feel sorry for them," Mary said.

"Totally."

"I'm starving," Mary said. "I haven't eaten in at least an hour."

Violet giggled. "Me too. Let's ask Sophie to make us a big fat burger. There's some chocolate milk in the fridge. We'll have to sneak or Dakota and Jubie will want some and spoil their dinner."

As luck would have it, Mary was seated next to Lisa and Pepper during dinner around the long table. Despite her intentions to the contrary, she immediately liked them both. They shared a gift for gab, leaving Mary to merely respond instead of having to think of anything to say. Throughout the meal, they asked her at least a dozen questions. When was the baby due, how did she meet Lance, had she lived here long? What was her favorite book to give as gifts? Had she ever seen a Broadway play? Wasn't Maggie simply the best singer in the entire world?

After dinner, most left the table to gather around the fire pit, but the three of them lingered at the table. While Mary nibbled strawberries dipped in cream and Pepper and Lisa sipped wine, she learned more details of the women's pasts.

Lisa had given up on her Broadway dreams and had gone home to Iowa about the same time Maggie had come home to Cliffside Bay. "I figured it was time for plan B, as Maggie and I called it. I went home to the land of the cornfields and good old-fashioned Midwest values. Sadly, I've been bored to tears. There's nothing interesting there, other than my family. And, I've given up all hope of ever finding a good man. I thought for sure *the one* would be somewhere in the middle of all that corn, but they're just as awful as the men I dated in New York."

"But tell her what happened last month." Pepper crossed her legs and leaned forward over her plate, obviously enjoying herself.

"Out of the blue I got a call from Reggie Prince, our old friend from college. Back then he was a bit of a dork."

Pepper shuddered and waved her waiflike arms like she was batting away a hornet. "A bit? He was awful. He had these clammy hands he was only too happy to share with any girl in near proximity."

Lisa smiled. Her mouth was the color of a pink rose. How could she eat without messing up her lipstick? "Now, he's a director. He's huge now, which we can't believe."

"He was a *dreadful* actor." Pepper fluffed her hair with her fingertips. "I had to do a love scene with him for a class and I swear it was nearly impossible to pretend he wasn't just creepy Reggie Prince."

"Apparently his true calling was directing," Lisa said. "He came out to Hollywood and somehow wormed his way into a mentorship with Hugh Hill."

"Hugh Hill? Isn't he the director that's in so much trouble?" Mary asked. According to the news, he was accused of harassment and rape of dozens of women, mostly actresses.

"Yes, that's how creepy Reggie ended up with the director job," Pepper said. "They ousted Hill and gave it to Reggie."

"Anyway, it's a miniseries for HBO. A period piece set in the Edwardian era," Lisa said.

"Really?" Mary asked, excited. "From a book?"

"No, it's a new script. A screenwriter out of England." A blond curl escaped from Lisa's ponytail and fell over her forehead. She tossed it away with a flick of her manicured finger.

"And he wanted Lisa for the main role," Pepper said.

"I came out last month for a screen test," Lisa said.

"They start shooting on Monday," Pepper said.

"So, here I am in California with an acting job," Lisa said. "It's the strangest thing. The minute I give up, a job comes."

The women spoke as if they were one person. What a riot these two were.

Lisa went on to explain that they would shoot the series in Los Angeles for a few months and then she'd decide what to do after that. "Maggie said I could come stay with them between gigs. That is, if I get any more gigs. One never knows."

"And what about you, Pepper? Are you still in New York," Mary asked.

"Well, that's an interesting story," Pepper said. "I've had a bit of trouble."

"Trouble?" Mary asked. "What kind of trouble?"

"Of the male variety," Pepper said. "As in, I fell for the wrong guy. Again."

"Pepper and I don't have good luck with men," Lisa said.

"I fell in love with my costar in the last musical I was in," Pepper said. "When I found out he was married, I had a little incident. Which, unfortunately, involved the law."

Mary suppressed a laugh. How little was this incident?

"I had no idea the candlestick was that heavy," Pepper said. "It was a prop, after all."

"Candlestick?" Mary asked.

"Yes. The one I hurled at his head." Pepper's dark gray eyes shimmered with mischief. "Who knew I had a throwing arm?"

"She took out his two front teeth," Lisa said. "So, he pressed charges. Actors, very vain, you know."

Mary didn't know, but she could imagine.

"Sadly, I couldn't press charges against him for being a pond-sucking-lying-lowlife," Pepper said. "The cops were entirely unsympathetic."

"They said being a cheater wasn't a crime," Lisa said.

"It should be," Mary said.

Pepper slapped the table. "That's exactly what I think. Anyway, I'm coming out west for a fresh start. I'll be living with Lisa in L.A. and looking for acting work. I've also pledged to give up men for one whole year. No dating sites. Not even one toss of a penny into a wishing pond. This is the new Pepper. I'll be crazy Auntie Pepper to Maggie's baby and give up on ever finding a man of my own. Honestly, I'm dying to love on that baby. Although, given the number of you knocked up at this point, I'm worried there's something in the sea air."

"It *is* suspicious." Mary patted her belly.

"Violet's having twins. So dreamy." Lisa glanced over at Violet. "I have a twin brother. He's back home in Iowa with his wife and kids, but we have a special bond no matter how far away I am."

A male figure emerged from the house and crossed the lawn. It wasn't until he was several feet from where they sat that Mary realized it was Rafael. She'd never seen him outside of his station at the Mullens' where he seemed almost frightening in his intensity. Here now, he looked like one of the guys, wearing cargo shorts and a t-shirt.

"Hi everyone." Rafael flashed a shy half-smile and shoved his hands in the pockets of his shorts. *He's shy, uncomfortable in social situations.* Mary could relate.

"Would you like to sit?" Mary asked after introducing Rafael to Lisa and Pepper.

"Um, sure, I guess. Maybe I should get a beer first," he said.

Mary pointed to the bin of drinks on the outside counter. "Drinks are in there."

He shuffled over to the bin and rummaged through until he came up with a beer.

"Where have the Dogs been hiding *him*?" Lisa spoke without moving her mouth. "I've never seen him around before."

"That's the Mullens' head of security," Mary said as quietly as she could. "I've never seen him at a social event."

"Lisa likes the dark and swarthy type," Pepper whispered.

"And I'm *not* giving men up for a year or otherwise," Lisa said.

When Rafael returned with a beer, he sat down at the table, nodding politely.

"What brings you out tonight?" Mary asked. "You're obviously not working."

Despite his square jaw and hard mouth, Rafael was soft-spoken with a respectful demeanor. Mary imagined him in another era, holding his hat in his hand in deference to the ladies. "I had the night off and Kara said I should come by. It took me all evening to decide."

"Why's that?" Pepper asked. "Are you afraid of people?"

He ducked his head with the same shy smile. "Something like that."

"Don't be afraid of us," Pepper said. "We're harmless."

"I am, anyway," Lisa said. "Pepper's been known to take out a man or two with a candlestick."

"One guy." Pepper held up her finger. "Just one. One man. One candlestick."

"As weapons go, there could be worse choices." Rafael took a swig of beer.

"It makes me think of that game, Clue," Lisa said. "Pepper on the set with a candlestick."

His dark eyes darted from Lisa to Pepper. Mary wished she

could rescue him. He wasn't used to witty, glamorous women that dazzled with their white teeth and clever tongues. She pictured them in a New York coffee shop, like Dorothy Parker and her crowd.

"Do you have a gun?" Pepper asked Rafael.

"Not now, no. But I wear one when I'm working."

"How does a person get into the security guard business?" Lisa flushed pink. "I mean, it's not really a business, but you know, a career."

Rafael curled his fingers around the beer bottle. "I used to be a cop."

"In Cliffside Bay?" Pepper asked.

He smiled and shook his head. "No. L.A.P.D."

"Why aren't you a cop anymore?" Pepper asked.

He patted his shoulder. "A bullet through my shoulder convinced me to do something a little less in the line of fire, so to speak. Plus, I like living here. The city's not for me."

"Weren't you a former Seal?" Mary asked. She was sure she heard that somewhere.

"That's right." Rafael said. "This is my third career."

"We know how that goes," Pepper said. "We've been waitresses, coat checkers, hotel maids, nannies, shop girls."

Lisa smiled at Rafael. "We're actresses."

"Kara mentioned that," Rafael said.

"She did?" Lisa asked.

He took a swig of beer and nodded. "It was on her list of why I should come to the party. Like most happily married women, she's concerned I'm going to die alone with my cat."

"You have a cat?" Lisa asked.

"Two, actually."

"I love cats," Lisa said.

"Doesn't everyone?" Rafael asked.

"I don't," Pepper said. "They're such jerks."

"Aloof. They only love you when they're hungry," Mary said. "Dogs love you and don't care who knows it."

"They say all humans can be classified as either a dog or a cat." Pepper pointed at Lisa. "She's a dog who likes cats."

"I don't want to be a dog, but it's true," Lisa said.

"Why?" Rafael asked.

"Why what?" Lisa swirled the wine in her glass and looked up at him through her lashes. *Flirting with the security guard.*

"Why don't you want to be a dog?" Rafael said.

She twirled her ponytail around one finger and looked up, obviously thinking it through. "I don't know. I suppose it's because they're so obvious. You never have to question if a dog loves you. They just do. Even when you don't deserve it."

"Which they usually don't," Pepper said.

Someone's phone buzzed.

"That's me." Rafael reached into the side pocket of his cargo shorts and pulled out his phone. A flicker of irritation crossed his face. "I'm sorry. I have to take this. Excuse me." He walked across the lawn and disappeared into the house.

"Holy God, that man," Lisa said.

"All dark and mysterious," Pepper said. "Just your type."

Maggie joined them at the table. She wore a pair of long cotton maternity pants and a linen shirt. Fair skinned with a million freckles, she almost never sat in the sun without proper coverage.

"You two aren't corrupting Mary, I hope?" Maggie slid into the seat next to Mary.

"We were discussing the abundance of babies," Lisa said. "Pepper's worried, even though she's sworn off men."

Maggie smirked. "I heard something about that last night."

"You say it like you don't believe I can do it," Pepper said.

Lisa spoke over Pepper. "But then we were interrupted by Brody and Kara's hot security guy."

"Rafael?" Maggie asked. "Yes, he's dreamy."

"That's one word for him," Lisa said.

The sound of raucous laughter drew their attention to Kyle

and his brother Stone over by the pool. Almost dark now, the lights of the swimming pool illuminated their faces.

"Who is *that*?" Pepper asked, staring at Stone in a way that gave no credence to her pledge of celibacy.

"Kyle's brother," Maggie said. "He's the contractor who built this house."

"That explains the muscles," Pepper said.

"New to town. Single. Hot," Maggie said. "But you're not interested in men, isn't that right?"

Pepper blinked, as if waking from a trance. "Correct. Yes. No men for a year."

"But in that time, he could be snatched up," Lisa said. "Good men don't stay single long."

"Not in this town," Maggie said. "If they're under seventy, especially."

Kyle and Stone headed in their direction.

"Keep your head," Lisa said to Pepper.

"No worries. I've totally got this," Pepper said.

Upon their arrival at the table, Kyle plopped next to Mary. He smelled like sunscreen and beer. "Lisa and Pepper, have you met my brother, Stone?"

"No, we haven't. I'm Lisa." She smiled up at him. "Maggie's best friend from college."

"Pleased to meet you." Stone remained standing as he shook her hand. Mary studied him for a moment. He looked like Kyle. Same intense blue eyes and hawkish nose and high cheekbones, only Stone had him by several inches in every direction. She guessed he was over six feet and built like a tank. His muscular torso stretched his soft, thin t-shirt taut over his chest. The span of his biceps could easily be the size of Pepper's waist.

"This is Pepper," Lisa said. "Our other best friend."

Stone's gaze flickered to the dark-haired beauty. He raised one eyebrow. "Pepper, like the spice?"

"Stone, like the soup?" Pepper asked without missing a beat.

He blinked, then laughed and took the seat across from

Pepper. "Stone soup requires more than a little pepper for flavor."

Lisa looked over at Mary and rolled her eyes. "A year, my butt," she murmured under breath.

Mary stifled a laugh.

"Nickname?" Stone asked.

"Guess." Pepper lifted her chin and glared at him.

"Given your sassy attitude, I'm going with nickname," Stone said.

Kyle stole one of Mary's strawberries and whispered in her ear. "This is going to be amusing."

"Wrong," Pepper said. "I'm named after my father's favorite spice."

Stone smirked and cocked his head to the side. "I highly doubt that."

Pepper widened her eyes in a look of innocence. "It's true. Ask my mother."

"Maybe I will," Stone said. "What's her number? I'll call her right now."

"She's unavailable at the moment." Pepper looked away briefly. Mary caught a hint of sadness in the tuck of her chin.

"Would you like a refill of your wine, or are you driving?" Stone asked.

"I don't drive," Pepper said.

"At all?" Stone asked.

"Never. I lived in New York City most of my life. I didn't need to."

"I see, a city girl."

Pepper's eyes flashed in the dim light. "What does that make *you*, Stone Soup?"

"That would make me a hick, ma'am."

Silence followed as the two stared at each other with slightly goofy smiles.

"How about you, Stone?" Mary asked. "Nickname or given?"

Stone looked over at his brother. "Would you like to tell them, or should I?"

Kyle crossed his arms over his chest with one of his characteristic smirks. "His real name's Stanley, but I couldn't say it when I was a kid, so it became Stone."

"Thus, a true badass was born," Stone said.

"You think Stone's a badass name?" Pepper asked.

"Isn't it obvious? I mean, look at me." Stone tapped his chest and winked at her.

"Looks can be deceiving," Pepper said.

"Not in this case," Kyle said. "This here's a full-fledged American hero. Three tours in Afghanistan."

"Thank you for your service," Lisa said, suddenly sounding very midwestern.

"You're welcome," Stone said.

Mary watched Pepper. Her eyes narrowed as she continued to look at Stone. A trace of wariness, almost fear, crossed her face.

Pepper jolted to her feet. "I hate to be a party pooper, but east coast time is suddenly catching up with me. Maggie, I'm going to head back to your house."

"It's almost dark. Take a flashlight," Maggie said. "And stay on the path."

"I will." Pepper smiled, but not like earlier. This was a fake smile, possibly learned. "It was great to meet you all. Good night."

With the quickness of a dancer, she leapt away and disappeared into the twilight.

"What did I say?" Stone asked.

Mary noticed Lisa and Maggie exchange a knowing look.

"It's nothing personal," Maggie said. "She's had a bad experience with military guys."

"Bad?" Kyle asked. "Like a broken heart?"

Lisa shook her head. "No." She looked over at Maggie. "It's not really our story to tell."

Maggie clasped her hands together on the table. "True. We aren't sure what to say when it comes up. She never talks about it."

"She was attacked when we were in college. On the subway," Lisa said. "By a group of navy guys."

"She's never been the same," Maggie said.

"Guys in uniform trigger her," Lisa said. "Especially if she likes him."

"Out of uniform too," Stone said.

"Yes, I'm afraid so," Maggie said.

"Poor thing," Kyle said.

"I should probably go check on her," Lisa said.

"I'll get Jackson and be right behind you," Maggie said.

No sooner had they left than Stone excused himself. "I've got an early morning, so I best get some sleep." He traipsed off in the opposite direction from the ladies.

"Where's he headed?" Mary asked.

Kyle explained to Mary that Stone had a trailer on the other side of the property where he'd been staying while he'd built their house.

Lance and Violet joined them at the table. Mary noticed then that Sophie, Janet, and Doc had left. She'd been so caught up in the moment, she hadn't noticed.

"What happened to your merry group?" Violet asked.

Kyle gave her the rundown. "Major sparks until I mentioned his military background."

"It's not your fault," Mary said. "There are some things that can't be forgotten."

A week later, Mary was finishing up with a customer when Janet Mullen came in to the shop. They greeted each other with a quick hug.

"I won't mince words," Janet said. "I came by to talk about Flora. Do you have time for a break?"

Mary looked around the shop. They had two staff members on today to deal with crowds of summer tourists. Lance said their revenue numbers for June had been a new record. Although it was only the middle of July, he felt certain they'd beat June's numbers. He'd been right about the café and soda fountain bringing business to the book section of the shop. What he hadn't totally predicted was how many people would buy coffees after they bought a book.

A line for ice cream spilled out the door. Hot summer afternoons made everyone scream for ice cream. A dozen or so folks milled about the bookshelves, stopping to read or look at back covers. Her two staff members seemed to have everything under control.

"I haven't taken a break yet today. Would you like coffee?" Mary gestured toward the coffee shop.

"No, I've had plenty for today. I don't suppose you'd want to take a short walk?" Janet's eyes went to Mary's stomach. With her due date a month and a half away, Mary's stomach had grown to the size of a watermelon over the past few weeks.

"I can still waddle down the street," Mary said. "A little slower than usual if you don't mind slowing your Mullen pace a bit."

"Dax is always commenting on how fast I walk."

"Lance does too. Normally, I can keep up with him just fine, but lately it's been a struggle."

Mary let her staff know she'd be back shortly. They exited onto the crowded sidewalk. The scent of sunscreen and sea mixed to create the smell of summer in Cliffside Bay. Weaving in and out of tourists, they meandered toward the beach. The crowds made it impossible to chat until they reached the beach. "Shall we wander down to the sand or walk on the boardwalk?" Janet asked.

"Boardwalk," Mary said. "I have to go back to work and the sand gets in my shoes.

The boardwalk was as crowded as town, but it was split in half, so that everyone on one side walked in the same direction.

"Lance came by yesterday," Janet said. "I've never seen him so content. You're a blessing to us."

"He's the best thing that's ever happened to me."

"Is Flora right that you two married because of the baby?" Janet asked. "I'm sorry to be so blunt, but I have to know if I'm right."

"We're in love. That's all anyone needs to know," Mary said. "How exactly we got there doesn't really matter."

"I suppose that's true," Janet said. "As long as you're both happy, then I'm happy."

"I feel joyful," Mary said. "For the first time in a long time."

They walked without talking for a minute or so until Janet brought up Flora again.

"Flora tells me you two haven't exactly made headway on forging a friendship," Janet said.

"Despite Lance's wishes, no." They skirted to the far right of the sidewalk to let a bicycle pass them.

"She can be trying," Janet said. "But she means well."

"I know." *So everyone keeps telling me.*

"She has her ways, and everyone just has to follow suit," Janet said. "Other than Kara, I've never seen anyone get her to back down."

"I wish I could be like Kara, but I can't think on my feet. Flora's too quick for me."

"Kara has a way with her. She has her convinced that the lasagna recipe she uses is the one Flora always made. I can tell you with great certainty that it is not."

"How does she do that?" Mary asked.

"No one knows. She has secret Flora powers. Brody's convinced Kara's a witch. She charms you with a potion or something. I don't suppose he's wrong, given the way Kara tamed him."

"Was he wild before?"

"No, just focused solely on football. There was no time for a serious relationship. I didn't think he'd ever get married."

"What about Lance? Did you think he'd be married by now?"

"I knew he'd want to be. He's like his father—made to be a family man."

"I feel lucky."

"His father was a great man to be married to."

"Did he ever cheat on you?" Mary asked. "I'm sorry, that was too personal."

"Don't be. I'm happy to answer any questions you might have. He did not cheat on me."

"How do you know?" Mary asked. "Didn't he travel a lot for his job?"

"Yes. And athletes are notorious for cheating. But not him. The way he felt about me and the type of man he was—he would never have hurt me that way."

"I feel that way about Lance, but sometimes a worry wriggles in there."

"It's only natural, considering the betrayal of your first husband."

"Maybe. But Lance deserves my trust."

"Over time, he'll earn it."

They turned back to head the other direction. The smell of grilled meat from a food truck made Mary's mouth water. Umbrellas were a dotted tapestry across the long stretch of beach. Children shouted and laughed as they played in the surf. *Summer in Cliffside Bay*. Next year, she might be there with the baby, teaching her how to dip her feet in the water.

There was a time not so long ago this scene would have pummeled her with pain. Today, she saw only possibilities of the future.

"Anyway, regarding Flora. I have an idea," Janet said.

"Do tell."

"You should ask her to teach you how to cook."

"I can't imagine anything worse," Mary said.

"I'll do it with you," Janet said. "Honor says she's in if you're in."

"For heaven's sake. You two are in cahoots?"

"Something like that."

Mary laughed. "We better do it soon before this baby comes."

"Excellent. I'll text her now."

Mary watched as Flora, wearing a scarf around her curly hair and a wide apron, wrestled a hunk of beef onto a cutting board. She cut it into one-inch squares, talking all the while about the importance of fresh herbs and red potatoes. None of those baby carrots from the bag, God forbid.

"Get carrots with the stem attached if you can. They're much better that way."

For the past three Sundays, Honor, Janet, and Flora have all met at Lance and Mary's kitchen for their cooking lesson. The first two Sundays they learned to make Lance's favorite red sauce for pasta, a whole roast chicken, green enchiladas, a traditional Caesar salad, and a chocolate cake.

For their third and final lesson, Flora would teach them how to make a proper beef stew. *None of that improper stew for Lance.*

They'd each been given a cutting board and knife. Mary cut celery. Honor diced an onion. Janet peeled carrots.

"Now here's my secret," Flora said. "The ingredient that takes this dish from ordinary to extraordinary." She reached into the bag of groceries she'd brought over and pulled out a can of Guinness.

"Beer?" Janet asked.

"Not just beer. It has to be Guinness," Flora said.

"All these years, I had no idea." Janet grimaced as she tugged on a carrot top.

"You had other things on your mind," Flora said. "Saving the world as a civil rights attorney." The pride in Flora's voice softened Mary a little. "Use a knife to cut the tops off. You'll hurt your hands that way."

Janet nudged Flora with her elbow. "Maybe I should've stuck with my law career instead of attempting to cook after all this time."

Flora raised one eyebrow. "It *is* perplexing, I admit."

"What's perplexing?" Janet asked.

"How difficult it is for you to catch on to the simplest of directions," Flora said.

Janet smiled and pointed to the wine cabinet. "Honor, open some wine."

Although they'd all learned a lot, Mary wasn't sure she would remember any of it when it came time to make the dishes on her own. Honor, not surprisingly, was the best pupil. Like with everything she did, she caught on right away. Mary and Janet rolled their eyes at each other every time Flora praised Honor's work. Mary wasn't sure she was making much progress winning Flora over, but she was bonding with her mother-in-law. They were both terrible cooks, loved books, and loved Lance. Last week they'd spent most of the lesson talking about Janet's latest book club pick.

While Flora washed potatoes at the sink on the other side of the kitchen, Honor pulled a cork from a bottle of wine and poured two glasses.

Janet took one, looking guilty. "Sorry to drink in front of you."

"Don't be. Five more weeks and I can join you," Mary said. "Right now, I'd take a milkshake over wine any day."

Mary yelped when the baby kicked her left rib. All three women stopped what they were doing and looked over at her. "Baby wants a milkshake too." She took Janet's hand and placed it on her belly. "Wait just a moment and she'll kick again." Sure enough, *boom* went the little foot.

"I want to feel," Honor said.

Mary did the same with Honor's hand. All was still. "I think she's done stretching," Mary said. "I'm sorry."

"It must feel amazing," Honor said softly.

Mary nodded. "It does."

Janet tucked Honor into a hug and looked over at Mary as if to say, *what do we say?* Mary shook her head. There was nothing *to* say. Every human life at one point in time was touched by loss and disappointment. There was no escape from this truth.

"I count my blessings," Honor said. "Think of everything I have."

"But you can still feel sad that you can't carry one of your own," Janet said.

"Just don't dwell on it forever. No one likes a crybaby," Flora said from the other side of the kitchen.

"Yes ma'am." Honor grinned. "I certainly don't want to be a crybaby."

Flora set a bowl of small red potatoes near the stove. "But I'll tell you what kind of baby they do like. Do you see these? Baby red potatoes. For this stew, they must be babies and cooked whole. That way they burst in Lance's mouth. He loves that."

Honor slipped back to her place beside Mary. "They burst in his mouth," Honor whispered in her ear.

"Don't make me laugh," Mary said under breath.

When Flora walked over to the refrigerator, Janet spoke barely above a whisper. "Stop causing trouble, Honor Sullivan. You're going to get us kicked out of here."

"You're such a suck up," Honor said.

"I'm afraid of her," Janet said. "And you should be too."

"Stop making me laugh. I'm the one who'll get in trouble," Mary said.

Flora returned with a brown bottle. "Worcestershire sauce. Gives the gravy a nice tang."

"Let me guess," Honor said. "Lance loves a tang."

Flora waved a spatula at her. "Young lady, you'll be happy you know the secrets when Zane falls even more in love with you after he tastes this stew. Your generation has no idea what power food has over a man."

"Is this an expectation for women? Still?" Mary asked at full volume. "We all have to learn to cook?"

Flora put her hands on her hips and glared at Mary. "How else will you feed Lance?"

"He hasn't starved yet," Mary said. "The microwave works really well for heating things up."

Honor kicked her. *Don't poke the bear.*

"The microwave? You've been using the microwave for his dinners?" Flora dropped the spatula onto the floor.

"I'll get it," Honor said.

She watched Honor's shoulders shake with silent laughter as she took way too long picking up one utensil.

"Not every dinner," Mary said. "I made a great steak on the grill one night. Sort of."

"Steaks are easily and often overcooked," Flora said.

That's the truth. She'd almost burned them. Damn grill. "I don't get it, though," Mary said, suddenly irritable. *Bossy old Flora.* "How come Lance isn't learning to cook for me?"

Flora opened her mouth to say something but didn't, the muscle in her jaw flexing with the effort of keeping quiet.

"He can cook for you and you can cook for him." *Janet, the diplomat.* "You can share the responsibilities. That's what Jon and I do."

"You cannot with a capital 'C' expect Lance to cook," Flora said. "He couldn't even make toast when he was in high school."

"That's because you always made it for him, dear," Janet said, not unkindly. "You never let the boys do much for themselves."

"Which may explain why Brody's such a big baby," Honor

stole a sip from the Guinness. "Seriously, he can barely order takeout."

"That's what he has you for," Janet said to Honor. "To negotiate deals and order takeout."

Honor flashed them all a cheeky grin. "That's job security right there."

Flora fixed her gaze on Honor. "Young lady, Kara is a wonderful cook. There's no need for takeout. She knows how to feed her man."

Honor laughed merrily and tore a paper towel from its holder. "Flora, no one in our generation gives two craps about feeding their man."

Flora sniffed. "Perhaps you should and there wouldn't be so many divorces. There's something sacred in making a meal for your family." She squinted at the one carrot Janet had peeled thus far and threw up her hands in obvious disgust. "Oh, for heaven's sake, give me that. We'll be here until midnight." She yanked the potato peeler from Janet's hands and stripped a carrot of its outer layer with precise, brutal flicks of her wrist.

"Zane cooks for me all the time." Honor wiped her eyes with the paper towel, crying from the onions. "He doesn't care about my culinary expertise, especially since we own two restaurants. But I do want to make nice meals for my family. That's the difference. I *want* to. I don't have to."

"Good attitude." Flora looked over at Mary's cutting board. "What in the world have you done to the celery? I told you to dice them not annihilate them."

Mary looked down. She'd cut the celery into very small pieces. Their juice bled onto the countertop. No wonder they had no calories. Nothing but water.

"That's like celery soup," Honor said.

"Not helpful," Mary said, stifling a giggle.

Flora put her hands on her hips. "I told you to dice them not mince them."

"You did?" Mary asked.

"What's the difference, again?" Janet asked.

"I know." Honor raised her hand.

"Teacher's pet," Janet whispered.

A peal of laughter escaped before Mary could hold it back.

Flora looked from Mary to Janet, shaking her head in a look of utter disappointment. "I can't say I'm sorry this is our last lesson. I'm not sure I have the energy to teach you how to coat the meat with flour before you brown it."

"Flora, that's very hurtful," Janet said. "After everything we've been through together, you're giving up on me?"

Honor raised her hand again and waved it around like an excited child. "Do you still want the answer to the chopped question?" Her mascara had smeared under her eyes from the onion tears, giving her a naughty clown look.

Even Flora had to laugh, which set them all off.

After they'd calmed down, Honor pointed to the empty pan on the stove. "How long does it take to cook? Shouldn't we get it in there? I'm starved. Maybe we should order pizza."

"Pizza? No. There will be no pizza," Flora said. "You three sit. Put a movie on. Something. Just stay out of the kitchen while I finish this."

"Now we're talking," Janet said, already half way to the couch. "Honor, bring the bottle."

Mary sat on the other end of the couch from Janet, grateful to rest her tired feet. She swung her legs onto the coffee table. "Look at my ankles." They were swollen to almost twice their normal size.

"You keep your feet up," Janet said. "I'll get you some ice water."

Honor, as usual, was ahead of everyone. She arrived with a tall glass of water for Mary and wine for Janet, then plopped beside them. "How about a Julia Roberts flick?"

"Great idea," Janet said. "*Pretty Woman* or *Runaway Bride*?"

"You're all totally hopeless cooks," Flora said from the kitchen. But her voice told a different story. She was glad to be there, taking over the meal preparations. She liked being indispensable. Mary had a sudden idea.

Mary called to her. "Flora, I was wondering if you'd cook dinners for us when the baby first comes. Just the first few weeks or so?"

"I suppose I should, given what I've seen of your skills in the kitchen. My poor Lance will need a good meal if he's going to take care of you properly. You make him do everything, you hear me? You're not to lift a finger other than to feed that baby."

"What do you two grandmothers want to be called?" Mary asked.

Flora's movements around the kitchen went silent. "Me?"

"Yes, you," Mary said. "You and my dad are going to be grandparents very soon and what she calls you is very important."

"I want to be called Grammie," Janet said.

"Grammie? That sounds like you're saying Jammie—something you'd spread on toast. But if that's what you want, I'll take Nana. I always wanted to be a Nana." Flora said with a slight quiver in her voice.

Janet patted Mary's knee. "My work here is done."

"You're the scary one," Honor whispered to Janet.

"Like a fox," Janet whispered back. "They say to never trust a lawyer."

15

Lance

FOR LANCE, the weeks sped by. He was busy preparing the nursery and arranging for someone to manage the shop during Mary's maternity leave. In the evenings, they followed the routine they'd established early on, but now with no secrets between them. Most every day, he would stop what he was doing and marvel at this new life with Mary. Now that she was free from her guilt, she blossomed in front of him. A burden had lifted from her shoulders and it seemed to Lance that she was lighter on her feet and quicker to laughter.

On a weekday in early August, Lance woke before his wife. Careful not to disturb Mary, he settled back against the pillows to read the news on his phone. The local headline startled him out of any residual drowsiness. Fires raged all over the state of California. This wasn't news. The entire state had been under siege for weeks, with blazes taking out entire neighborhoods. So far, they'd been safe, although plagued with smoke. However, due to strong winds, the one just south of them, between Cliffside Bay and San Francisco, had worsened overnight. The fire had jumped the highway, burning hundreds of acres. Because of dense smoke, authorities advised staying indoors and to be on high alert for evacuation.

Evacuation? How were they supposed to evacuate? The highway that took them into the city was blockaded as the firefighters fought to contain the fire. This complication took a moment to fully sink in to his consciousness. They were essentially trapped.

Violet and Maggie were due any day now. Maggie wasn't as much of a concern, as Jackson and Doc could deliver her baby. Violet's twin birth would be more complicated, possibly a C-section. Kyle and Violet had planned to leave this very morning for San Francisco to stay at Brody and Kara's condo in the city. Violet was supposed to be induced within the next few days. Twins were always considered risky births, but in a hospital, the babies would most likely be fine. Here in Cliffside Bay under the care of a general practitioner and without the sophistication of a state-of-the-art hospital, the risk was greatly increased.

He texted Jackson, asking if he'd seen the news and if Violet and Kyle left for the city yet. When he didn't get a response, he sent a text to Maggie. Seconds later, he received one back from her.

Violet went into labor this morning. Jackson and Doc are with her at his office. If she can't deliver naturally, he's going to have to perform the C-section himself.

Does he know how to do that?

He's been trained, but he hasn't performed one on a mother of twins since medical school.

Should I be worried?

I am. Also, I'm feeling a little funky.

Funky? Like labor funky?

Maybe. Small contractions, I think.

Crap.

It's okay. I'll walk around a little and see if the contractions keep going.

Call or text if you need us.

Mary stirred and opened her eyes. "What's wrong?"

He filled her in.

"We should tell Maggie to time the contractions," Mary said.

"Yes, right. Hang on."

Another text alert buzzed on his phone. Maggie again.

My water just broke.

"Her water just broke," he said.

Mary threw back the covers and lumbered over to the dresser. "Get some clothes on and tell her we'll be right there."

Stay put. We'll come get you and take you to the office.

As he pulled jeans and a shirt on, he thought through the situation. If she wasn't already in labor, Maggie would have to be induced. He knew this from the book. After a woman's water broke, risk of infection was too high if she didn't deliver within twenty-four hours. How was Jackson supposed to deliver three babies in his small practice?

Fifteen minutes later, they knocked on Maggie's front door. She answered, looking disheveled and frightened. "Contractions are coming in regular intervals. I haven't been able to get Jackson on the phone. He won't know we're coming."

"He'll know soon enough," Mary said.

Lance escorted Maggie to the car and helped her into the front seat, then helped his wife into the back. Thankfully his car was roomy. He kept that thought to himself.

He drove down the hill, watching Maggie out of the corner of his eye. She groaned and squeezed her eyes shut. "Another one."

"Breathe. Nice and steady," Mary said from the back.

"Hang in there. Jackson will know what to do," Lance said. He talked to himself silently. *Stay calm. Everything will be fine. Jackson and Doc know what they're doing. Kara will be there to help. She worked in a trauma unit for years.*

He parked in the lot behind Jackson's practice. Doc's car was parked next to Jackson's. Kara's was there too. Three doctors for three babies. That was enough, wasn't it?

Maggie was in the middle of another contraction. He waited until the pain ceased before he helped her out of the car and up the steps to the front door of the doctor's office. Zane and Honor were in the waiting room. Kyle must have called them. Honor rushed to them.

"Maggie's in labor," Mary said.

"Are you sure?" Honor asked.

"We're sure." Maggie leaned heavily against Mary.

"Jackson, Doc and Kara are all in there with Violet," Zane said. "We don't know what's going on."

"We heard screaming." Honor looked like she was about to cry.

"Kyle's with her," Zane said, as if that needed to be explained.

"Where are the kids?" Mary asked.

"With Flora," Honor said.

Maggie doubled over and moaned.

Mary led her over to a chair with wooden arms. "Get on your knees. Squeeze the arms." She knelt by her, talking her through the contraction, reminding her to pant. When the contraction ended, Maggie slumped against her.

"What do we do?" Zane asked. "Wait until they're through with Violet?"

"I think this baby's coming soon. Like really soon," Maggie said.

"We need to get her into one of the exam rooms," Honor said.

Mary agreed. "You guys stay here. Honor and I will stay with her. The minute Jackson is done with Violet, send him to us."

Lance didn't have time to agree. The women disappeared behind the closed door. He looked over at Zane, who was gray under his tan.

"What do we do now?" Zane asked.

"Wait, I guess."

"We're useless. I hate being useless."

Another scream came from the examination rooms. Was it Maggie or Violet? Overhead, they heard the roar of an airplane. How close was this fire?

16

Mary

ONCE INSIDE THE examination room, Mary and Honor helped Maggie climb onto the table. She found a box of gloves on the counter and pulled them onto her sweating hands. "Honor, you do the same."

Maggie was curled up in fetal position on the table, panting and moaning. "I think she's coming now."

Mary, with the gloves on, waited for the contraction to end, then spoke in a calm but firm voice to Maggie. "I don't know exactly what it looks like, but I remember the nurse used her fingers to tell me how dilated I was. Four fingers meant I was ready." She looked up at Maggie. "You okay if I feel?"

Maggie nodded and opened her legs. Mary asked her to scoot down and put her feet in the stirrups.

Mary gasped. "It's…it's the baby's head. Right there."

"Holy shit," Honor said. "Red hair. I see red hair." She ran to the cupboards. "We need towels, don't we?"

Maggie sobbed. "I'm scared. What do I do?"

Honor ran to Maggie's side. She wiped the palms of her hands on the front of her shorts. "Mary, what does she do?"

Don't show Maggie how scared you are. Act like you know exactly what you're doing. "You're fully dilated. Do you think you can wait until we get Jackson before you start to push?"

Maggie moaned as another contraction came. "No, I have to push now."

"*Can* she push?" Honor asked. "We can't wait, can we?"

"I don't know. Get one of them in here," Mary said.

Honor ran out of the room.

Mary told Maggie to squeeze her hand and pant. About twenty seconds in, she wasn't sure it had been a good idea. Her hand might never be the same.

The contraction subsided. Sweat soaked Maggie's hair. Crying, she begged, "I have to push next time. Please."

"Just wait for Jackson. Honor's getting him."

Maggie's face contorted in pain. "It's another one."

This baby wanted to come now. Mary would have to deliver this baby. There was no other option. And there was no way in hell she was letting anything happen. *Please God, be with us.* "Can you bear down like you need to poop? Give it everything you have." Mary didn't know if this was the right instruction. Meme had been so small the delivery had been easy.

Maggie's face reddened with the effort. Another inch of the baby's head appeared.

"Won't be long now," Mary said, amazed at how calm she sounded when inside there was a turmoil of uncertainty. "One more push should do it." She lied, having no earthly idea if that was true or not. Where was Jackson? Why hadn't Honor returned? When the next contraction came, Maggie bore down again. This time the baby's head shot out like a ball out of a cannon. *What do I do? What do I do? What do I do?*

A man's voice, gentle and calm, came to her. *Guide the rest of the baby out, like you saw on the video.*

Mary slipped her hand under the baby's head. She could feel a shoulder and tugged gently. Like in the video, the baby slipped out. A great gush of blood followed.

Honor burst back into the room. "Jackson's coming. He had to wash up. Holy God, it's too late." She froze for a split second before darting to the counter and grabbing one of the towels. "You need this, right?"

Mary nodded and took the towel from Honor. As gently as she could, she wiped the blood from the baby.

"Is she all right?" Maggie tried to sit up, brushing her wet hair from her face. "I want to see her."

"She's perfect." Honor said.

Mary placed her in Maggie's arms.

"Oh God, oh God, she *is* perfect," Maggie said.

"Is she breathing? Are we supposed to spank her?" Honor asked.

The baby howled in response. "No, she's just fine." Maggie looked down at her bundle, tears running down her cheeks. "She's going to be a singer like her mama."

"She might need some vocal lessons to work on that tone," Honor said.

Maggie looked up at them. "You guys, we did it. We got her out."

"You did most of it," Mary said. *With a little help from God.*

"Is there supposed to be all that blood?" Honor asked.

"I think the nurses usually do stuff to get rid of it." Mary's legs felt like they might collapse under her. "What just happened?"

"You just delivered a baby," Honor said.

"I feel like I'm going to pass out," Mary said.

"Put your head between your legs," Honor said.

"I can't. My giant stomach's in the way."

They burst into hysterical laughter and clutched each other to keep from falling.

Conversely, Maggie had calmed completely. With a blissful

expression plastered on her sweaty, pink face, she stared at her baby. The little one continued to howl.

"There's nothing wrong with her lungs," Honor said.

"Try nursing her," Mary said. "While we figure out what to do next."

The ropy umbilical cord stretched out like a snake over Maggie's stomach. "We need to cut the cord," Mary said.

"How do we do that?" Honor asked. "With like regular scissors?"

"I don't know. And we have to deliver the placenta."

"There's more going to come out of there?" Honor pointed at Maggie's lower regions.

Jackson rushed into the room. "No, no. I missed it?" He tore off bloody gloves and froze just inside the doorway. "Maggie?"

"The baby came." Maggie smiled up at him. "She came so fast. Mary had to deliver her."

He stumbled over to his wife and child, crying. "Red hair. I knew she'd have your hair."

Mary stepped aside, staring at the bloody mess all over the floor and exam table. "Thank God you're here. We didn't have any idea what to do next."

Jackson perched on the side of the examination table and wrapped his arm around his wife. "Get my dad or Kara in here. I need help."

Mary followed Honor out the door and down the hallway just as Doc came running from the other direction. "Is she all right?"

"Yes, but Jackson says he needs you," Honor said.

He strode toward the examination room. Mary and Honor followed closely behind.

"How's Violet?" Mary asked.

"She's remarkable," Doc said. "She didn't need a C-section. The babies were in the right direction. She delivered them one after the other like a champ."

"And the babies?" Honor asked.

"Both five pounds and change. They're perfectly healthy, if a little small. Nothing to worry about." He disappeared into Maggie's room.

They stood outside the door and stared at each other, too stunned to move.

"She delivered them one after the other," Mary said. "How is that possible?"

"It's all that yoga," Honor said.

"I really need yoga," Mary said.

"Not with that belly."

This made them laugh again as they stumbled into the lobby.

Brody had joined Zane and Lance during their absence.

"Cliffside Bay officially has three more residents." Honor told them of Maggie's insanely fast delivery and relayed what Doc had told them in the hallway.

"You should have seen Mary," Honor said. "Cool as could be. Delivered that baby like a boss."

"I was scared out of my mind," Mary said. "Trust me. But all those shows Lance and I watched of actual deliveries really came in handy. Who knew reality television was useful?"

"I knew there was a reason we were addicted to those." Lance wrapped his arms around her. "I'm beyond proud of you."

She rested her cheek against his chest and breathed in and out. Lance, her oxygen.

"Unlike Mary, I was a hot mess." Honor sank into a chair.

"You were not," Mary said.

Zane sat next to his wife and rubbed the back of her neck. "I bet you were awesome, baby."

"Nope, totally not true. You guys say I'm never flustered, but we found my kryptonite," Honor said. "I never thought there would be so much blood."

"No worries, Lady Macbeth, it's all over now," Brody said.

Honor laughed. "If I'm wandering around the house muttering about a damn spot you'll know I have PTSD."

"My legs are still shaking," Mary said. "I should probably sit."

"It's not every day your friend delivers a baby in like five minutes." Lance escorted her over to a chair and helped her sit.

Kyle seemed to fall rather than walk into the lobby from the hallway. Mary had never seen him look even remotely disheveled, but his wife delivering twins in a town trapped by fire had done a good job of it. His eyes were blood shot and he needed a shave, not to mention his hair stood straight up like a chia pet after a binger. Fatigue did nothing to dull his joy. He raced around the room hugging each of them in turn. "Violet's the strongest most incredible woman that's ever lived. It was unbelievable. She was like, 'Hell no, you're not cutting me open if they're facing the right direction. I'll get them out the natural way.' You should've seen her—totally focused and breathing though the contractions."

"It's the yoga," Honor said. "I knew it."

"That's what she said. All I know is my granola girl kicked butt," Kyle said. "Jackson, Doc, and Kara were phenomenal." He slapped his forehead. "Oh, God, I'm forgetting the most important part. They're not both boys. One of them is a girl. The doctors were wrong."

"Shut the front door," Honor said.

"No way," Brody said.

"Can you believe our luck?" Kyle was clearly running on new dad adrenaline. He picked Honor up and swung her around the room. "We have a baby girl and a baby boy. Two for the two we have at home. Violet started laughing when the second one came out and Jackson told her it was a girl. She said she'd finally gotten used to the idea of two more Kyles. Do you want to see the babies?"

"Yes, but only if it's all right with Violet," Honor said.

"She's asleep. Exhausted." He ran his hands through his wild hair. "Kara's bringing them out for you to see."

A second later, Kara came in with both babies nestled in the crooks of her arms. "This little guy is Chance Brody Hicks." Kara pointed at the baby on her left. "And this is Hope Honor Hicks."

"We chose middle names of two people we love and admire. If our babies are even close to the people you are, we'll be blessed," Kyle said. "But we thought a first name should be just theirs."

"Plus, it would get confusing with two Brodys and two Honors." Brody grinned, clearly pleased.

"God knows one of each of us is enough," Honor said.

The women cooed as they looked down at the babies. Kara gave Chance to Mary and his sister to Honor. The weight of the warm bundle made Mary want to cry. Soon she would have her own warm baby to hold.

"Chance and Hope," Lance said. "What great names."

"Given everything, Violet and I thought they were appropriate."

Kara excused herself. "I need to check in on Maggie and Jackson."

"Send Jackson out with the baby," Honor said as she placed Hope into Lance's arms. "Is it just me or do they look like Kyle?" Honor asked.

"Let's hope they take after their mother and not my ugly mug," Kyle said.

They spent a good fifteen minutes passing the babies around, until Jackson and Doc arrived in the lobby. Jackson held his daughter in his arms. "Hey everyone. Meet Lily Mae Waller. We named her after our mothers."

"Look at that hair," Zane said. "Just like our songbird."

"Is Maggie all right?" Mary asked.

"Yes, my dad got her all fixed up," Jackson said. "And, I got to cut the cord even though I missed the actual birth."

"I'm sorry about that, dude," Kyle said. "I feel terrible."

"No one could've predicted how fast Lily came," Jackson said. "I'm glad Mary and Honor could think on their feet."

"It was all Mary," Honor said. "I screamed like a little girl."

"Maggie said you were both incredible," Jackson said, tearing up. "I can't thank you enough."

"Somehow I thought towels would help," Honor said.

"They always say that in movies," Brody said. "Get towels and boiling water."

"Boiling water is never needed," Kara said.

Mary watched as the friends took turns holding the babies, all talking and laughing at once. She hung back, marveling at the miracles this day had brought to them. After all they'd been through, each with their own losses and tragedies, they'd made it to this day.

She looked over at Lance who smiled back at her. She should have had more faith that her life would get better.

Faith.

Lance wrapped his arms around her and spoke into her ear. "You're the strongest person I've ever known. I'm the luckiest man in the world."

She looked up and into his eyes, her stomach a barrier between them. "I know what we should name the baby."

17

Lance

AFTER THE DRAMA of Lily's birth, Lance and Mary moved into Brody's condo in the city a few weeks later. The fires were under control by then, but Lance felt better being close to the hospital. Doctor Freddie wanted them close to the hospital in case Mary went into premature labor. They spent the days enjoying the city, going to movies and restaurants. At the beginning of her thirty-seventh week, Mary started experiencing dull cramps. Doctor Freddie assured them the baby was now considered full-term. "Any time Mary goes into labor at this point will be just fine." She took the cerclage out and sent them home to enjoy what little time they had left as a party of two.

Two days later, Mary wakened to a painful contraction. Knowing the drill, given Lance's obsessive re-reading of the chapter on delivery, they stayed at home until the contractions had strengthened and were coming at regular intervals. They grabbed their already packed overnight bag and sped to the hospital. Doctor Freddie was not on call that night. One of her colleagues examined Mary and checked her into the hospital. By 3 a.m., Mary was comfortable after an epidural and they waited through the contractions by watching a movie.

Mo, the nurse assigned to them, was a stout woman in her fifties. With gray hair and a serious countenance, she moved about the room in efficient, determined strides. The floor squeaked under her shoes, as if in protest. When Lance asked her how many babies she'd help deliver, she just shook her head. "Too many to count."

Around seven that morning, Mo declared Mary to be fully dilated and ready to deliver. Doctor Freddie had arrived at the hospital by then. Lance stood around helplessly as Mo and Doctor Freddie bustled around the room. There seemed to be a thousand instruments that gleamed under the lights. How had Mary delivered Lily without any of this?

The pushing process went on for an hour without much progress. "I'm sorry," Mary said to Lance. "Maggie did it with two pushes."

"You're doing fantastic," he said.

Mo shot him a look of approval.

"I'm tired. I don't know if I can do it," Mary said.

"You can. Just hang in there for a few more. We're almost there. A few more pushes and we get to meet our daughter."

His words seemed to strengthen her. After three more pushes, the head slipped out. Another one brought their baby girl into the world. Red-faced with fists clenched and legs flailing, she let out a lusty cry.

"Is she okay?" Mary asked.

"Right as rain," Mo said as she placed her on Mary's chest. Lance leaned closer, amazed by the perfection of her tiny body.

Mary stared at the baby in her arms and sobbed. "I can't believe she's here."

Lance perched on the delivery table next to his wife, almost blinded by his own tears. "She's so small," he said.

"But perfect," Mary said.

"Dad, would you like to cut the cord?" Doctor Freddie asked.

He wiped his eyes and took the scissors Mo offered. "Are you sure it won't hurt either of them?"

"No sir," Mo said. "Just clip it like a hotdog."

A hotdog? Who clipped hotdogs? He placed the scissors on the spot Mo instructed him. He cut through the cord, feeling nauseous as the cord dropped away, leaving the baby with a bloody stump. Black spots danced before his eyes. He handed the scissors back to Mo.

She laughed. "You need smelling salts?"

"No, I'm fine," he said.

"You best stay up near Mary's head for the rest of this. Placenta delivery isn't nearly as much fun as cutting the cord."

He was only too happy to oblige.

Mo snapped her fingers and asked for the baby with an indulgent sparkle in her eyes. "We need to give her a little bath, do some eyedrops, and weigh and measure her. Then you can have her back." Mary handed her to Mo, who strode across the room on her squeaky shoes.

Doctor Freddie had Mary give her another quick push. Lance was careful to remain fixated on Mary's face and not on what was happening below.

Mary's eyes shone as she looked up at him. "Thank you."

"You're the one who did all the work."

"For being here. For insisting on being here."

"You've made me the happiest guy in the world." he said.

From the scale, Mo called out to them. "Six pounds, two ounces. Twenty-one inches."

"Is that good?" Lance asked.

"Yes, quite good." Mo diapered the baby and wrapped her in a blanket before bringing her back to them. "Does she have a name?"

"Faith," Lance said. "No middle name. Just Faith Mullen."

"Faith, all by itself, is enough." Mary said.

Perched on the side of the bed, his heart throbbed with love. *Thank you, God, for keeping them safe*. Had there ever been a more beautiful baby than this?

"I agree," Mary said as if she heard his thoughts.

"She's perfect," he said. "Our Faith."

"It suits her, don't you think?" Mary asked.

"I do."

"Do you want to hold her?" Mary asked.

"She's so small," he said. "I'm afraid I'll hurt her." An arm popped out from under the blanket. He marveled at the perfectly formed fingernails.

"You can't hurt her," Mo said. "She's tough. She'll grow even stronger in your arms."

"You've been waiting to do this." Mary beamed up at him. "She's finally here."

"And the doctor has more lady business to do on your wife," Mo said. "So you step over to the window with your daughter."

Lance took the baby into his arms. She was no bigger than the span of his two shaking hands. "Hello, little love."

Faith stared up at him with glassy eyes. Her dark hair was sparse and did nothing to cover the soft spot in her skull. Pink splotches on her face told the story of her long and difficult birth. A layer of downy hair covered the tips of her ears. He peeked under the blanket. Her legs were scrawny, and her skin seemed thin and much too soft to survive in this world. He wrapped the blanket more tightly around her. This was his job now. He must keep her safe. She must always feel supported and loved. The task daunted him. He couldn't lie, especially to himself. But it didn't matter if he was afraid. He would do it. There was no other option.

"All right, Mary, you're all taken care of now," Doctor Freddie said. "I'm going to keep you overnight, but you should be just fine to head home tomorrow." She looked at her watch. "That's my cue. I've got to go. Another baby is ready to join the world."

Lance crossed over to her and held out his hand. "Thank you. Thanks for everything."

"My pleasure. I'll see you when you come in for baby number two," she said.

"Let's see how we do with one," Mary said.

"You'll do just fine." Doctor Freddie gave them each a nod and scampered off to her next delivery.

Lance continued to hold Faith while Mo asked Mary what she should order for her from the cafeteria. Mo suggested Mary try nursing her. Faith latched on right away. He'd been worried about that, given what the baby books had said. However, mothering seemed to come naturally to Mary. He knew that no matter what came their way, she would be a phenomenal mother.

After they moved Mary and the baby to another room, the nurses chased him away so he could eat something and Mary and the baby could rest.

On his way, he called Brody. His brother didn't answer. Lance left a message. "Baby came. She's perfect. Mary's doing great. Call me when you get this."

He bought a sandwich at the cafeteria, suddenly ravenous, and walked outside to sit on the patio. He chose a table in the sunshine and let the autumn rays warm him. Red and orange leaves of a maple fluttered in the crisp air. His father had appreciated days like this. They represented everything he loved, he'd told Lance once. Football and days with his family in the backyard. His dad had been a family man. A *nice* man. Simple in his tastes and desires. *Like me.*

He remembered then—the memory that had escaped him. His father, that last morning of his life, as they wheeled him away, had grabbed Lance's hand. "Best days of my life were when my sons were born."

"Not winning the Super Bowl?" Brody had asked, teasing.

"Not even close. Listen, you boys remember something. The measure of a man is not in his outward successes but how he treats people, most especially his wife and children." He'd drifted to sleep as the nurses wheeled him away.

Lance closed his eyes as the stinging tides of grief engulfed him. He wanted his dad. He wanted him to see his baby girl and his beautiful wife.

His father's voice came to him, as if there was indeed a line from here to heaven. *I'm here. I'll always be here.*

Lance used the paper napkin to wipe his eyes. He must get back to his wife and child. *I'm a husband and father now. Nothing else will ever be as important.*

The next day, he drove his little family home. When they arrived, Brody's car was in the driveway. Kara and Brody came running down the steps before they were even out of the car. Brody went around to the passenger side to help Mary while Lance grabbed the baby seat from the back. Kara peeked into the carrier and immediately started cooing. "Hello sweet Faith."

"Come inside," Brody said. "We brought dinner."

Mary walked gingerly toward the house with her arm linked into Kara's. "The grandparents are all on their way as well," Kara said. "I made them all promise not to overstay their welcome."

From behind them, Lance saw Mary and Kara exchange a knowing glance as they climbed the steps to the porch. "Thank you."

"Sisters have to stick together," Kara said.

Freckles bounded up to greet them the moment they walked in the front door. He did one of his joyous half flips when he saw Mary. She patted the top of his head and scratched behind his ears. "Did you miss us?"

The dog licked her arm to tell her how much. "We've come back with a baby."

Freckles barked.

"There's no need to be jealous," Mary said. "We'll still love you just as much."

Lance set the baby carrier on the floor and knelt to pet his dog. He was almost knocked over by the force of Freckles' wagging tail. "This is Faith," he said to Freckles. "Your job is to help protect her." Freckles sat on his haunches and looked down at the baby, who slept peacefully, not yet knowing she would have a furry best friend. He whined, then lay on the floor, with his head near Faith's feet.

Lance chuckled as he stood and picked up the carrier. "Come on, boy. You can protect her over here."

Lance got Mary settled on the couch with Faith, so she could nurse. Freckles lay on the floor as close to Mary's legs as possible.

Kara brought Mary a glass of water and some apple slices. "Are you hungry? Do you want anything?" Kara asked.

"I'm fine," Mary said. "But I do have a few questions." Mary spoke to Lance. "Honey, why don't you and Brody catch up over a beer. I need to ask Kara a few girl questions."

"A beer and a cigar are certainly in order," Brody said.

The weather was as nice as the day before. They sat on his deck with their beers and looked at the blue sea. The faint sound of seagulls' cries and crashing waves broke the silence of the autumn afternoon.

They clinked their beer bottles.

"I wish Dad was here," Lance said. "Can you imagine him with a little granddaughter?"

"I can." Brody lifted his beer up to heaven. "I know he's up there watching, though."

They watched the afternoon sun lower over the horizon. A beer had never tasted as good as it did this afternoon.

"For years now, I've been trying to remember the last thing Dad said to us," Lance said. "It was like this black hole in my memory. But yesterday morning, after Faith was born, it came to me."

"Yeah?" Brody's gaze didn't move from the sea, but his fingers fluttered.

"He said the best days of his life were when we were born. And you joked, not the Super Bowl?"

"And he said, not even close," Brody said.

"That's right."

"I was such an idiot back then I had no idea how anything could be better than winning the Super Bowl. But I was wrong."

Lance lifted his beer in a toast. "Here's to growing up. To fatherhood."

"Here's to Dad. May we do it half as well as he did."

"Amen, brother."

The grind of cars pulling into the driveway beckoned to them. They went inside to join their families.

18

Mary

THE GRANDPARENT BRIGADE, as Kara had called them, descended like the grasshoppers on the prairie grasses in the *Little House* books. Except the grasshoppers didn't bring presents like grandparents did. Flora and her dad brought a darling knit hat with a pink crocheted flower. They insisted on putting it on her immediately, even though the hat dwarfed Faith's tiny head. Janet and Doc were equally enamored and seemed pleased they'd brought an entire outfit rather than just a hat.

While they passed Faith around from one to the other, Mary slipped into the dining room to grab a few bottles of wine to go with the lasagna and salad Kara had brought for dinner. She stared at the wine cabinet, unsure what to choose. At the sound of footsteps, she turned. Brody smiled and gestured toward the wine. "Need some help?"

"That would be great. I have no idea what goes with lasagna."

"I'm not sure what he has in here, but I bet we can find a nice Merlot or Malbec." He strolled over and ran his fingers down the rows of bottles, like the labels were in braille. She'd noticed this before. Brody Mullen was a tactile man who seemed to read the world through the connection to his flesh and muscles. He and his cerebral brother were different in this way and many others, yet they shared the same qualities of decency and curiosity.

She watched as he picked one bottle and then the other. "I need to send some decent wine over here," he said.

"There's nothing good? I don't know anything about wine."

"Decent, but not great." He smirked as he set the bottles on the dining room table. "We like great in this family."

She met his gaze with a smile. "Such high standards. I don't know that I'm worthy."

"You are." He opened a drawer and pulled out a wine opener. "Does he have a decanter anywhere?"

She pointed to the cabinet below the wine. "In there, I think."

He knelt and came up with two. At the table, he yanked the corks from one bottle then the other. "I'm sorry for all the stuff I said that night. I feel like a heel."

"I didn't exactly give you a reason to like me," she said.

"Even so, I acted like a jerk when I should've been supportive of my brother's choices. It was like I couldn't see anything but red. Not a nice red like this wine—more the color of hot coals."

Red. That was a great way to describe the rage she'd felt when her dad had decided to upend his life and marry a woman he hadn't seen for forty years. "I know what that's like."

"Flora and your Dad?"

"I'm not proud of how I've acted. All I can say is it felt disloyal to my mother to accept anyone else in my dad's life."

"Kara assured me it's no excuse, but I've always been protective of Lance, especially after my dad died. And, truthfully, he's never had the greatest taste in women." He tipped the bottle of merlot into one of the decanters. The wine gurgled as it filled the glass container. "Until now, that is. Bottom line, you make him happy and that's all I care about."

"We fit together, strange as it seems."

"I see it now." He tipped the second bottle into the waiting decanter. "All I wanted was for Lance to have what I have with Kara. The way this all went down made me worry that wasn't the case with you two."

"Honestly, I can understand exactly how you felt. A marriage of convenience is not what I would want for someone I loved. But it's not that way between us. It never really was." She flushed, embarrassed, but continued, knowing how important it was that Brody understand. "I'm a hard person to love. I've *made* it hard anyway."

"I get that. Ask Kara how I acted when we first met."

He grabbed two wine glasses and poured them each a small amount of the merlot. "Here, we should try these and make sure they haven't turned. I told him to get a wine fridge, but he said they were pretentious."

She laughed. "Yet, he loves to fly first class."

"My brother's nothing if not a walking dichotomy. Maybe I'll get one for you as a wedding gift."

She sniffed the wine in her glass. The scent was pungent. "I might get drunk from the fumes."

Brody lifted his glass. "Here's to a fresh start for you and me."

"To family."

They clinked glasses. She took a tentative sip and almost choked. "I haven't had alcohol for a long time, so I have no idea if this is good or not."

He chuckled and drank from his glass. "Tastes fine."

"When I think about how much has changed for me since I moved here, it's hard to get my head around it. But I'm grateful to Flora for bringing me to your family, to Lance. Even though it was a lot of change, it's exactly what I needed."

"I hate change."

"Just when I get used to things a certain way, they change." Mary set aside her glass. She might have more at dinner but right now, it didn't taste good to her. "It's hard to find my footing."

"I feel you." Brody poured a small amount from the other decanter into his glass. "This year's been tough that way. I've felt like a wanderer in a strange land. Maybe a bit like Gulliver, confused and clumsy."

"Have you decided what you want to do next?" she asked.

"I'm in talks with a few of the networks about becoming a football commentator. There are also a few offensive coordinator coaching jobs I have my eye on. Depending on how the season plays out, there could be turnover. All that said, those jobs would require a lot of travel. Kara doesn't want me away from home that much. Especially now."

Lance poked his head inside the doorway. "Are you two hoarding all the wine?"

"You need a wine fridge," Brody said.

"You need your own jet."

"Good idea." Brody offered his arm to Mary. "May I escort you to dinner?"

Kara's lasagna melted in her mouth. Mary ate hungrily, despite worrying that her stomach still looked pregnant. After she finished her piece, she eyed the glass casserole dish that held the remainder. Should she?

Lance, like he did, knew her thoughts. "Honey, it's been one day. You can't expect to immediately be back in your regular clothes. Eat the pasta."

She grinned and did as suggested. Still, she thought longingly of her former wardrobe, waiting impatiently for her to come back to them.

Kara distracted her from this line of thinking when she cleared her throat and said they had an announcement.

"We found out we're having a boy," Kara said, beaming.

"Oh, how wonderful," Janet said. "I loved having boys."

"Great news, kids," Doc said.

"They'll still grow up together, even if Faith's a little older," Kara said. "Just like we wanted."

"I'm so glad," Mary said.

"Zane and Honor's baby will be along around the same time," Brody said. "We almost have enough for a football team."

"Violet and Kyle have certainly done their part," Lance said.

"You two will simply have to catch up," Flora said. "There's no reason to let that rascal Kyle Hicks get the better of you."

"Last time I checked, it wasn't a competition," Brody said.

Flora shrugged, nonchalantly. "All I'm saying is they've gotten quite a head start on the rest of you. Not to mention, Zane has Jubie plus another one on the way. One baby each seems paltry."

"If I didn't know you were kidding, I'd be horrified right now," Lance said, laughing.

"I don't think she is," Brody said.

"The Mullen boys shouldn't be outdone. I'm merely thinking of your mother. She's waited such a long time for grandbabies," Flora said. "That's my only point."

Dax shook his fork at Flora. "Didn't we talk about how some things should be kept inside your head, not spoken out loud?"

"I have no idea what you're talking about." Flora turned her attention back on Lance. "You haven't had a bite of salad, young man."

Lance picked up his fork and stabbed a cucumber. "If I eat three bites can I have dessert?"

"Four," Flora said.

Everyone burst into laughter. Mary stole quick glances at the faces gathered around their table. This was family, community, a tribe in which to belong. Home. She imagined all the events to come. Football games on the lawn at Thanksgiving, visits to Santa, Easter egg hunts, trick or treating. There would be pirate and princess birthday parties and first dates and graduations. It was no longer only the two of them like it had been since her mother had died. The Mullen family had returned them to life.

"I've been thinking," Flora said. "That perhaps Lance and Mary might like a wedding."

"We had a wedding," Lance said. "With Elvis. Hard to beat that."

"But wouldn't you like your mother to have a real wedding?" Flora asked.

Lance turned to his mother. "Do you want a wedding?"

Janet lifted one shoulder in a noncommittal way. "It's whatever you kids want."

Her dad caught her eye. "What about you, sweetheart? Do you want another wedding?"

Did she? The last one had been rushed and, well, fake. A real wedding with everyone they loved in attendance might be nice. There was the dress. That beautiful dress.

"I might like to wear the dress again. If it ever fits again." She looked over at Lance. "What do you want?"

"I'd like to see you in that dress again." Lance winked at her.

"There was a dress?" Flora scowled at Lance. "You had a wedding with a dress? That doesn't sound like an elopement to me."

"Lance arranged it rather quickly," Mary said.

"I'm a detail, guy," Lance said. "I wanted Mary to have a dress."

"He made it happen when no one else could've," Mary said.

"I'd like to get married in our little church in town," Lance said.

"I'd like to see my little girl walk down the aisle toward the right man," Dax said. "If she were so inclined to indulge her old dad."

"If it would mean that much to everyone," Mary said. "Then let's do it."

"And then a reception at our house," Kara said.

"We'd have to wait until spring," Mary said. "Until after our nephew comes."

"Why?" Kara asked.

"Because if you were to say…accept my request to be my maid of honor…it might be nice to be done with pregnancy for a while."

"Really? You want me?" Kara asked.

"Who better than my sister?"

Kara flew around the table and pulled her into a hug. "It would be my absolute honor, and yes, it would be much better to be able to fit into a regular sized dress." She patted her bump as she returned to her seat. "Right now, things are going the opposite direction."

"It's settled then," Flora said. "We'll have to start planning right away."

"Mary's going to be busy with the baby," Lance said. "And the shop."

"No worries. I'll take care of everything," Flora said. "I need a little project to keep me busy while Dax golfs with Doc all the livelong day."

Mary made a face at Kara. *Rescue me.*

"As her maid of honor, I'd like to help too," Kara said. "And Mary probably has ideas of what she wants."

"We can all do it together," Janet said, clearly catching on. "But yes, whatever Mary wants, we will do. We'll be your minions, sweetheart."

"Something small and simple will be fine," Mary said. "When the flowers bloom."

Faith burbled from the cradle. Lance shook his head when she moved to get up. "I've got her. You eat." He gathered the baby and held her against his chest, smiling down at her. "It's a pity Elvis won't be there for this wedding."

"We could fly him in," Brody said.

"I think we can do without him," Mary said.

"As long as you're sticking with the same groom, I don't care what you do," Lance said.

"No one else will do," she said. "Not even Elvis."

19

Lance

ON A DAY in the middle of October, Lance held Mary's hand as they made their way across the parking lot of Zane's new brewery. Near the entrance, they stopped to peer at the signage above the double doors.

The Dogs Brewery.

Before they went in, Lance turned to look at the expansive lawn, flattened for warm weather activities such as frisbee, volleyball, and badminton. Further out, a baseball field lay waiting for its young players. Stone paths led to several gas fire pits. Picnic tables were interspersed across the lawn.

Beside him, Mary shivered. The weather had cooled the past few weeks, especially at night, but Mary had insisted on wearing a sleeveless dress. It was the only one from her pre-pregnancy wardrobe that had a forgiving middle, she'd said after a few tears and a pile of dresses lay in wreckage on the bed. He'd had to talk fast to convince her that she was beautiful, and after all, it had only been a month since she'd given birth, and she'd be back to her normal weight in just a few more weeks.

In truth, she'd never looked lovelier. If there was a little extra flesh around her middle, he couldn't see it. He loved her in the red and flowy dress she wore. Those strappy sandals showed off her slender legs.

This was their first night away from the baby. Mary had only ventured out of the house to visit Kara or do a quick run to town for groceries, and always with the baby attached to her. Their days and nights consisted of feedings and changings and naps. Not that he minded. The days had passed in a happy, dazed, exhausting blur.

Four weeks in, they weren't hopeful that a full night's sleep was happening anytime soon.

He rubbed his hands over her arms, hoping to warm her. "You've never looked prettier than you do tonight."

"It feels good to be out and dressed, wearing makeup with clean hair." She stuck her bottom lip out in a mock pout. "I'm sorry I've been such a mess."

"You've not been a mess. You're feeding another human being." He kissed her. "To me, you're always beautiful."

"Do you think she's okay? Should I call Flora to check?" she asked.

"Flora will have her potty trained by the time we get home."

She laughed and tossed her hair behind her back. "You're right. Let's just have fun."

"Tequila?"

"Very funny."

He opened the wide door and held it for her as she passed by him.

"Oh, Lance, look at it."

He almost ran into her as she stopped abruptly just feet from the doorway, clutching her handbag to her chest.

Zane had decided on a casual, almost industrial feel for the interiors, leaving the space open so that patrons had only to look up to see the shiny surfaces of the actual brewery. A long bar ran the length of the room. Both family style and intimate bistro tables were scattered about or set in front of the large stone fireplace. Lance knew from his earlier tour that there were enclosed spaces for private parties to the left, as was the kitchen. Out back a covered patio with the same stone from the entrance provided more spaces to dine or drink.

The official opening was tomorrow, but Zane had asked the Dogs and their wives to come for a preopening party. They were the last to arrive. Not surprising, given the tears and pile of dresses they'd left behind.

Their friends were gathered around the fire. The moment the ladies spotted Mary, they all descended, exclaiming how pretty she looked and asking if she was dying for wine.

He let the girls lead Mary away with strict instructions to Violet to make sure she had some fun.

"Challenge accepted," Violet said.

Honor stayed back as the others walked toward the bar. She planted a kiss on his cheek. "I love you. I hope you know that."

"What's that for?"

"I don't know. It's just the passage of time these days. "Time slips away. I want to make sure I tell people how I feel when I still can."

"You think you love me now, just wait. I have a little surprise for you." He motioned for his brother to join them. Brody bounded over.

He'd called Brody earlier to tell him the news. They'd reached the goal on Honor's secret fund. It was time to tell her.

"What's the surprise?" Honor asked.

"Should we get Zane too? He's her husband now," Lance said. "Fifty-fifty and all that."

"Good point." Brody called over to Zane, leaving Kyle and Jackson alone around the fire. They were immersed in a discussion and didn't seem to notice.

"Let's go in one of the private rooms," Lance said. "We have a financial matter to discuss with you."

"Sure." Zane led them around the bar, down a skinny hallway, and into a private dining space.

"You two might want to sit down for this," Lance said. God, he felt like a kid at Christmas.

They all took seats at the table. Lance couldn't. He had to pace while he told them. "Brody, you start."

"Okay, well you know how a few years ago Lance invested some money for us?" Brody asked.

Honor smiled. "Yes, it's still building. My little twenty thousand has grown quite nicely."

"Yeah, well, I thought back then that it might be good to start a little retirement account for you. In case I had to retire early, and our time together was cut shorter than we hoped."

Honor's eyes widened. "You're not firing me, are you?"

"What? No," Brody said. "Obviously we've still got work to do together. But anyway, I put some money in a fund for you, Honor. I did the same for Lance. We agreed at the time he'd invest it in higher risk stuff. If it ever reached four million, we'd give you the opportunity to cash out. Or not. Depending."

"Yeah, anyway, things have gone better than I expected," Lance said. "The initial amount has grown to four million. So, it was time to tell you."

Honor was staring at him like he had two heads. "What are you talking about?"

Zane closed his eyes, almost like he had a headache. "He's saying that he made four million dollars from the initial retirement fund that Brody set up for you."

"Retirement fund? I'm not following," Honor said.

In all the years they'd been friends, he'd never witnessed Honor not understanding a situation.

"Your fund is at four million dollars. All yours," Lance said.

"Thanks to my little brother being some kind of savant when it comes to investing," Brody said.

"You guys, it's too much," Zane said.

"Now, don't get too excited," Lance said. "It's not that much, really, when you think about it. You could blow it all really fast if you do something stupid."

"No." Honor shook her head. "No, we'll just keep it with you. Maybe invest a tad more conservatively. But we don't need it now." She looked over at her husband. "Right?"

Zane nodded. "Right."

"I mean, I have a lot of shoes," Honor said.

"She has a lot of shoes," Zane said.

Honor's face contorted as she tried not to cry. "I don't know what to say. This is…just unbelievable." She turned to Zane. "I wish your dad was here. He'd be so happy for us."

Zane nodded, but didn't say anything, evidently overcome.

Honor leapt to her feet and threw herself into Brody's arms. "Thank you for being so generous." She hugged Lance next. "And thank you for being so clever."

"Listen, I don't know what's going to happen with me," Brody said. "The endorsements and all that are already drying up. It might be time to consider looking for another athlete to manage."

"Maybe," Honor said. "I don't know if I want to work for anyone but you."

"If you decide you want to give up work for a while and be with the kids," Brody said, "you can live on the dividends."

"Not to mention this place," Lance said. "I think it's going to be a huge success."

"And we still own The Oar," Zane said.

Honor looked at each of them in turn. "I've never had the freedom to think like this. It might take some time for me to decide."

"Once the baby comes, things will be different," Lance said, stifling a yawn. "Faith's kicking our ass."

"You're scaring me," Honor said.

"Me too," Zane said.

"Whatever you decide, I wanted you to have something to show for all the ways you grew my wealth," Brody said. "I would never have been able to do it without you."

"We're not done yet," she said. "We've got an announcer job to bag first."

Brody tweaked her ear. "Always such a slave driver."

Honor wiped under her eyes. "You guys, the best decision I ever made was walking into The Oar for the first time." She kissed the heart locket she wore around her neck and looked heavenward. "Rest in peace, Hugh."

After dinner, the Dogs stood in a straight line on the back patio. Each had a lit cigar. The outside heaters warmed the chilly air. A bottle of scotch and five tumblers were on the low table behind them. Brody was in the middle, with Kyle and Zane on either side of him. Lance and Jackson were bookends, like they'd always been. Cool and steady compared to the fire of the three in the middle.

The sound of Mary's laugh from inside warmed Lance like a heater never could.

"Man, I'm the luckiest guy on earth," he said.

"Me too," Jackson said.

"Me three." Zane blew out a puff of smoke.

"Me four." Kyle zipped up his jacket with his free hand.

"Me five," Brody said.

"For longer than I can remember, this brewery was my dream." With his cigar between his teeth, Zane slapped Kyle and Brody's shoulders. "Obviously, I couldn't have done it without you two agreeing to invest."

"Do you ever wonder what to do after everything you ever dreamed of came true?" Brody asked.

"Dream new dreams?" Jackson asked.

"Bigger ones?" Zane asked.

"Or small fat ones, like more babies," Lance said.

"Violet's cut me off," Kyle said in a mournful tone. "No more babies."

"Four *is* probably enough," Zane said.

"'A ridiculous amount' is how she phrased it. However, it was three a.m. and Dakota was puking, so her judgment might be skewed."

They all laughed.

"There was a time we wouldn't have found that humorous," Jackson said.

"It's still not *that* funny," Zane said.

"Especially at three a.m.," Jackson said.

They smoked their cigars, the scent thick in the cool night air. A sliver of a moon appeared between the trees at the far end of the lawn.

"I thought I'd have more time," Brody said. "More years to play. Without football, I wonder what I'm supposed to do next. I get that it's a new season. I'm a husband and will be a father. My dad always said those were the most important roles in a man's life, and I agree. But still, there's this feeling inside me that there's more to do." He tapped the end of his cigar. "I wonder what the purpose of my career was. Like, yeah, I won the Heisman and the Super Bowl, but what does that mean? What have I done with my life that's important, that wasn't all about my drive and ego? God blessed me with a physical gift, so I've just been damn lucky my whole life. Is that it? I'm just a lucky son of a bitch."

"The same could be said for any of us," Lance said.

Kyle's voice was soft and slightly gruff. "Everything I ever wished for has come true. When I trace everything back to its origin, I find one common denominator. You guys. I don't know what my life would've been like without you."

"You didn't need us," Brody said. "A man like you finds his way."

"I don't know about that," Kyle said. "When you think of where I started, it's hard to imagine I'd end up here. Each of you helped form the man I am today. So, when you wonder, Brody, what you've done with your life, what purpose your career served, look no further than the people right in front of you. You gave me my first loan with your football money. Without it, I couldn't have started my business. Yes, my ambition and ego drove me toward success. I could think that everything I did was just to serve my own desire for money and prestige. I worked hard and was clever and now I'm rich and that's the end of it. Yay for me. But you have to think of how one action leads to another. Violet taught me this. It started with your loan. Fast forward ten years and think about how many people I employ, how many families are taken care of because of my business. We can never really know how our actions affect others. But in your case, it's pretty clear."

"You helped me build this place," Zane said. "And look what you did for Honor."

"She earned every cent of that money," Brody said. "Plus, Lance did that."

"Without your investment, I couldn't have," Lance said. "Your generosity was the seed. Without it I couldn't have grown anything."

"I haven't done anything for Jackson," Brody said.

"That's because he never needed anything," Zane said. "He always knew exactly who he was and what he wanted."

Jackson smiled. "All I ever wanted was to be Cliffside Bay's doctor and to marry Maggie Keene and have little red-headed babies." He paused. "But you're wrong that you never gave me anything. You know that."

"Nah," Brody said.

"You know how low I was that first year. Without you guys, I don't know if I'd be here," Jackson said.

Silence stretched out as far as to the moon and back until Kyle spoke.

"I have a new dream," Kyle said. "But I need you guys to do it. You guys know how it was for me as a kid, right?"

They all nodded. Lance could see it all in his mind. The rundown trailer and lack of hot water to wash clothes and bodies. The mean kids at school taunting him, nicknaming Kyle Pig. He wished he could go back in time and beat the crap of everyone who hurt his friend. But there were no time machines except in the sci-fi books in their shop.

"I got out but only by the grace of God via a scholarship to USC where I met you guys. But what about the kids who don't? The poor, the bullied, the kids who don't quite fit in? Who's looking out for them?"

"Or the kids in foster care like Honor was," Zane added.

"What if we look out for them?" Kyle asked. "Not all, obviously, but as many as we could? We could establish a scholarship fund for college scholarships. That's where you come in, Lance. You could grow our initial investment. We could have a camp in the summers where they were taught leaderships skills, coping skills, how to become strong physically. Brody, that would be under your direction. Maybe we could give them jobs here at the brewery as busboys and dishwashers, so they had money of their own to build a future. We could teach them how to become the kind of men who make a difference in the world."

"Where do we find them?" Lance asked. He knew they existed everywhere, but how would they identify them?

"I think that's where Honor fits in," Kyle said. "If anyone can figure out how to do that, it's her. I've already talked it through with Violet and she wants to take over the fundraising portion. You know how she loves a good cause. With all your connections to wealthy people, Brody, she thinks we could easily raise money. Maggie and her actress friend Lisa can also be an attraction, not to mention the most famous quarterback of all time. We can hire staff to run the program and the camps later, but we would make up the board. It would be our vision. A combination of all our talents could make something special."

"Where would this camp be?" Zane asked.

"This is the weird part. Do you remember where Mel took the kids? That rundown cabin? Well, that land's for sale. It would be perfect for a summer camp. We'd hire Stone to build the cabins and dining hall, that kind of thing."

"You've really given this a lot of thought," Jackson said.

"I have," Kyle said. "Does it sound crazy?"

"Not at all," Brody said. "A little daunting, but not crazy."

"So, are you guys in?" Kyle asked.

"Hell yeah," Zane said. "I'm all the way in."

"Me too," Jackson said.

"Me three," Brody said.

"You had me at growing the initial investment," Lance said.

"Let's toast to it." Brody put out his cigar on the bottom of his boot and grabbed the bottle of scotch. When they all had a glass, they formed a circle.

"To our new purpose," Brody said.

"Wait, before we toast, I have one more thing I want to run past you," Kyle said. "How would you feel about naming it the Hugh Shaw Foundation?"

Zane bowed his head. "He'd be honored."

"It's a perfect tribute to a great man," Jackson said.

"Couldn't agree more," Lance said.

Kyle raised his glass. "To Hugh."

"Long live the Dogs," Zane said.

"And God bless the Wags," Jackson said.

"For saving us from ourselves," Kyle said.

They all clinked glasses. Perhaps it was the moon pulling them, but they all returned to their former positions, lined up in a row at the edge of the patio.

"Why do I feel like an era's ending and another's starting?" Jackson asked.

"I think that train has passed," Kyle said. "We're already there."

"It's a new era, but the Dogs will always be the Dogs," Brody said. "We'll always have one another."

"Through thick and thin," Zane said.

"Do you think we'll ever get back to our poker games?" Kyle asked.

"If you'd stop having babies," Zane said.

"I'm cut off, remember?"

The moon rose above the sycamores and pines and shed silvery light over the lawn. In the distance, an owl hooted a long, high note in harmony with the rounded ripples of their wives' muted laughter. A sudden gust of wind brought the scent of the briny sea. Tall yellow grasses in the decorative pots at the edge of the patio swayed like graceful dancers.

Lance smiled as he glanced at the familiar faces of the men who'd helped one another survive in this often cruel, always unpredictable, yet beautiful chaos called life. Shoulder to shoulder, they formed a line like a fortress against all foes, brothers in this life of chance and hope and faith, stronger together than apart.

Images of the college boys they once were played before him. It was Jackson's eyes he remembered, glassy blue with grief, regret, and the certainty that something bad was about to happen as he waited up for one of them to come home from a party. Kyle, as thin as the shirt he wore, scrunched over schoolwork, fueled by ambition and hunger. Zane with that proud, clenched jaw, serving lunch from behind the counter at his job in the cafeteria. Brody, exhausted from practice, asleep on the floor with a book covering his face.

Lance lifted his face to the light of the uneven moon. The missing sliver made it imperfect, like the men that stood together now. That slice was the cost of living. Pain, regret, and loss chipped away until one became like the imperfect moon, shining and shining through the darkness until the sun once again rose in the east to set them free.

A note from Tess…I hope you enjoyed Lance and Mary's story. To read a novella about a few Christmas miracles, download The Season of Cats and Babies here!

Then, the Cliffside journey continues with Missed: Rafael and Lisa here! Will Rafael be able to keep his beautiful actress safe once he becomes her bodyguard?

Sign up for my newsletter at https://tesswrites.com/ and get a free copy of my holiday novella The Santa Trial.

ALSO BY TESS THOMPSON

CLIFFSIDE BAY

Traded: Brody and Kara

Deleted: Jackson and Maggie

Jaded: Zane and Honor

Marred: Kyle and Violet

Tainted: Lance and Mary

Cliffside Bay Christmas, The Season of Cats and Babies (Cliffside Bay Novella to be read after Tainted)

Missed: Rafael and Lisa

Healed: Stone and Pepper

Cliffside Bay Christmas Wedding (Cliffside Bay Novella to be read after Healed)

Chateau Wedding (Cliffside Bay Novella to be read after Christmas Wedding)

Scarred: Trey and Autumn

Jilted: Nico and Sophie

Kissed (Cliffside Bay Novella to be read after Jilted)

Departed: David and Sara

BLUE MOUNTAIN SERIES

Blue Mountain Bundle, Books 1,2,3

Blue Midnight

Blue Moon

Blue Ink

Blue String

EMERSON PASS

The School Mistress of Emerson Pass

The Sugar Queen of Emerson Pass

RIVER VALLEY

Riversong

Riverbend

Riverstar

Riversnow

Riverstorm

Tommy's Wish

River Valley Bundle, Books 1-4

LEGLEY BAY

Caramel and Magnolias

Tea and Primroses

STANDALONES

The Santa Trial

Duet for Three Hands

Miller's Secret

ABOUT THE AUTHOR

Tess Thompson Romance...hometowns and heartstrings.

USA Today Bestselling author Tess Thompson writes small-town romances and historical romance. She started her writing career in fourth grade when she wrote a story about an orphan who opened a pizza restaurant. Oddly enough, her first novel, "Riversong" is about an adult orphan who opens a restaurant. Clearly, she's been obsessed with food and words for a long time now.

With a degree from the University of Southern California in theatre, she's spent her adult life studying story, word craft, and character. Since 2011, she's published 25 novels and 6 novellas. Most days she spends at her desk chasing her daily word count or rewriting a terrible first draft.

She currently lives in a suburb of Seattle, Washington with her husband, the hero of her own love story, and their Brady Bunch clan of two sons, two daughters and five cats. Yes, that's four kids and five cats.

Tess loves to hear from you. Drop her a line at tess@tthompsonwrites.com or visit her website at https://tesswrites.com/

facebook.com/AuthorTessThompson

twitter.com/tesswrites

bookbub.com/authors/tess-thompson

pinterest.com/tesswrites

Made in United States
North Haven, CT
17 November 2022